DYING IN STYLE

JOSIE MARCUS, MYSTERY SHOPPER

Elaine Viets

A SIGNET BOOK

SIGNET
Published by New American Library, a division of
Penguin Group (USA) Inc., 375 Hudson Street,
New York, New York 10014, USA
Penguin Group (Canada), 90 Eglinton Avenue East, Suite 700, Toronto,
Ontario M4P 2Y3, Canada (a division of Pearson Penguin Canada Inc.)
Penguin Books Ltd., 80 Strand, London WC2R 0RL, England
Penguin Ireland, 25 St. Stephen's Green, Dublin 2,
Ireland (a division of Penguin Books Ltd.)
Penguin Group (Australia), 250 Camberwell Road, Camberwell, Victoria 3124,
Australia (a division of Pearson Australia Group Pty. Ltd.)
Penguin Books India Pvt. Ltd., 11 Community Centre, Panchsheel Park,
New Delhi - 110 017, India
Penguin Group (NZ), cnr Airborne and Rosedale Roads, Albany,
Auckland 1310, New Zealand (a division of Pearson New Zealand Ltd.)
Penguin Books (South Africa) (Pty.) Ltd., 24 Sturdee Avenue,
Rosebank, Johannesburg 2196, South Africa

Penguin Books Ltd., Registered Offices:
80 Strand, London WC2R 0RL, England

First published by Signet, an imprint of New American Library,
a division of Penguin Group (USA) Inc.

ISBN: 0-7394-6088-9

PUBLISHER'S NOTE
This is a work of fiction. Names, characters, places, and incidents either are
the product of the author's imagination or are used fictitiously, and any resemblance to actual persons, living or dead, business establishments, events, or
locales is entirely coincidental.

The publisher does not have any control over and does not assume any
responsibility for author or third-party Web sites or their content.

This book is dedicated to the American shopper—those brave women who line up at the Target stores in the chilly dawn the day after Thanksgiving, the veterans of the August White Sales, and the fearless souls who face their peers seminaked in the dressing rooms at Loehmann's.

Acknowledgments

I live in Fort Lauderdale now, but setting my new series in my hometown of St. Louis gave me a terrific reason to visit my favorite friends and places.

So many of you helped with this book. I hope I can remember everyone.

Special thanks to Jinny Gender and Janet Smith, who gave me their valuable local expertise. Photographer Jennifer Snethen took detailed pictures of Maplewood and the surrounding areas.

Thanks also to Susan Carlson, Karen Grace, Diane Earhart, Rita Scott, and Anne Watts for their help and advice. Also, thanks to Valerie Cannata, Colby Cox, and Kay Gordy.

Special thanks to the law enforcement men and women who answered questions on police procedure and lie detector tests. Particular thanks to Detective RC White, Fort Lauderdale Police Department (retired). Some of my police and medical sources had to remain nameless, but I want to thank them all the same. Any mistakes are mine, not theirs.

Thanks to the librarians at the Broward County Library and the St. Louis Public Library who researched my questions, no matter how strange.

Thanks to public relations expert Jack Klobnak, and to my friend, Carole Wantz, who loves books and bookselling.

I also want to thank Emma, a special friend and expert on nine-year-olds, since she used to be one last year. Emma gave me deep background on what it's like to be nine years old in St. Louis: what you wear, where you shop, what you eat and study in school. I wish I could use her name, but the world is a dangerous place these days for young women.

I also wanted to thank the many moms who generously took time to answer my questions about their hopes, needs and fears for their children. Their replies were useful and touching. They include author Laura Burdette, romantic suspense writer Allison Brennan, Amy, Cindy Bokma, Stephanie Elliot, Jennifer, Kelly, Kristin Billerbeck, author of the Ashley Stockingdale books, Lisa, Chris Redding, author of *The Drinking Game*.

Thanks also to Susan McBride, author of *The Good Girl's Guide to Murder*.

Special thanks to my agent, David Hendin, and Kara Cesare, one of the last of the real editors, as well as the Signet copy editor and production staff.

Last but never least, I want to thank my husband, Don Crinklaw, for his extraordinary help and patience.

Chapter 1

"You're going to kill me," he said.

He was young, maybe twenty-five. He'd followed her outside with a sensual swagger, his Armani suit clinging to him like a wicked woman.

Fear wiped away the ugly sneer he'd had five minutes ago in the store. Now he was alone with Josie Marcus in a mall parking lot in suburban St. Louis. They were lost in a sea of empty cars baking in the fall sunshine. The auto audience didn't care what happened to the man. Neither did Josie.

"I'm begging you," he said. "Don't do it." His full lips trembled. They were such nice lips when they pleaded for mercy.

Josie tried to feel sorry for the man. But she remembered the way he'd scorned her in the store. His upper lip had curled like a salted slug when he'd noticed her cheap jeans. He'd made her feel sexless and unfashionable. He'd practically elbowed her out of the way to chase after a bottle blonde with jacked-up boobs.

How many other women had he treated the same way? Josie wondered. He deserved what was going to happen to him. A quick, painless termination was too good for him.

"I'm sorry," Josie said. "You've made too many mistakes. I have my orders."

He grabbed her hand. He reeked of fear, sweat and cologne.

Josie snatched her hand back, but not before she noticed his was softer and smoother. "Don't touch me," she said, "or it will be even worse."

"Wait!" he said. Sweat slid down his forehead. "I don't know what they pay you, but I can pay you more. How much do you want? You want my next commission check? It's yours. And the one after that. Please, please, don't write that report. They'll terminate me for sure."

She looked at his Save Chic name tag. "I'm sorry, Patrick," she said, "but you know the rules. You are supposed to wait on every Save Chic customer, no matter what we wear. Save Chic knows that the modern jewelry buyer may not dress like a millionaire, but she could spend like one. I deliberately wore cheap jeans and a T-shirt, as the company instructed. But I had a Movado watch. That's quality merchandise, Patrick. You should have noticed."

She continued his indictment. "I was supposed to be greeted at the door with 'Welcome to the Save Chic Shop.' Instead, you sneered at me. You made me feel inferior, Patrick. I couldn't get you to wait on me, no matter how hard I tried.

"Meanwhile, you fell all over that young blonde in the gaudy Versace. She didn't buy a thing, did she? But I got the two-hundred-fifty-dollar sterling silver Heart Stopper necklace."

(The necklace was a rip-off of the famous Tiffany Heart Link necklace, fifty bucks cheaper than the original, but it wasn't polite to mention that.)

"I had to beg you to take my money, didn't I, Patrick?" Josie looked him in the eye. Patrick cringed. He knew it was true.

"At the cash register, you were supposed to tell me about the sale on eighteen-karat gold earrings, but you didn't. You were supposed to say, 'Do you have the Save Chic Discount Card? For only twenty-five dollars, you'll get a ten percent discount on every purchase.' You cut it short."

"There was a long line," Patrick said. His languid

boredom had turned to fast-talking desperation. "People hate that stupid spiel. They want to buy and get out."

"I'm sorry, Patrick," Josie said. "My job is to make sure you follow corporate sales procedure. How did you know I was a mystery shopper?"

"Only mystery shoppers want to hear the whole Save Chic Discount Card thing," Patrick said. "Everyone else tries to shut us up as soon as we start."

Patrick dropped to his knees. Ugh, Josie thought, he's going to grovel.

"Please, I'm begging you," he said. "Don't turn in that report. You have absolute power. You can save me. I'll be fired. I'm already on probation. The boss is looking for an excuse to get rid of me. She's old and she hates me."

She's thirty-five, you twit, Josie wanted to say. She's only four years older than I am, but supervising people like you is aging her fast.

"Please, my mother is sick," he said. "She needs an operation. I'm all she has. If I'm out of work, I can't help her."

"Get off your knees, Patrick," she said. "You'll ruin your suit. You'll need it for your job interviews."

"Bitch!" Patrick said, brushing off his knees.

"I bet you say that to all the girls," Josie said.

She watched him lope off toward the mall. Sick mother indeed. Josie had been busted only three times in nine years. Each time it was by a man, and each time he'd claimed to be the sole support of his sick old mother. Josie suspected Patrick was really supporting a fat old credit-card company. He was probably in debt up to those pretty ears for boy toys: a state-of-the-art sound system, plasma TV, hot car, cool clothes. Her report would put a crimp in Patrick's style.

He shouldn't have dissed Josie Marcus, mystery shopper, she thought.

The mystery shopper is the suburban spy. I make my living shopping. I get paid to do something other women do for fun. It beats my other choices. I'm an ordinary-

looking woman with three years of college and no special training. I could work retail, shovel fries, or clean houses for a living.

Mystery shopping is the most exciting job I could have. People think it's so glamorous. That always makes me laugh, especially at the end of the day, when my feet hurt from walking ten miles in the malls, and my neck and eyes ache from hours on the road. I sometimes drive three hundred miles a day.

So why do it?

Josie loved the drama.

Like any good spy, Josie could change her appearance. She had a closet full of disguises. One day she was a haughty lady in Prada, shopping the designer boutiques. The next day she was a hillbilly in a halter top, slouching through concrete-floored discount stores. She loved the disguises, even though some of them embarrassed her mom.

Josie loved the danger.

Store employees resented mystery shoppers. The last time Josie had been busted, she'd caught a cashier red-handed in a returned-goods scam. The crooked employee figured out Josie was a mystery shopper, followed her to the parking lot and threatened to beat her up. Josie dialed 911 on her cell phone and the clerk ran off. Neither the store nor Josie ever saw the guy again.

Okay, she wasn't James Bond, but her job had more thrills than working the cash register at Kmart. Mystery shoppers had been threatened, bribed and beaten up. Just the thought gave her a little thrill. She'd die of boredom in most other jobs.

Besides, Josie had a strong sense of duty. She felt it was her job to protect and serve the average shopper.

Like that one, Josie thought. She watched a woman about forty years old, struggling with her bulky shopping bags. She was nice looking, in neat khaki pants and a pink sweater, but salesclerks like Patrick wouldn't give her a second look. The woman shoved the bags into her blue minivan, rearranging hockey sticks and baby car seats to make them fit.

Mrs. Minivan was the unsung shopper, the backbone of the American economy, the butt of a thousand jokes. Mrs. Minivan got up at five the morning after Thanksgiving so she could be first in line for the Christmas toy bargains at Target. Mrs. Minivan braved the surly post-Christmas crowds to buy holiday decorations at 75 percent off. Then she stored them away for next year.

This was the woman Josie mystery-shopped for. She thought Mrs. Minivan deserved the best. Usually she didn't get it. In Josie's nine years as a mystery shopper, she'd filled out enough paperwork to cover the Mall of America.

What had become of her reports? Nothing, in most cases. She suspected many companies simply filed them away. But not always. Mystery shoppers were overworked, underpaid and despised by the stores they served. But sometimes they had absolute power. That's when heads rolled. Incompetent managers lost their bonuses because of her reports. Rude clerks lost their jobs. If the stores were really serious about changing their ways, Josie's report was final. There was no appeal.

The Save Chic had a serious personnel problem. After being named in the *Wall Street Journal* as one of "America's Ten Rudest Chain Stores," its stock fell seven points. The chain hired mystery shoppers. Patrick the rude clerk was right. Corporate would hit the roof when they saw her report. He was one of the sales associates who'd ruined the chain's reputation. He'd be fired.

Josie didn't feel guilty. There were plenty of good salespeople who could do Patrick's job. Josie had to think about Mrs. Minivan.

Mrs. Minivan, her packages safely stowed, checked her watch, hopped in the driver's seat and roared off. She was late for something.

Josie looked at her own watch. One o'clock. She'd better get moving. Too bad she didn't get to keep the $250 silver bangle from this Save Chic. She would have to return it to another Save Chic. People thought mystery shoppers got to keep those designer clothes and shoes they bought in the line of duty. No way. Discount store T-shirts, jeans and kids' clothes, maybe. But expensive items went back, often to test a store's return procedures. If Josie got a shopping allowance at all, it was embarrassingly small. Sometimes the hardest part of her job was trying to spend $25 in a gilded boutique.

Before she started the car, Josie locked the doors, then pulled out the hot-pink Save Chic bag. She opened the velvet jewelry box, stared at the silver necklace and sighed. The sterling silver shone like moonglow.

Ten years ago, Nathan had bought her necklaces like this. She'd had so many pretty things, so many good times. Now it was all gone. All she had left of their love was Amelia, her nine-year-old daughter.

Amelia was the major reason why Josie was a mystery shopper. The pay was lousy. She was harassed by her boss. She could have gone back to college and gotten a better job. But being a mystery shopper had one major advantage: flexible time. Josie wanted to be with her daughter. She couldn't give Amelia a father, but Josie could give her daughter her own time. Most days Josie could take Amelia to school and pick her up. They had time to do homework, eat dinner and even do fun things, provided Josie didn't sit in mall parking lots sighing over the past.

She closed the pink box and headed for the Save Chic at the St. Louis Galleria. She would feel like an idiot returning that necklace an hour after she bought it. The clerk would see the time on the sales slip.

Except she didn't. The minute Josie walked into this Save Chic, she knew things would go well. The hot-pink carpet was freshly vacuumed. The mirrors gleamed. The black-lacquered showcases were fingerprint free. The chandelier didn't have a single cobweb.

A slender African American woman with a name tag that said CAROLEENA welcomed Josie at the door. The pink bag in Josie's hand meant thankless paperwork, but Caroleena still waited on her. "It's a woman's prerogative to change her mind," she said. "Now, is there anything else I can show you today?"

Caroleena would get a rave review. Josie liked this part of her job—rewarding good people. Caroleena would take proper care of Mrs. Minivan.

It was after two o'clock by the time the return paperwork was completed and Josie was back in her car. She barely made it to the Barrington School for Boys and Girls in time. She pulled up the long, curving drive and took her place in the pickup line behind the other mothers. Josie from Maplewood couldn't believe she had a daughter in the city's classiest private school. She loved the Barrington's redbrick buildings with their pristine white trim. They promised a bright future. Amelia would be a doctor, a lawyer or a CEO. She would not be a mystery shopper like her mother. Josie's daughter would have a profession. Nobody said, "I want to be a mystery shopper when I grow up." It was something people— mostly women—fell into when they had kids and needed money.

"Amelia Marcus," the principal announced, and Josie's daughter came running out, hauling her dark green backpack. Amelia's long hair was flying. Her blue pants had grass stains on the knees, and her shirt was untucked. Josie hoped her daughter had not been in a fight.

Amelia flopped into the car, dragging her backpack and jacket behind her.

"Do you have a lot of homework tonight?" Josie asked.

"The usual," Amelia said.

"Then I think it's time for a guerrilla gorilla expedition."

"Sweet!" Amelia said. She had a thing for the Jungle of the Apes exhibit at the St. Louis Zoo. They could practically walk to it from their home. Well, maybe that was an exaggeration, but it was darn close. Josie didn't have time for many daylong trips, so they started making unplanned one- and two-hour stops at the zoo after school. Josie called them guerrilla gorilla expeditions.

"Let me call your grandmother and tell her where we'll be," Josie said, opening her cell phone.

"She's going to tell us not to ruin our dinner by eating junk at the zoo," Amelia said.

"You can predict the future, oh wise one," Josie said when she hung up the phone.

"Grandma always says that," Amelia said seriously.

Josie scored a free parking spot on the street near the zoo. They crunched through the fallen sycamore leaves to the leafy, glassed-in ape habitat. The bare barred cages were long gone. These gorillas lived in a make-believe forest. Amelia could spend hours watching the big silverback male and his female companions.

"The apes are sweet," Amelia said.

"Personally, I'm a penguin person," Josie said.

"Don't you like the little baby gorillas?" Amelia said.

"They're cute," Josie said. But she couldn't bear to look at the adults' sad eyes.

They watched the gorillas for nearly half an hour. Then mother and daughter wandered outside and ate hot pretzels and frozen Cokes while the sea lions sunned themselves. The day was warm, but Josie could feel the cold underneath as the sun started to sink.

"Put on your jacket, Amelia," she said. For once, Amelia didn't fight her.

"At school they said our zoo is one of the best in the whole wide world," Amelia said.

"They're right."

"Even better than the one in New York?" Amelia asked.

"New York looks like a dog kennel compared to us," Josie said.

Amelia didn't laugh. "I thought New York had every-thing good."

"It doesn't have you or me or the St. Louis Zoo," Josie said.

Finally Amelia giggled. "How was your day?" she asked, with one of those sudden switches into adulthood.

Josie answered her daughter with equal seriousness. "Good and bad. The good part was I met a really nice sales associate and I'll get to give her a good report. But I met a real jerk at another store. He followed me out to the parking lot."

"Were you afraid?" Amelia said. A tiny frown marred the soft skin on her forehead. Josie wished she hadn't blabbed. Amelia was a natural worrier.

"I fear no man," Josie said, holding her frozen Coke aloft like a sword. "Or woman, either, except for your grandmother. So wipe that pretzel mustard off your mouth, or she'll know we've been eating zoo junk."

"She'll know anyway when we don't eat dinner," Amelia said. "What did the bad guy do when he followed you out to the parking lot?"

Her child could not be sidetracked. She got that from her father.

"He tried to get me to change my mind and give him a good report."

"You didn't do it, did you?" At nine, Amelia was obsessed with right and wrong.

"I don't change reports," Josie said. "Not ever. Not for any reason, no matter how much trouble it causes. Right is right."

Josie would remember her answer in the weeks to come, when three people were dead. If she hadn't been so stubborn, if she'd softened her report a little, would any of them be alive today?

Fortunately, Amelia never asked her that question.

Chapter 2

Josie pulled the sheet out of the fax machine in her home office and read her secret assignment.

> Danessa. Plaza Venetia. Between 10 and 10:30 A.M.
> Danessa. The Mall at Covington. Between 11:30 A.M. and 12:30 P.M.
> Danessa. The Shoppes at Greenhills. Between 1:30 and 2:30 P.M.
> Shop two days in a row. Reverse times from bottom to top on second day.

This must be important if her boss faxed it himself. Hush-hush, too. Otherwise Harry would make his secretary do it. Josie had never seen him put a finger on a fax machine. Josie was being sent to the Danessa stores at three of the plushest malls in St. Louis County, two days in a row. What was going on? She bet it was the Creshan deal. She checked the client information. Yep. That was it. The story had been all over the news for two days.

Danessa Celedine, a high-profile local beauty, created exquisite purses and sold them at her three stores, along with other designer handbags.

Danessa was the star of St. Louis social events. She showed up beautifully accessorized, accompanied by her Russian lover, Serge. Her purses could cost five thousand dollars or more, and had a star-studded clientele that reached far beyond the city. Reese Witherspoon had been photographed in *People* clutching a Danessa bag. Gwyneth Paltrow carried a silver Danessa purse to the Oscars.

Josie didn't know anyone who opened her wallet for a five-thousand-dollar purse, but Danessa did. She understood the market so well, her stores were about to be sold to the Creshan Corporation. They planned to turn them into a national chain.

The conglomerate wanted to give Danessa Celedine a personal services contract to remain their spokeswoman. The *St. Louis City Gazette* said the contract was for fifty million.

What the papers—and Danessa—didn't know was that the Creshan Corporation had hired Suttin Services, Josie's company, to secretly shop Danessa before the deal was closed. Josie couldn't suppress a little thrill. She had power. Fifty million dollars was riding on Josie from Maplewood. The fate of the richest woman in the city depended on a nobody from a nowhere section of town.

Josie knew which disguise she had to wear when she shopped Danessa. She would be a Fashion Victim. Ugh. It was her least favorite role. That disguise hurt from head to toe. Especially toe.

No pain, no paycheck, Josie told herself.

She shoved her plain brown bob under the hot, heavy blond wig. Then she carefully put on her makeup. Next she wiggled into control-top pantyhose. Double ugh.

Josie's red Escada pantsuit was covered in gold braid and buttons. I look like a Michael Jackson impersonator, she thought.

For the final torture, Josie squeezed her feet into needle-nosed Prada slingbacks. She winced as her toes were squashed into an isosceles triangle. Lord, those shoes hurt, and the pain would only get worse. She'd be walking for miles on marble.

Josie looked at herself in her bedroom mirror.

Pretty damn good, she thought. Almost worth the pain. At thirty-one, she was still young and thin enough to pass for a trophy wife, if she remembered to swing her hips and flip her shoulder-length wig.

"Not bad," she said out loud. "At least I won't get thrown out of Plaza Venetia."

"So how many careers are you ruining today, Josie?"

Josie jumped. Her mother, Jane Marcus, stood at the bedroom door, hands on her hips.

"Oh, Mom, I don't ruin careers."

"Yes, you do." Jane set her jaw in the strong line that meant there was no arguing with her. "My friend Edie said so. She works at Bluestone's. Not because she has to. Edie just needs to get out of the house."

"Right," Josie said, as she clipped on her gold earrings. "Every woman of sixty loves standing in a department store forty hours a week."

Josie's mother ignored her. "Edie knows for a fact that a sales associate at Bluestone's was fired after the mystery shopper came through. Just because she said she was too busy to show her the cashmere sweaters. She was with Bluestone's twenty-seven years and that's the gratitude she got."

"Mom, Mom," Josie said, "you're getting all worked up over nothing. I don't mystery-shop for Bluestone's."

"You're like the CIA, doing your dirty work in secret with no accountability."

"That's me, Mom. Josie Marcus, mall moll, licensed to kill. I have to get going or I'll be late."

Josie looked at her mother, her face set in its stubborn lines. Her heart melted. Jane was a fighter. She'd fought hard for Josie, but it was difficult for fighters to stop. They swung at everyone and everything.

"GBH, Mom," she said.

"I don't want to," her mother said and stuck her lower lip out like Amelia.

Josie laughed. "You have to. Family rules."

"GBH" stood for "Great Big Hug." Since Josie was a little girl, if a family member said "GBH," you had to give her a Great Big Hug. It was a sacred rule. GBH had stopped many a family fight.

Jane laughed, too. Josie held her mother, breathed in her shampoo and Estee Lauder bath powder, saw the age spots on her hands. "Thanks, Mom. I appreciate everything you do for me."

Jane sighed. "I didn't make all those sacrifices so you could work as a company spy."

"My job is to help customers. I make sure they get proper service."

"No good will come of this sneaking around," her mother said. "I could get you a job at the bank, Josie. A nice job where I could be proud of you."

Josie knew she couldn't win this argument. "I need to see if Amelia has finished her breakfast. My first assignment is way out west. I have to leave early."

"It's not right to rush that child," her mother said. "Breakfast is the most important meal of the day. Let her digest her food. I'll get her to school on time. You go on."

Josie could never stay mad at her mother for long. Jane's generosity made their odd household work. They lived in her mother's two-family flat. Her mother had the upstairs apartment and Josie and Amelia lived on the first floor.

"Thanks, Mom," Josie said. "Bye, Amelia! Your lunch is in your backpack. I love you." She ran to the kitchen to kiss her daughter, then bolted for her car.

Moms. You can't live with them, and you can't live without them, Josie thought. Her mother's words still stung. The old regrets were roiling in her brain. I will not brood on this. I will live my life, not my mother's.

Josie got into her anonymous gray Honda Accord— even she had trouble finding it in parking lots—and headed out Highway 40. Oops. I-64. Like most St. Louisans, Josie lived a little in the city's glorious past. When something was renamed, she still used the old name. This made it difficult for outsiders to find anything, but St. Louis was an insider's city.

Highway 40 was the gateway to the rich western suburbs and the three malls where she'd be shopping today.

The malls were why she had squeezed into control-top pantyhose. Josie had her own theory: the more upscale the mall, the thinner the customers. Seventy-five percent of adult Americans might be overweight, but not at the high-priced malls. Fat was the ultimate social sin for the rich.

Her first stop was Plaza Venetia, "where the best people shop the best stores."

Josie didn't know if the people were the best, but they were definitely the whitest. Plaza Venetia was whiter than a Klan laundry. The mall looked like *Gone With the Wind* gone wild: massive rotundas with white pillars and pointless balconies, French doors that opened onto nothing, Palladian windows that overlooked parking lots.

Inside were one hundred exclusive shops and restaurants, including Danessa.

That's when it hit Josie.

Her mother was a fervent fan of Danessa Celedine. What if Josie had to give Danessa a bad report? Thank God her work was confidential. Jane would never know her traitorous daughter was spying on her beloved Danessa.

Jane thought Danessa was St. Louis's answer to Martha Stewart and Princess Di—before their disasters, of course. Danessa was known for her charity. Danessa won Jane's undying devotion when she donated a thousand dollars to her church's organ repair fund. After that, Jane had joined the growing choir that sang Danessa's praises.

Danessa was headlined in every local newspaper and magazine, and some national ones, including the *New York Times*. Girls at Amelia's school kept Danessa scrapbooks. Not her own daughter, thank God. Living with Jane's hero worship was hard enough.

"So elegant," Jane would sigh when she saw Danessa's photo in the paper.

"So generous," Jane said when the TV news showed Danessa signing a check for a children's home.

"So intelligent," Jane said when she read about the Creshan deal. "Danessa made something of herself."

Josie heard the rest of that unspoken sentence: And you didn't.

Take that, Mom, Josie thought. I'm sitting in judgment on the great Danessa. But she couldn't say anything. She wouldn't, either. Josie had her principles. Besides, she wasn't expecting trouble. She'd never heard a whisper against Danessa. Then again, she'd never been in a Danessa store. She couldn't afford to walk in the door.

Josie pulled into the Plaza Venetia parking lot and checked her watch: 10:02 A.M. She noted the time on the questionnaire, and the weather conditions: sunny and hot. In St. Louis, late September felt like August. Even the carefully tended mall grass was brown around the edges and the impatiens looked exhausted.

Then she checked the questions. Josie wasn't allowed to take the questionnaire into the store, or even the mall. But it helped to review the questions.

Was the store clean and neat?
Were the displays well put together?
Were the counters, shelves and display cases free of dust and fingerprints?
Was the basket of Danessa's autographed photos displayed in a prominent position?
Was the rest room tidy? Was there paper in the stalls and towel dispenser?
Were you greeted when you entered the store?
Was the greeting friendly?
Were the sales associates properly dressed?
Were the sales associates familiar with the merchandise? Could your sales associate answer these three questions about the product:

(1) Designer or country of origin?
(2) Price?
(3) Special features?

When you made your purchase, did the sales associate
   check your driver's license and ask for your
   phone number?
What was the name of your associate?
Did the sales associate thank you for shopping with
   Danessa?

   All reasonable questions. Even her mom would agree.
   Josie would also have to rate her shopping experience
from Poor to Excellent, then write a short summary. She
had twenty-five dollars to spend in each store.
   What on earth can I buy at Danessa for that amount?
she wondered. Certainly not a handbag. Well, she'd figure out something.
   Josie vamped into Plaza Venetia on her high, sleek
heels and felt instantly energized. Some upscale malls,
like some casinos, pumped in oxygen. The Muzak was
actually playing a tune from when she was a teenager.
Josie got tired of the forty-year-old "most of us are
dead" bands the boomers loved.
   Plaza Venetia was done in tasteful shades of cream
and beige that were constantly repainted. It was exces-
sively clean. Venetian glass chandeliers, great iridescent
saucers suspended by heavy silver chains, shimmered
and sparkled in the light. Sound-absorbing jungles
sprouted from marble planters. Fountains trickled
quietly.
   The Zen of shopping.
   As she climbed the stairs, Josie contemplated the im-
portance of the purse. The shoe may be a woman's sexu-
ality, but the purse is her self. Is she young and flirty?
She has a small, sexy purse. Is she older and burdened
with the cares of family life? She has a fat grandma
purse, filled with every comfort from Band-Aids to baby
pictures. Is she all business? Her Coach bag shows it. If
she's fashionable, she must decide whether Prada, Gucci
or Kate Spade suits her style best.
   Josie checked her watch again, then prepared to shop
the target.

Danessa looked more like an art gallery than a purse store. There was none of the cheerful jumble of the discount stores. The walls were painted flat white. Hyperexpensive purses were exhibited on Lucite pedestals, like the artworks they were.

Josie admired the clever beading and cunning clasp of the evening purse in the window. She nearly choked on the discreet price tag—"5000" was all it said, but that said plenty. The purse was this moment's color: citrus green. What happened next year, when it wasn't the color? Did you give an outdated purse that cost five grand to charity or hold a funeral for it?

An autographed photo of Reese Witherspoon carrying her Danessa bag hung over that exact same model. Another photo showed Madonna schlepping a Louis Vuitton Takashi Murakami bag. The bag was on a Lucite pedestal. Josie thought it bore an unfortunate resemblance to the matronly purse her mom bought at Marshalls.

Danessa's own line of belts and purses all had the distinctive diamond D clasp. Josie examined them and found some of Danessa's purses carelessly constructed for such expensive merchandise. One had a poorly sewn strap that looked like it would break easily. The beading on an evening purse was dull. Cheap plastic beads, Josie thought, sold at glass-bead prices. A third leather purse had crooked stitching. She peeked inside the purse. The tag said MADE IN ITALY, home of fine leatherwork. I don't think so. Well, it wasn't her job to rate the merchandise.

A purse shaped like a Chinese takeout carton sat on another Lucite pedestal. Josie choked when she saw the "3900" price tag. She also noticed something odd about the Lucite stand. It was almost gray with fingerprints, especially at toddler level. And what was that pink lump on the side? She bent forward for a closer look. It was a wad of bubble gum.

Maybe it was some sort of superhip statement. Josie looked again. Nope. Somebody had parked her old gum there. Yuck.

"May I help you?" a small, dark-haired woman asked. Her hair was in fashionable spikes. Her accent was exotic. She was sleek as a cat and just as self-satisfied.

"I was looking at the Chinese purse," Josie said.

"It's kicky," the woman said. Her accent sounded Eastern European. "I say that right, yes? My name is Olga Rachmaninoff, like the composer."

"Pretty purse," Josie said. "But a child left fingerprints on the display cases." Josie expected her to apologize, or reach for the Windex.

"You Americans," Olga said. "You are crazy about cleaning. I sell. I don't scrub like a peasant. Where I come from in Russia, we show customers the goods and they buy. If a customer doesn't like them, we say, 'Go to the shop down the street.' Then we laugh. There is nothing in the shop down the street, either."

"Right," Josie said. That probably explained why this Danessa store was empty.

"Can I show you the purse?" Olga asked.

"I'll just browse for a bit," Josie said. She was happy to see a basket of eyeglass holders for $22.99 near the cash register. Good, she thought. I'll get one for Mom. She's always losing her glasses.

Olga rang up the purchase. She did not thank Josie for shopping at Danessa. Maybe a twenty-three-dollar purchase didn't rate a thank-you in Russia.

Josie noticed that the basket of Danessa's autographed photos was empty. She'd have to put that in her report, too.

"Can I use your rest room?" Josie asked.

Olga pointed at a door.

At least the rest room passed muster, Josie thought, back in her car. The rest of the survey was one thumbs-down after another. Perhaps this Danessa store was having a bad day. Josie still had two more.

By two-thirty Josie was fighting the traffic on Clarkson Road and wondering what she was going to do about her report. The highest rating she could give any store was Fair. At Covington, a jumble of purses sat on the store floor, as if they'd been dumped out of a packing box, and there was a burned-out lightbulb in the rest room. The clerk sleepwalked around the store, not bothering to greet her. Josie thought she could have walked off with the stock and the woman wouldn't have noticed.

At the exclusive Greenhills store, Josie found a half-eaten candy bar next to a thousand-dollar clutch. The sales associate picked it up and said, "Sorry, my lunch." That was the only thing she said to Josie.

When Josie went back to check the rest room (no paper in the stall), she noticed that the door to the loading dock was unlocked and ajar.

Danessa had serious management problems.

I still have tomorrow, she thought. Maybe it will be a better day. If I can give all three stores an Excellent rating tomorrow, my report won't be so bad. And if I grow six inches and lose twenty pounds tonight, I can be a supermodel.

Josie's report would be an unpleasant surprise. The Creshan Corporation would not be happy. Neither would Danessa. There was nothing Josie could do about it. What had she told her daughter yesterday? *I don't change reports. Not ever. Not for any reason, no matter how much trouble it causes. Right is right.*

I saw what I saw, and I'll probably see more of the same tomorrow. There's going to be hell to pay. What if my report kills the Creshan deal?

Then a thought struck Josie that was so frightening it took her breath away.

What if Mom finds out?

Chapter 3

"What am I going to do with three eyeglass holders?" Josie's mother said. "I've only got one pair of eyes."

Right now, they had an angry glare. The St. Louis glare was a powerful citywide weapon, and Jane didn't hesitate to use it on her daughter. Her eyes bored into Josie like lasers. Josie knew her mother could see right through her.

She tried to fend off the glare with soothing words. "Mom, these are holders for your sunglasses, your reading glasses, and your distance glasses. You leave your glasses all over your home and mine. I got these for you at Danessa. You love Danessa Celedine."

Any argument with Jane was three against one: Josie was fighting with her mother, her landlord and her babysitter, all at the same time.

"I like Danessa personally," Jane said, "but I could get the same thing on the Home Shopping Network for half the price. You're just paying for the name. If you were at Danessa's shop, why didn't you get me an autographed picture? Those are free."

"They were out," Josie said.

Her mother turned the glare on her full force. Josie tried to shield her face. "You're spying on Danessa, aren't you?" Jane said. "You're going to give her a bad report. Danessa has a major deal in the works and you're going to ruin it. I'll never forgive you, Josie Marcus. Danessa saved our church."

"Mom, I can't discuss my assignments. You know that."

Jane kept glaring. It was a preview of Josie's own face in thirty years. Josie knew she would get the same trenches from her nose to her lips, the same crinkles on her neck, the same sag in her jaw.

"Mom, I'm a professional—and that's how I'll behave. If you need me I'll be in my office."

Some office. It was one corner of Josie's bedroom. It didn't have a door to slam or a wall for privacy. Josie's office was a cranky secondhand computer, a fax and a printer on a two-dollar yard-sale table. The wooden chair was uncomfortable, but that was deliberate. It kept Josie from falling asleep after a long day.

As Josie headed for her office, she tripped over the foot massager her mother had bought on the Home Shopping Network. The darn thing nailed Josie on the shinbone, then landed on her shoe-squeezed toes.

"Ouch. Ouch. Ouch." Josie hopped around the bedroom, rubbing her bruised foot. That was the only decent massage she'd ever had from the contraption. She didn't have the heart to tell her mom it didn't work.

Josie could hear her mother calling down the staircase, "I'll be praying my daughter doesn't ruin the woman who's done so much for this city. Danessa has fifty million dollars riding on your words."

Josie could feel the glare a whole floor away.

She woke up the next morning, as hopeless and leaden as the sunless September sky. She chose her disguise for the second day at Danessa with care. She didn't want the staff to recognize her. Fat chance. They'd acted like she was invisible yesterday.

Josie picked an even more outrageous rich-lady outfit: a pink-and-red Versace suit with clamdigger pants. Josie had found it at an estate sale for twenty-five bucks. She plopped a red wig on her head and crammed her feet into the same toe-squashing Prada shoes.

Josie slipped out without seeing her mother that morning. Jane's words from last night were still ringing in her ears. She gave Amelia an absentminded kiss and dropped her off at the Barrington School.

She approached the first Danessa store with resigned dread. At the Shoppes at Greenhills, there was no half-eaten candy bar on the counter. Today, an exquisite blonde was slurping a blueberry yogurt. She put it down when Josie entered, but only because her cell phone rang. "You want to fix me up with Barry?" the blonde howled into her phone. "That creakazoid has to be forty."

As Josie roamed the store, the blonde raged about her aged date.

Using sign language, Josie indicated she wanted an eyeglass holder. The clerk rang her up, still talking on the phone. "I don't care if Barry is rich. Old guys have saggy butts."

At Covington, the sleepwalking clerk was replaced by a young woman with dead white skin and crimson hair. Her eyes were outlined in black and her lips were blood-red. The effect was intriguing. The young woman was listening to an iPod, but she unplugged the earbuds when Josie walked in.

Josie picked up a yellow satin purse. "Can you tell me its country of origin?"

The cool woman with the crimson hair shrugged. "Taiwan? Tibet? Something Third World," she said.

"How much is it?" Josie said.

"It's a cheapie," Ms. Cool said. "Five hundred dollars, give or take fifty." The price was too insignificant to check.

"Any special features?" Josie said.

"It's a purse," Ms. Cool said, and shrugged again.

Josie opened it. Inside, a tiny light illuminated the interior.

The sales associate had her iPod back on.

By one-thirty, Josie was at Plaza Venetia. This time, the beautiful saucer chandeliers and the plashing fountains failed to soothe her. Josie knew the Plaza Venetia store would be the worst. It didn't disappoint her.

The store was empty. No customers, no staff. The gum was gone, but the gray patina of fingerprints still covered the Lucite stand with the Chinese takeout purse. Josie saw a snakeskin belt coiled like a hissing cobra on another stand. The price tag had real fangs: "2700."

"Hello?" Josie said.

Silence.

Josie went through the AUTHORIZED PERSONNEL ONLY door into the back area, a dreary section of concrete and cardboard boxes. "Anybody here?" she said.

"You're not supposed to be back here," said a blond giant in tight black leather pants. The woman's arm muscles were as thick as her accent. She had to be at least six two.

"You're not supposed to be back here, either," Josie said. "You're supposed to be on the floor, waiting on me. I'm a customer."

The Amazon looked Josie up and down and sneered, "I'm sure you are," as if she knew Josie's Versace was from an estate sale.

I'll get this rude creep, Josie thought. How many other innocent shoppers has she shriveled with that look?

"I want to see some merchandise right now," Josie said.

"What?" the woman said insolently.

Josie picked the display that would be most difficult to reassemble. "That snakeskin belt," she said. "The twenty-seven-hundred-dollar one."

The woman sighed audibly.

"I didn't catch your name," Josie said.

"Mzm," the woman mumbled.

"Excuse me?"

"Marina."

"You're Russian?" Josie remembered from her history classes that Marina was the name of Lee Harvey Oswald's Russian wife.

"Mmph," the woman grunted. Josie took that as a yes.

A twenty-seven-hundred-dollar belt felt just like a twenty-seven-dollar one, Josie decided, except that the clasp was harder to figure out. She looked at herself in the mirror. Were her hips really that wide?

"I don't think so," Josie said.

Marina sighed with all the warmth of a Russian winter.

"I'll take this instead," Josie said. She bought yet another eyeglass holder.

Marina did not thank Josie for shopping at Danessa. In fact, she didn't say anything after her last monumental sigh.

What was going on? How did this store survive with no customers?

Josie's friend Alyce Bohannon might know. Her crowd shopped at Danessa. Maybe she'd noticed its decline. Alyce had the life Josie was supposed to have: the handsome husband at a high-powered law firm, the country-club membership and the stunning house. Still, Alyce was always eager to slip away from her perfect life and go mystery-shopping with Josie.

Alyce lived in the Estates at Wood Winds, a subdivision of mansions in far West County. Her neighbors included two TV anchors, a major league baseball star, enough lawyers to stock a courthouse—and the St. Louis power couple Danessa Celedine and Serge Orloff.

Josie speed-dialed Alyce's number.

"Help!" Josie said. "I need information, but I can't talk about it on the phone. Can I stop by your home?"

"I'm not there. I've just finished a committee meeting at the Junior League. How about meeting at Plaza Frontenac? Our usual place?"

"Will you have the baby?" Josie said.

"Justin is with his nanny."

"You're still my best friend," Josie said, "even if you do have a nanny and natural blond hair."

Josie and Alyce always met at the movie house. They'd duck inside, buy popcorn and rot-your-teeth movie candy, then sit at the tables in the mall. Josie arrived first. She bought an espresso and popcorn: conflicting doses of caffeine and serotonin.

Josie spotted her friend by her gliding walk. Alyce didn't move like other people. She seemed to float. She had slate-blue eyes and the softest, silkiest blond hair. It floated, too. She'd gained about thirty pounds with the baby, and the extra weight made her miserable. Josie wished her friend had been born a hundred years ago, when people appreciated a little poundage.

Alyce tortured herself with a bottle of water. "What's going on?" she said.

Josie swore her to secrecy, then told her what she'd found. "The Danessa stores are an absolute mess." She crunched a handful of popcorn.

"I'm not surprised," Alyce said. "Ugly rumors are floating around Wood Winds. I'm hearing that Danessa is short of money. She's been firing staff right and left. If she doesn't get that Creshan deal, she's dead. There's trouble on the home front, too. Danessa and Serge are fighting. They've had some real battles, but we can't figure out what they're about. Danessa's housekeeper would know, but she's not talking."

Josie reached for more popcorn. Alyce watched her.

"I know Serge has been straying," Alyce said. "Danessa caught him with Amy the Slut at the country club and made a big scene. No smart woman ever does that. Amy's not worth it. You can't take her seriously. Sex for her is like a handshake. Danessa dragged her out of the women's locker room by the hair and bitch-slapped her in front of everyone."

"Good heavens," Josie said. "Why hasn't any of this been in the papers?"

"Because Danessa has a good public-relations machine, and it constantly cranks out press releases and glamorous photos," Alyce said. "How many Danessa stories have you read in the last month?"

"None," Josie said. "I don't have to. Mom reads them to me. I'd say six hundred seventy-eight stories on Danessa have appeared in the last thirty days. I'm not counting the quotes from Serge."

"You couldn't," Alyce said. "The machine spits out

Serge-isms by the hour. The man is a walking sound bite."

"Photogenic, too," Josie said. "He looks like a young Omar Sharif with that curly black hair."

"I noticed the wide shoulders and narrow hips," Alyce said. "Big hands, too. Do you think the size of a man's hand tells you about the size of his thingie?"

"Alyce!" Josie said.

"Well, his is huge. His hand, I mean," Alyce said. She eyed Josie's popcorn like Oliver Twist. Josie poured half on a napkin and pushed it toward her.

"Here. I can't stand it," Josie said.

Alyce didn't bother with polite protests. She grabbed a handful.

"I'd think some of this would make the gossip columns at least," Josie said.

"Danessa is a major advertiser," Alyce said. "The media will never attack her. I don't know why you're so surprised. Did you know that Martha Stewart was a gold-plated bitch until her indictment? That woman had an ass double."

"A what?" Josie said.

"Whenever she bent over on TV to get her soufflé out of the oven, that was the ass double's rear end. We never saw Martha's own rear. For that alone they should throw her butt behind bars."

Josie couldn't stop laughing.

"There's a long tradition of prettying up women entrepreneurs," Alyce said. "Did you know Leona Helmsley was the Queen of Mean until she was sitting in the dock? Leona and Martha had the same thing as Danessa: good public-relations people."

"So nobody you know would be surprised by an unfavorable report on the Danessa stores?" Josie said.

"They'd be surprised if you said anything good," Alyce said and finished the last of the popcorn. "Anything else?"

"Yes," Josie said. "Can you use three Danessa eyeglass holders?"

That afternoon Josie finished her report. She was sick with dread as she typed. She wasn't used to this kind of pressure. She would have some protection. Josie's reports were anonymous, so the stores she shopped would never know her name. Some people would be discouraged by the anonymity of her job, but Josie liked being a fly on the corporate wall.

That's what made the Danessa assignment so unnerving. Everyone would know the results, especially Josie. She knew Patrick the Rude would probably be fired after her Save Chic report, but she'd never see him getting the ax. If the Creshan Corporation killed the Danessa deal, it would be all over the news. Her mother would know, too. Josie would never hear the end of it.

I was fair, she told herself. I was impartial. I fairly and impartially destroyed the woman my mother most admires.

No, I didn't. I didn't create those dirty stores or hire that surly staff. The Creshan Corporation executives looked at the books and took the VIP store tours. But they suspected something was wrong.

Now Josie was about to hand the Creshan Corporation a dynamite report—one that could blow up and hurt a lot of people. Including herself.

Josie called her boss, Harry Bolrman, to warn him.

Harry lived up to his name. He had curly black hair all over his head, ears, nose, even his hands. More hair peeked through his shirt. The man looked like a werewolf at moonrise. Harry was perpetually fifty pounds overweight. Josie thought he could lose ten if he shaved.

She talked with Harry almost daily, but she rarely came into the office. He faxed or mailed Josie her assignments. In between, Harry talked about his Atkins diet. He was crunching something when he answered his phone.

"What are you eating, Harry?" Josie said. She'd never known anyone on a diet who ate such fattening food.

"Bacon," he said. "I've lost two more pounds."

Crunch. Crunch.

"Congratulations," Josie said. Harry was always losing two pounds. The same two, over and over.

"When are you gonna get on this diet with me?" he said. Crunch.

"Sorry, Harry, I'm a carboholic. I can't give up my bagels."

"Those things are unhealthy," Harry said as he munched nitrates and nitrites. "You should be on the Atkins diet. It's the only way to go." Crunch. "Serge, Danessa's boyfriend, lost fifty pounds on it."

Josie saw the ruthless-looking Russian sitting down to a whole roast bear with a side of oxen. He probably shot and skinned his own dinner.

"Didn't he say that the Atkins diet was really invented by the Russians?" Josie said.

The savagely handsome Serge claimed to be a member of the Russian aristocracy. From what Josie could figure out, half the Russian immigrants were royalty and the other half were mobsters. Serge could have been both.

"Was that last week or the week before?" Harry said. "I can hardly open an issue of the *City Gazette* without seeing something Serge said."

"This week he ranted that American prescription drugs were too expensive and Russia had a better health-care system," Josie said.

"Don't they?" Harry said. Crunch.

"The Soviet Union has collapsed, Harry," she said. "There is no health-care system."

Why am I defending the U.S. drug companies? Josie wondered. They're all crooks.

Crunch. Harry bit into more bacon. He must have eaten half a pig while she'd been on the phone.

"How did the Danessa shopping go?" he said.

"Not good, Harry," she said. "I wanted to warn you before I sent in my report. The stores are dirty and disorganized and the staff is rude."

Crunch. "Hey, that's what our client paid to know."

"Harry, the highest grade I could give any Danessa store was Fair."

Crunch. Crunch. "Write the truth, Josie," he said. "And send that report ASAP. Creshan wants it today."

"Brace yourself," Josie said. "Danessa won't be happy."

"That's her problem," Harry said. "You let me deal with it. You just write your report. Let 'er rip."

Josie did. She e-mailed her report to Harry, dreaming of a cold margarita and a hot bubble bath. She wouldn't get either. Amelia had a Spanish test tomorrow. Spanish always gave her trouble.

Now Josie's daughter stood at her bedroom door, digging one toe into the carpet. "Mom," Amelia said, "I need help with my Spanish."

Josie marveled at her daughter's gorgeous skin and dramatic nose. She looked like her handsome father, not her ordinary mother. Someday, Amelia would be a beauty. Right now she was a little girl, struggling with her lessons.

"Why do I have to learn this?" Amelia whined. "I'm not going to live in Spain."

Josie didn't feel like giving her "Americans are isolated" speech. They'd had this argument a hundred times, and it was only September. Tonight, Josie was too tired to reason with a nine-year-old.

"Why, Mom?" Amelia's whine was a wire in her ear.

"Because I said so," she snapped. Josie was horrified. She sounded like her mother. Amelia didn't notice.

Josie scurried back to the safety of the Spanish lessons. "We were looking at masculine and feminine nouns," Josie said. "Is 'traitor' masculine or feminine?"

"That doesn't make sense, Mom," Amelia said. "It's both. Men and women can betray people, can't they? But in Spanish, a traitor is masculine. How come they do that, Mom?"

"Men are better at it," Josie said.

Amelia rolled her eyes. "Oh, Mom." She had no idea how true her mother's words were.

Tomorrow, Josie would get a lesson in masculine betrayal.

Chapter 4

"Young lady, you are not leaving the house in that outfit."

"Oh, Mom."

"What kind of example are you setting for your daughter?"

Josie was wearing a pink tube top with WHITE TRASH written in rhinestones, purple short shorts that looked like they'd been applied with a paintbrush and red high-heeled sandals. Her Dolly Parton wig was down to her rear.

Josie thought the temporary tattoo on her right breast and the barbed wire tat around her ankle were the finishing touches.

"I'm an example of a working mother, and that's one Amelia needs to see. I'm shopping General Cheeps chicken today, Mom, so I have to wear my white-trash outfit."

Amelia cheered. "Cool! The General's coming for dinner! We're CHEEP! CHEEP! CHEEP!" Her daughter knew all the corporate slogans.

"Fast food is full of fat and preservatives," Jane said.

"That's why it's so good, Mom. A few chemicals won't kill the kid. She eats healthy most of the time."

"Soy burgers are dorky," Amelia said. "I want Five-Star Curly-Crisp, Mom."

Definitely my daughter, Josie thought, and a true St.

Louisan. This city was settled by the French, who poured sauce on everything, and the Germans, who fried their food, sugared it, or both, then served it with beer.

St. Louis culinary specialties had a heart attack in every bite. The innocent-sounding toasted ravioli were deep-fat fried. Gooey-butter cake was a baked stick of butter and a box of powdered sugar in a little square pan.

The St. Louis food philosophy was: "Might as well enjoy yourself. Nobody gets out of here alive."

Josie's daughter ate grease with gusto, like her mother. Amelia thought salad greens belonged in leaf bags. She liked cheeseburgers with onions and ketchup, macaroni and cheese, and fried peanut-butter-and-banana sandwiches, "just like Elvis." She also liked Elvis, but that was thanks to her grandmother. Jane openly disapproved of the child's diet. Josie secretly encouraged her daughter's renegade eating habits.

"If you're going to bring that junk home for dinner, at least get some vegetables and salad," Jane said.

"Will do," Josie said. Just because it was on the table didn't mean she had to eat it. Living in the same house with my mother keeps me young, Josie thought. Now I'm acting Amelia's age.

Amelia groaned. "I hate salad."

"Josie, wear a raincoat if you're going out dressed like that so the neighbors won't see you," Jane said.

"I'll roast in a raincoat, Mom. It's ninety degrees."

"Sweet tattoos, Mom," Amelia said. That was high praise from a nine-year-old.

Great, thought Josie, as she ran out the door, Amelia in tow. My daughter will grow up to be white trash, thanks to her mother.

"Hi, Josie." Oh, Lord. It was Stan the Man Next Door.

"Stan's waving," Amelia said helpfully. "I think he likes you, Mom."

"Get in the car. It's seven thirty." Josie wished she had the raincoat. "We're going to be late for school."

She looked down and saw that her tube top had slipped. Josie pulled it up and saw Stan staring bug-eyed at her chest.

"Need any help?" he asked. "I mean, around the house?" Stan was an incurable handyman, and Josie wasn't above taking advantage of his skills.

"The living room air conditioner is wheezing and rattling," she said. "But I have to run Amelia to school and I'm late. I don't really dress like this. I'm working."

Stan's ears turned bright red and Josie blushed. There was no point trying to explain. She threw the Honda into reverse. It lurched backward and Stan jumped out of the way.

"Mom, you nearly ran over Stan," Amelia said.

Josie needed coffee in the worst way. But first she had to get Amelia to school before eight.

"You know how you always tell me to act more like a lady and not a boy?" Amelia said.

"Yes," Josie said warily.

"Well, it's not easy. Dresses are really uncool. Nobody wears them to school. But I like them. I'm just telling you this because sometimes I want to act more like a lady, but I can't." •

"I understand," Josie said solemnly. Amelia was so serious one minute, so silly the next, it hurt her heart. Josie treasured these car confessions. She didn't know how much longer Amelia would tell her things.

"Can I turn the radio on 101 The River?" Amelia said.

"Go ahead," Josie said. She could stand listening to Hilary Duff for the trip to school. She knew it was important to Amelia's social life to hear The River in the morning.

There was no way Josie could afford the Barrington School for Boys and Girls. She had a small legacy from her Great-Aunt Tillie, but even so, the tuition was more than Josie made in a year. Fortunately, her daughter had her father's brains. Amelia was a scholarship student with top grades in everything except the dreaded Spanish.

Amelia got the scholarship because she fit the school profile. Josie suspected it was because they lived in Maplewood, which was practically the ghetto by Barrington standards. It was an old suburb of St. Louis that looked like a city neighborhood. The homes were brick and limestone, built early in the last century.

Josie's Honda was creeping along Manchester Road through Maplewood's main shopping district. Josie thought Maplewood looked like an old-fashioned small town. They passed the Paramount Jewelers, with its clocks and cuff links in the window. Penzey's Spices had the best pepper. She would take Amelia in there and say, "Snort!" and they'd breathe in the good smells until they were laughing too hard. The Switch Stand sold model trains, but Josie could never get Amelia interested in them. Josie was a sucker for train villages with water towers.

The shopping district's plate-glass windows sparkled in the morning sun. So did the sidewalks. Some kids in Amelia's school had never walked on a sidewalk. One boy called sidewalks "little patios."

There were big patios, new decks and in-ground pools for most of the Barrington students. Mother and daughter drove through the old-money suburb of Ladue along wooded roads just starting to get a bit of fall color. Cicadas made their sad end-of-summer sound, and Josie thought she felt the cold winter under the last summer heat.

At 7:50, Josie flicked on her blinker to pull into the long driveway of the Barrington School. Her daughter shouted, "Stop, Mom! You can't!"

Josie slammed on the brakes, her systems on full maternal alert. "What's wrong?"

"You can't go to school like that," Amelia said.

The kid was right. Josie's yellow tush-brushing wig and rhinestone tube top would shock the Lilly Pulitzer crowd down to their pedicured toes.

"I'll stay in the car," Josie said. "I promise."

"They'll still see you."

Amelia's agonized plea made Josie remember when her own mom had picked her up at school wearing a baggy brown knit hat. Jane's hat looked like a cow patty, as that nasty Heather told Josie—and everyone else at school. Snotty girls chanted, "Patty, patty, hi, patty" whenever Josie's mom drove up. Her mother innocently wondered who the popular Patty was, while Josie prayed for death in the seat beside Jane.

She wasn't going to do that to her daughter. Josie pulled over and whipped off the wig. Her respectable brown bob was hopelessly flattened. "Now I look like I have terminal bed head."

Amelia looked relieved and Josie knew she'd made the right move.

"Sorry, kid, I can't do anything about the tube top and the tattoo," Josie said.

"You can hunch down a little," Amelia said.

"Good idea. They'll think your mother is the Hunchback of Notre Dame. Assume the Quasimodo position."

Josie hunched. Amelia laughed. She sat with her monogrammed backpack on her lap, ready to launch herself out of the seat before anyone noticed her embarrassing mother.

Josie was pretty sure none of the other car-pool moms saw her tube top. They wouldn't believe it if they did. White trash didn't go to the Barrington School.

Who am I kidding? she thought. I'm the closest thing to white trash this school has. They probably think I dress like this for real. Josie didn't fit in with the other Barrington moms and she knew it. But she wanted her daughter to have the best schooling.

Amelia was the love of her life. The best mistake she ever made.

Thanks to mystery shopping, Josie picked up some cool clothes for her daughter that she could never afford otherwise. Josie used to troll the garage sales in rich neighborhoods for high-priced children's clothes. Now that Amelia went to Barrington with the kids who had those garages and the palatial homes that went with them, Josie couldn't risk buying their castoffs.

The job provided other perks. Josie mystery-shopped cruise lines and amusement parks for free vacations. Rating ritzy restaurants gave Josie and Amelia a taste of the good life.

Her mother watched Amelia when Josie was stuck on a job. Jane could be summoned by cell phone with the emergency code 666—MOM.

What did moms do before cell phones? Josie wondered. What did moms do before coffee? She badly needed some after her white-trash near disaster at Barrington.

Josie pulled into the parking lot of Has Beans and checked herself in the mirror. Her brown hair was still flat. She stuck it under the flossy blond wig. It was total trash time.

Josh whistled when she walked into the coffee shop. "Nice outfit," he said. "Can I take out the trash?"

"Forget it, Josh," she said. "I'm working."

"On the Stroll?" That was the city's prostitution zone.

Josh was three years younger than Josie and the handsomest coffee hustler in Maplewood. He wrote science fiction. So far he was unpublished, but Josh was sure someday he would be the next Orson Scott Card.

"What would you like?" Josh said.

It wasn't quite a leer, but Josie knew Josh's intentions were strictly dishonorable. He was as bad for her as a caramel cappuccino, but she craved him anyway.

Why can't I feel this way about sensible Stan next door? Josh would never fix my air conditioner or do anything else useful. Josh would also never wear short-sleeved drip-dry shirts and a hangdog look.

Josh was her mom's worst nightmare, down to his pierced tongue. The man was bad—in a good way.

"Earth to Josie," Josh said. "What can I get you?"

"Double espresso," she said.

"Whoa, breakfast of champions."

"I need the 'feine," she said.

"What are you doing today for truth, justice and the American consumer?" Josh asked.

"Checking out General Cheeps chicken."

"Ah," Josh said, "now I understand the outfit. Very clever."

"It's my favorite disguise," Josie said.

"Mine, too," Josh said. "Your rich suburban lady outfit is low on my list. Makes you look like a total tight-ass."

"It's supposed to," Josie said, finishing off her espresso. She was wired and ready for work.

The first General Cheeps was way up north in Florissant, near a trailer park. No one raised an eyebrow when she sauntered into the chicken store in her WHITE TRASH tube top. Compared to the other customers, Josie looked like she was dressed for a Junior League luncheon.

She hit ten chicken stores. As she drove around the St. Louis area, Josie listened to eighties music. U2 was her favorite, and she sang along with the plaintive "New Year's Day" and "With or Without You." Even though she sounded more like a horny cat than a lovesick singer, Josie didn't care and sang freely. No one heard her.

By two o'clock, Josie had a stack of reports, most of them favorable. General Cheeps was a well-run franchise. Her car was loaded with buckets of chicken, mashed potatoes and corn bread. On the seat next to her sloshed a double tub of green beans, a tribute to Jane. Josie hoped her mom didn't notice the fatback bacon floating in the vegetables.

Josie checked the dashboard clock and breathed a sigh of relief. If the highway traffic kept moving, she'd have enough time to drop the food at home, change into something decent, and pick up her daughter at school.

Her cell phone rang. She scoped the number on the screen. It was her boss, Harry.

"I need you at the office right now," he said.

Office? Josie could count the times she'd been in the Suttin office.

"Harry, I've been shopping General Cheeps in my white-trash outfit. I smell like a giant fried chicken. My car is filled with buckets of Curly-Crisp. Let me go home and change first. It will only take ten minutes."

"I said *now*," Harry shouted. "Don't stop for anything, not even the red lights. Get your ass in this office."

Josie's heart froze. Something was wrong.

Chapter 5

"This cheap tart tried to ruin my fifty-million-dollar deal?" Danessa looked at Josie and laughed.

Mom was right, Josie thought. I should have worn the raincoat.

The fiercely elegant Danessa had charged into the ratty office of Suttin Services, scattering a whirlwind of papers. Chairs overturned in her wake. Office equipment slid off the stands. Staffers crouched down at their desks. She was followed by a small, pale creature in owlish glasses and a beige suit a size too big. The personal PR woman.

Harry, Josie's boss, had been munching something meaty when Danessa burst through his door. He covered it with a stack of reports, but there were grease specks on his shirt and shiny smears on his mouth and fingers.

His lips trembled in fear, but no sound came out. Josie would have to defend herself.

"Who are you calling a cheap tart?" Josie was in full Maplewood fighting mode. It took guts to say those words with WHITE TRASH on her chest.

Danessa stepped in front of Josie. She was nine feet tall in witch-pointy stilettos. Her eyes were the color of a summer storm. Her simple black dress was the down payment on a house. Her dramatic necklace cost even more. It was a dragonfly in amber. Josie couldn't stop staring at the trapped bug.

Josie's fried-chicken fumes overpowered Danessa's

subtle perfume. Please God, don't let her notice the WHITE TRASH on my tube top, she thought.

She glanced down. God had answered her prayer. The WHITE TRASH wasn't showing because Josie's tube top had rolled down to her nipples. Josie yanked it back up.

"For your information, I am dressed properly for my current shopping assignment," she said. "Just as I was dressed properly when I shopped your stores. I produced a report that was fair, balanced and accurate."

Josie thought she sounded dignified yet fearless, which was more than she could say for Harry, that trembling blob. Was this the man who told her, "You let me deal with it. You just write your report"? Now he sat at his desk like one of those lifelike people statues. Harry could at least have chimed in with a "Yeah, that's right."

Danessa turned a glare on Josie that should have shriveled her soul. Fortunately, Josie had been rendered glare-resistant by her mother.

"Accurate!" Danessa said, in the voice God used when she was displeased. "You call that report accurate? It was a tissue of lies."

Josie pulled her eyes away from the long-dead bug around Danessa's neck. Amazing. She'd never heard anyone say "tissue of lies" when she meant "full of shit." Josie had to admit Danessa was magnificent in her rage. Her anger was a force of nature.

"I am Stephanie with Reichman-Brassard Public Relations. We have found numerous discrepancies in your report," the PR creature said. She pulled out a beige leather folder and handed a thick packet to Josie and Harry, along with six eight-by-ten glossies.

"My stores are not dirty," Danessa said. "My displays do not have fingerprints and my counters are not covered with half-eaten candy bars. You made that up."

"Our professional photos show no sign of fingerprints or debris," Stephanie said.

"Of course not," Josie said. "You cleaned the Lucite stands before you took the photos."

"Shut up!" Danessa said. Josie didn't know if she was speaking to her or to the pale PR creature.

"You're a jealous little nothing from Maplewood. Maplewood!" Danessa spat out the word. "I wouldn't let someone like you work for me, much less shop at my stores. You couldn't buy one of my purses without taking out a loan, but this thing"—she waved a talon at Harry—"allowed you to tell lies about me.

"And here's the worst lie: You said there was a rude saleswoman named Marina at my Plaza Venetia store."

"There was," Josie said.

"Liar! There is no Marina on my sales staff. I've never, ever employed anyone by that name. No one."

Danessa slammed her hand down on Harry's desk. A pork chop jumped into the air. Harry sat there, a speechless lump of meat. Did he think he was watching a reality TV show?

"That's the name the sales associate gave me," Josie said. "The woman wasn't wearing a name tag, but she was a tall blond Amazon who had what sounded like a Russian accent. This Marina was about six feet two inches tall and her straight blond hair was down past her shoulders. She wore black leather."

"No one by that description works at any of my stores."

Stephanie the PR person presented a printout as thick as a phone book to Danessa. Danessa threw it at Josie. She meant it to fall on the floor and fan out all over. Josie caught it in midfling.

"Here's the staff list," Danessa said. "Find her on there. Do you see any Russian names?"

Josie scanned the list, holding the printout with both hands to control the shaking. I'd like to walk out that door, she thought. But I have a daughter. I have to keep calm and keep this job for Amelia's sake.

"Well, there's Olga," Josie said. That name was as Russian as roulette.

"Olga is five feet two, weighs a hundred pounds and

has black hair. No one in her right mind would call her an Amazon."

Right. Olga like the composer.

The PR person produced a yellowed *Plaza Venetia Times*, open to an ad. It featured a photo of the shop's sales staff.

"That's me at our grand opening," Danessa said. "And that's Olga." She pointed to a pixielike brunette who barely came to Danessa's elbow. "See any blond Amazons in that store?"

"So you hired Marina later," Josie said. She checked the paper's date. "You've been at that location seven years. Retail staff comes and goes. The woman who told me her name was Marina lied. She's on that list. She's called something else."

Josie shrugged her shoulders and sent the tube top rolling downhill toward the fake tattoo. "The tall blonde I talked to had good reason to lie. She was rude to me. She probably thought I wanted her name so I could call your office with a complaint. So she gave me a false name."

Stephanie pulled out a packet of photos. "These are the pictures that we have with every employee application. We have not hired any sales associates over five ten."

"No one answering that description works at any of my stores," Danessa thundered, and the ceiling light fixtures swayed.

"I saw her. I talked with her," Josie shouted back. She was not afraid of anyone who had a trapped dead insect as a fashion accessory. Danessa had wasted good money to wear a prehistoric Roach Motel.

Danessa snapped her fingers. The PR person pulled out a copy of Josie's report to the Creshan Corporation. "This report says you were in my Plaza Venetia store between one thirty and two thirty in the afternoon, Josie Marcus. Here's the staff schedule for that date. You read it and tell me who worked that afternoon."

Danessa threw the schedule down on Harry's desk. Josie's boss backed away, as if it might bite him. Josie picked it up. It seemed authentic, right down to the thumbtack holes in the corners.

Josie read the neat boxes marking each day: "Olga: 10 to 5 PM Monday. Tuesday. Wednesday. Thursday. Friday. Noon to 10 PM. Saturday—Sunday Off." Someone named Tiffany worked ten to five p.m. Josie suspected Tiffany did not have a Russian accent.

"Olga worked afternoons all this week," Danessa said, "and she'll swear that in court. There was no Marina. You were never in my store. You made up that evaluation. I have the proof."

Josie could be fired for a fraudulent report. She would be blacklisted in her profession. She felt like she was standing on the edge of a cliff while the ground fell away under her.

"You made up this Marina," Danessa said. "Who paid you to ruin me? Who bribed you?"

"No one," Josie said. "Don't you dare say I've been bribed. Ever. My reputation is impeccable."

It was Danessa's turn to stare. Josie bet she didn't often hear someone in a WHITE TRASH tube top say "impeccable."

Josie waited for Harry to say she was a model employee, but he was silent as a side of beef.

The pale PR person pulled at her too-long beige sleeves.

"My report was the truth." Josie was so frightened and angry, her words came out at half speed. "Your display stands were gray with fingerprints. There was a chunk of chewed bubble gum on one. It was pink, for your information. And your staff was rude. Just like you.

"As for your so-called proof, anyone can create a schedule in a computer. You can deny that Marina exists. You can also bribe Olga to say what you want."

Danessa pointed an exquisitely painted nail at Josie's eye. "You listen to me. You retract that report or I'll sue you so fast you'll never afford another rhinestone. You got that?"

"Never!" Josie said, like the heroine in a melodrama. "I'll retract my report over your dead body."

She shouted her noble words to Danessa's back. The businesswoman stalked out, the PR person trailing behind her. Josie wondered what kind of positive spin Stephanie could put on this encounter. St. Louis's sweetheart had a temper like a rabid mud wrestler.

There was an awkward silence, then everyone in the Suttin offices began talking nervously.

Harry cleared his throat and searched his desk for his pork chop. "Well, glad that's over. You handled it pretty well, Josie, but I think I'd better put you on unpaid leave for your protection." He began gnawing nervously on the cold pork chop.

All that bacon had turned Harry into a swine, Josie thought. She wasn't going to let Danessa destroy her reputation and take her job. She was not going on leave, paid or unpaid. Harry was a coward and a bully. Josie knew how to deal with him. She had to bully him right back.

"Listen here, Harry," Josie said. "I did a proper report. I told you it might be a problem before I turned it in. I warned you Danessa wouldn't be happy. I have that all on tape. And what did you say? 'Let 'er rip.'

"Well, it ripped. You put me on unpaid leave now and I'll sue you for unlawful termination and endangering the welfare of a minor child under Section 131-B of the 1996 Federal Female Employment Code. I'm a single mother, remember. It's double indemnity."

Harry gulped, but not because he was chewing on the pork chop.

"Let's not be hasty, Josie," he said. Sweat broke out on his low, hairy forehead. He'd been threatened with two lawsuits in two minutes. "I was trying to work out a reasonable solution. I can't have you shopping at our high-fashion stores until this problem is resolved."

"Fine," Josie said. She was happy to forgo pantyhose and toe-pinching shoes for a while. "Send me apartment shopping. I can do discount stores or restaurants. I'm good at restaurants. You've never had any complaints on my restaurant work."

Harry looked relieved. "Well, I guess you can do our Fifty Is Nifty promotion at Pleasin' Pizza. But you'll have to front the fifty-dollar reward money. It's going to cost you two hundred a day minimum, and the Pleasin' Pizza people are slow to reimburse. You won't get your cash back for six to eight weeks."

"I'll take the job." Josie grabbed the assignment sheet from his greasy fingers. Harry was chomping the pork chop like a toddler with a teething ring.

She started to breathe easier. She was going to walk out of the office with her job. That was a minor miracle after the scene with Danessa and her spineless boss.

She hoped Harry didn't check out her threat. There was no such thing as the Federal Female Employment Code. She'd made up all that stuff. The year, 1996, was Amelia's birth year. As for Section 131-B, with any luck Harry wouldn't realize Josie lived at 131 Phelan Street, Apartment B. She hoped he never asked for the tape. It didn't exist, either.

Josie was almost out the door when he said, "One more thing." His voice was hard now. Josie looked into his small, porcine eyes.

"If you want to keep your job, you better find that Marina woman," Harry said. "Because if it turns out that Amazon with the Russian accent doesn't exist, you'll never work again."

Josie yanked up her tube top and walked out.

Chapter 6

A cheap tart. A liar. A bribe taker.

Danessa had called Josie all those things, had accused her of deceit and corruption, while Harry cowered with his pork chop. Her pig of a boss didn't say one word in Josie's defense. He let Danessa verbally beat her up.

Josie marched across the hot pavement with short, furious strides, her cheap red shoes sinking into the melting blacktop.

She yanked her car door open and broke a fingernail. The seat burned her bare legs, but it was no match for her flaming anger. Josie cranked the engine and started to peel out of the parking lot. She wanted to be away from Suttin Services as soon as possible.

Danessa had insulted her character, her integrity, even her home. What had she called Josie?

Oh, yeah, a "jealous little nothing from Maplewood." Josie slammed on the brakes and skidded across the lot. Maplewood. Danessa knew where Josie lived. She knew her name, too. She'd said, "This report says you were in my Plaza Venetia store . . . Josie Marcus."

Even the client wasn't supposed to know the name of the mystery shopper. That was confidential, for Josie's protection. But someone gave Danessa her name and told her where Josie lived.

Josie knew who did it, too: Her scumbag boss. Danessa—or her lawyers—had applied a little pressure and Harry had cracked like an egg. He'd sold her out.

She couldn't complain to Harry's boss at headquarters. She was cheap help, easily replaced.

Josie was shaking so badly she was afraid to drive. Deep breaths, she told herself. Take deep breaths. You can't help your daughter if you're arrested for road rage. Josie checked her watch. It was two thirty. She'd never make it to the school by three to pick up Amelia. She took out her cell phone.

"Hello, Mom. I got called into the office unexpectedly. Can you pick up the kid?"

"Office? You never go into the office. There's trouble, isn't there? It's Danessa." Josie's mother had an irritating way of being right. "There's a big stink over your report, isn't there? You slammed poor Danessa."

"Mom, poor Danessa just tried to get me fired," Josie said.

"Good!" her mother said. "I told you not to attack her, but you didn't listen to me. Since this problem is your fault, I'll pick up my granddaughter on one condition. You have to go out with Stan. He stopped by today to look at the air conditioner and asked if you'd be interested in a date."

Ha, Josie thought. He wasn't looking at the air conditioner. He was hoping her tube top would roll down again. Too bad he didn't make anything move for her. Stan was a friend, not a lover. Everyone but her mother could see that.

"Mom, that's blackmail."

"It's for your own good, Josie. Now, am I going to pick up Amelia or not? It's two thirty-five. At three fifteen, she goes into the extended school day. That will cost you an extra twenty-five dollars. Don't expect me to pay it."

Twenty-five bucks would make a serious dent in Josie's pay.

"You wouldn't leave your own granddaughter stranded in after-school playtime." Amelia would be mortified. She knew it was mostly for the work orphans, the kids who'd been abandoned by their ambitious parents. Poor

Amelia wouldn't even have the comfort of a parent who was a high-profile lawyer or doctor. Her parent checked out chicken franchises.

"If it meant giving her a future, I would," Jane said.

Josie wished she had a video screen on her phone so she could see her mother's face. If Jane's jaw was set in that bulldog line, nothing would change her mind.

"Stan has a steady job at the VA hospital. He would make a good husband," Jane said.

"So marry him, Mom."

Stan would make a terrific husband for a woman of sixty-eight. He drove twenty in a thirty-mile zone. He saved his pennies in a Mason jar on his dresser. He clipped coupons and shopped for the best values. He'd once talked to Josie for twenty minutes about paper towels, detailing the differences in price versus absorbency.

"What's it gonna be, Josie? This is for your own good." Josie saw her daughter languishing in the extended-day play class.

"Okay, Mom, I'll go out with Stan." I just won't say when, Josie thought.

"Good. I'll tell him you'll go out with him Thursday night. I'll call him before I pick up Amelia."

Josie was trapped as surely as the dragonfly around Danessa's neck. The date with Stan would last aeons.

She sat stalled in traffic, nearly suffocated by General Cheeps fumes. She'd left the chicken in the hot car when she'd had her run-in with Danessa. Josie thought she could hear the salmonella spawning in the buckets. She knew the food wasn't safe to serve for dinner anymore. She'd have to throw it all out. There wasn't a General Cheeps on her route home. Josie would have to stop somewhere and pick up dinner. She sure wasn't cooking after the day she'd had.

It was another hour before Josie made it home. She arrived, hot and frazzled, with an armful of fries and burgers.

"I like onions and ketchup on mine—no pickles," Amelia said.

"I remembered," Josie said.

"Did you remember the vegetables?" Jane said.

Josie tossed a pile of ketchup packets on the kitchen table. "Here you go, Mom. President Reagan said ketchup was a vegetable. If it's good enough for the president, it should be good enough for you."

After that declaration of war, Josie knew it was only a matter of time before she and her mother engaged in battle. She longed for a bubble bath, a good book and a margarita. She knew there wasn't a chance for any of them.

At least Josie had time to shower and change into jeans and a plain white shirt. She buttoned it higher than usual after her day of wrestling with the tube top. The evening settled into an uneasy quiet while Josie helped Amelia with her homework at the kitchen table. Amelia worked on perfecting her cursive writing.

"So what do you think, Mom?" Her daughter proudly showed her a page. "Does it look grown-up?"

"Your writing is so much better than mine. You don't have your mother's chicken scratches."

Josie admired the faint cinnamon sprinkle of freckles across her daughter's nose and her straight black hair. Amelia hated her own nose. She thought it was too big, but Josie knew it would give her daughter's face character. Josie's nose was a hopeless pug. The nicest thing anyone ever called it was cute.

Tonight, Amelia's slightly slanted hazel eyes were worried. She knew there was a fight brewing between her mother and her grandmother.

"Amelia, you know that your grandmother and I love each other. But you can love someone and still disagree with them sometimes."

"It's your mystery-shopping job, isn't it?" Amelia said. "Grandma says she still has some pull at the bank. You'd have a pension and benefits."

Josie could feel the walls close in on her. Her mother had worked at the same job, worn the same navy suits and eaten the same tuna-salad lunch for twenty years. Josie couldn't do it. She couldn't sit at a desk all day.

"The bank was a good place for Grandma, but not for me."

"A mystery shopper is a sweet job, Mom," Amelia said. "Emma thinks so, too."

Emma was her best friend at Barrington.

"Thanks," Josie said. "You're sweet, too." She kissed her daughter's forehead.

"You're not using it right," Amelia said. Slang had strict rules at age nine. "Can I call Emma, Mom, before it gets too late?"

"Go ahead."

Amelia raced to her room, dodging Jane in the kitchen doorway. Josie's mother had her arms folded defensively across her chest. She was still angry. Josie noticed her mother's gray hair had a yellow cast and straggled down her neck. Jane hadn't made her weekly visit to the beauty shop.

"Are you really going to get fired?" Jane said.

"I don't know, Mom. Danessa said I lied on her report."

"And did you?"

Josie was hurt. "How can you say that?"

"Because I know how much you resent Danessa. You're jealous of her."

"I don't resent her." Right now, Josie burned with resentment for what Danessa had said and done to her, but she hadn't when she wrote that report. "Her stores were a mess, Mom, and I said so. Harry told me to tell the truth and I did. Then that coward hung me out to dry. He sat there while Danessa screamed at me. So, yes, I may get fired."

"I never did like that man," Jane said. "He's low-class." That was her mother's worst insult. "But so much of what you do in that job is low-class. Look how you left the house yesterday. Mrs. Mueller saw you. She mentioned your outfit to me. She said it wasn't decent for a woman your age to dress like that."

"She's the worst busybody on the block," Josie said. "She's disappointed that I don't have any boyfriends who stay overnight. Then she'd really have something to disapprove of."

"She's concerned," Jane said. "We don't have many women of her caliber in this neighborhood. She's president of the St. Philomena Sodality. She's an important person, Josie. Lived here forty years. She cares about this neighborhood. Of course she's worried when one of her neighbors dresses like a prostitute."

"A what? I'm a hooker because I wore a tube top? And you sat there and let her say that?" First her boss, then her mother.

"I most certainly did not, Josie Marcus. I told her you were in a play. But I hope you do get fired. Maybe then you'll get a decent job. You could have worked your way up to vice president at the bank by now. You're so smart." Josie could see the tears in her mother's eyes. She didn't want to hurt Jane. She just couldn't live her mother's life.

"GBH, Mom," Josie said.

Her mother submitted stiffly to a hug.

"Josie, I never doubted you," Jane said. "I just want a better life for you."

What all mothers want, Josie thought. Including me. But tonight Jane's love felt like a smothering blanket. "Mom, we're out of milk. I'm going to run to the store, maybe go for a drive. Amelia's in her room talking on the phone with Emma."

"I'll keep an eye on her. She can watch TV with me," Jane said.

"Thanks, Mom," Josie said and kissed her again.

She stopped by her daughter's room. "Amelia, it's a school night. You have to be in bed by nine o'clock. Start your bath by eight thirty if I'm not back."

"Why do I have to take a bath at eight thirty?" Oh, God. Amelia looked just like her grandmother when she put her jaw in that locked-down pout.

"Because I'm the mom; you're the kid."

Josie stopped, too horrified to continue. Another mother phrase had slipped out of her mouth. She fled in the middle of Amelia's "Oh, Mooom."

Josie drove in circles, worrying about her life, her daughter and her job. Love is fear, she decided. Her love for Amelia was a different kind of love than what she'd had for Nathan, her child's father. That was over. Josie hoped someday to feel that same wild love again. But she could live without it.

But if anything happened to Amelia, Josie would feel an emptiness she couldn't fill ever, no matter how many other children she had. When she became a mother, she gave birth to a whole new crop of fears, some rational, some irrational.

Josie was afraid she'd say or do something that would screw up her daughter's life forever. She was worried she'd die and Amelia would be raised by her mother and turn into a little old lady. She was afraid Amelia would get some dread disease, like cancer or leukemia.

Those were rational fears. Well, fairly rational.

Then there were the irrational fears. When Josie saw someone arguing about stamps at the post office, she started looking for places to hide Amelia, in case the fight went postal.

When Amelia rode the big roller coaster at Six Flags, Josie stayed on the ground, wringing her hands, afraid the track would break and her daughter would fall to her death.

When Amelia went to a swimming party at Emma's, Josie had visions of her daughter dead on the bottom of the pool.

When Amelia crossed the street alone, Josie saw cars rushing to run over her, kidnappers waiting in dark vans, gangbangers racing around the corner, spraying bullets.

It was ridiculous, she told herself. It was irrational.

But these tragedies had happened to other parents, ordinary people like her.

Every time Josie heard sirens on her street, her heart stopped. She knew the police were coming to tell her something bad had happened to Amelia.

Josie fought those worries, because she wanted her daughter to be happy and normal. I'm doing a fine job of being a mother, driving all over St. Louis, she thought.

Josie looked at the dashboard clock. It was nine forty-five p.m. She'd been driving aimlessly for two hours. Or maybe it wasn't so aimless. She found herself at Plaza Venetia.

I need to get back home to Amelia. I am a woman with responsibilities. But Mom's watching her and Amelia is in bed by now.

Josie remembered there was a chocolate shop on the mall's second floor, the Queen of Chocolate. She wasn't going to get that hot bath and margarita tonight. She deserved a chunk of dark chocolate.

The shop drew Josie like a magnet. She could smell its rich perfume two stores away. She bought three ounces of dark chocolate for herself and a milk chocolate dog for Amelia, who loved canines in any form. Her mother liked white chocolate, which Josie considered unnatural. But she got Jane a strawberry dipped in white chocolate.

"Thank you for shopping with us," the woman behind the chocolate counter said. Her name tag said she was Libby.

Josie would have given Libby an excellent rating if she was mystery-shopping this store. She was polite, helpful and attentive.

Josie had left home without a dime, so she put her purchase on a credit card. Ten bucks for chocolate, she thought. One more bill I can't pay.

"You look tired," Libby the Chocolate Lady said. "I am, too. I've been here since noon."

"It has been a long day," Josie said. "And yours isn't over yet."

The chocolate-shop bell rang and a stampede of customers rushed in. Josie picked up her purchases and left.

Right across from the chocolate shop was the Danessa store. Maybe Marina was working a ten-hour shift, too. Maybe Josie could verify that the Russian giant really was there. She went into Danessa's.

The store was absolutely quiet.

"Hello?" Josie said. "Anyone here?"

No one answered. As usual, she thought. She wished Harry could see the store now. No salesperson greeted her, just like in her report.

But there had been major changes since Josie's visit to the store yesterday. Now the Lucite stands were gleaming. The pink lump of gum was gone. The basket of autographed photos was replenished.

"Hello?" Josie said again. No one answered. Josie checked her watch.

The store closed in three minutes. The salesperson must be busy in the back room.

Josie wanted to go back there, but decided against it. After her fight with Danessa, she could be accused of shoplifting or vandalism. She should get out of the store.

Might as well take an autographed photo of Danessa as a peace offering for Mom, she thought, and stuffed one in her purse.

Then she took a second Danessa photo. For her dartboard.

Chapter 7

"Josie, wake up."

"Huh, what? What time is it, Mom?"

"Six a.m."

Josie groaned and rolled over in bed. She hadn't fallen asleep until three in the morning. She felt like she'd spent the night on a park bench. Jane had obviously showered, dressed and had her coffee. She was indecently alert.

Her mother flipped on the overhead bedroom light. It was like a searchlight in Josie's eyes. She winced and threw the covers over her head.

"Go away, Mom. I don't have to get up until seven."

This was what it was like to get Amelia up in the morning. Josie was regressing.

"Mom, why are you breaking into my bedroom?"

Thank God I wore a T-shirt to bed, she thought. The last time her mother had caught Josie sleeping naked, she had to listen to the "What if there's a fire?" lecture. Her mother had said, "Suppose this place goes up in flames and the firemen see you naked, Josie?"

"Then I'll get rescued first, Mom," she'd said.

Too bad there hadn't been any lectures called, "What are you doing with a naked man in your bed?" Josie couldn't remember the last time she'd spent the night with a man. It wasn't likely to happen anytime soon— even if she could get Amelia out of the house for a weekend. Not with her mother bursting into her bedroom.

"Wake up," Jane said. "We have an emergency."

Josie sat straight up. "Where's Amelia? What happened? What is it? A terrorist attack?"

"Your daughter is asleep," Jane said. "Your problems are a lot closer to home than terrorists. Danessa is dead. And so is Serge, her boyfriend. I saw it on TV. The cops are going to come looking for you after that fight you had with her yesterday."

"What? What do you mean dead? Both of them? How dead?"

"Very," Jane said.

"I mean, how did they die?" Josie said. Her mother flipped on the bedroom TV and cranked up the volume. The sound exploded like a dynamite blast. "ST. LOUIS POWER COUPLE MURDERED," the announcer shouted.

Josie leaped out of bed and turned the TV down to a level that didn't crack the plaster. "Shhh. You'll wake Amelia," she said.

Footage of Serge and Danessa at some society event at the Ritz flashed on the screen. Danessa glittered. Serge glowed. They belonged together, a super couple who lived in a rarefied world. They were taller, thinner and better dressed than ordinary mortals. Danessa waved to the bystanders as if they were peasants lining up to see the city's princess.

Next Josie found herself staring at morning show anchor John Pertzborn on Fox 2 News. John was one man Josie could stand this early—but only at a distance, on the tube.

"Danessa Celedine, thirty-one, and Serge Orloff, forty-two, were murdered last night," John P. said. He looked seriously sincere. "The St. Louis couple were found dead within an hour of each other."

Josie listened, but it was hard to wrap her mind around the words. Danessa was dead. That was good, wasn't it? A dead person couldn't sue her. A dead person couldn't take her job.

She should be ashamed of those thoughts, but little scenes from that nasty fight had replayed in her head all night: Harry's pork chop jumping in the air. Danessa's nail pointed at her eye. Danessa's threats aimed at her career. Harry's revolting passivity.

Josie had been so angry, she'd put Danessa's photo on the dartboard on the bedroom door. She stuck it to the cork with a dart through Danessa's forehead.

It didn't help. Josie still felt Danessa's own darts, when she'd called her a liar, a slut and a bribe taker and declared Josie unfit to work at her store. Oddly, the one that hurt the worst was when Danessa said Josie would need a loan to buy one of her purses.

Probably because that charge was true.

About midnight, Josie had decided it was time to quit hurting herself and start hurting Danessa. She began thinking of ways to kill Danessa. It beat counting sheep.

First, Josie pushed Danessa off a cliff. Then she pushed her under a bus.

She stabbed Danessa with her own witchy black stiletto heels. Then she strangled her with that dead dragonfly necklace.

She kidnapped Danessa and made her wear a pink polyester pantsuit until she died of shame.

She spent an hour deciding whether to shoot Danessa neatly with a .22 or blow her to hamburger with a .357 Magnum.

By two o'clock, she'd decided not to shoot Danessa after all. Josie wanted the personal satisfaction of a hands-on death. Danessa should die slowly and painfully.

Josie fell asleep sometime around three a.m., as she was force-feeding Danessa buckets of General Cheeps chicken. Danessa had been strong-armed into a tube top and tube socks.

Now Danessa was really dead. Yesterday Josie would have howled in gleeful triumph. Today, confronted with the actual fact, she was dazed, numbed and curiously flattened. Under the numbness, she felt fear. It was a faint fear, a tiny smoldering fear fire, but Josie knew it would soon be raging out of control.

John P. was still talking on the TV. "Danessa Celedine was found dead in the stockroom of her upscale Plaza Venetia store last night," he said.

We had our fight at the office that afternoon, Josie thought. Omigod. Mom's right. I could be the chief suspect.

The tendrils of panic smoke burst into little flames. Josie tried to tamp them down. You don't know how Danessa died yet, she told herself. Danessa could have been mugged, carjacked or shot by a jealous lover. The police may already have a suspect in custody.

"The police officials have not released the cause of the deaths, pending the autopsies," John P. said.

Now an important-looking police officer was talking to a horde of reporters shouting questions. "Were both murders committed by the same person?" a hair-sprayed man asked.

"I can't comment on that at present," the police official said.

"Do you have any suspects for these murders that rocked the city?" a hair-sprayed woman asked.

"No comment," the cop said.

They're going to get me, Josie thought. I'll wind up in prison. Amelia will be raised by my mother. She'll wear pajamas to bed and eat soy burgers and work at the bank. I'll see her on visiting day once a month.

"Josie, are you watching this, or are you staring into space?" her mother said.

Josie turned back to the TV and John Pertzborn's report. "In a bizarre twist, Serge Orloff was found dead at the couple's palatial West County home at eleven thirty last night, when homicide detectives arrived to inform him of Danessa's death. The Russian-born Orloff was Danessa's longtime companion."

The tape showed a small herd of police, plain clothes and uniform, standing around looking serious. The brass preened for the TV cameras. Yellow crime-scene tape swayed in the wind. Two uniformed attendants opened massive dark wood doors and wheeled a gurney down the stone stairs. The black body-bagged mound on the gurney was not as big as Josie expected.

Serge Orloff had been larger in life.

The camera pulled back to show Serge and Danessa's home. It was a palace. Actually, it looked like it had been put together from palace spare parts. There were turrets, balconies, bay windows, Spanish tiles and French doors.

John P. looked so earnestly at his TV audience that Josie was glad she was wearing a T-shirt. He said, "The body of Danessa Celedine was found at ten thirty p.m. when a security guard noted that the shop's doors had not been locked after the mall closed for the evening."

Ten thirty? That's less than half an hour after I left the shop, Josie thought. The fear fire was building again.

I wonder if Danessa was already dead when I was in her store. My God, her body was probably in the back room when I was grabbing photos. I left my fingerprints on the counter. Josie felt hot with terror.

It's not that bad, she thought. The store was empty. No one was inside. No one saw me in that store.

Except Libby the Chocolate Lady. Smart, alert Libby. She would probably remember the conversation they'd had about Josie's long day.

Josie had had other conversations that day, and they were even more memorable. Dozens of people had heard her yelling at Danessa. She'd had the fight in the Suttin office in front of countless witnesses.

Her porky boss had tried to dump Josie at the first threat of a lawsuit. He'd do everything possible to save his bacon if Josie was involved in a murder.

Once again Mom was right, Josie thought. The Danessa job was a disaster. I didn't fight with Danessa. I threatened her. I told her I'd retract that report over her dead body.

On TV, Danessa's body was being wheeled out of Plaza

Venetia. She was wearing black this time, too. It was full length and zipped up the front, but no one would call a body bag elegant.

Josie's fear fire burst into a raging conflagration. It raced through her gut and melted her bones. She ran for the bathroom and began a hot, ugly retching.

"Josie!" Her mother pounded on the door. "Are you okay?"

"I'm fine, Mom," Josie said, her arms wrapped around the commode.

"You're not pregnant, are you?" Jane said.

"If I am, it's an immaculate conception, Mom."

"That's not funny, Josie."

"You're telling me, Mom."

Josie tried to wash the bitter taste out of her mouth. She felt clammy and sick. She was leaning against the bathroom wall when she heard John P. say on the TV, "A special police task force has been formed to investigate the murders."

The doorbell rang.

"It's six ten in the morning. Who'd visit us at this hour?" Josie asked.

"I'll get it," Amelia shouted. They could hear her bare feet on the living room floor.

"Wait!" her mother and grandmother cried.

Both women charged for the front door. But they were too slow. Amelia came running back, her eyes as shiny as Christmas morning.

"Mom, Homicide's here to see you."

Chapter 8

"Josie Marcus?"

She nodded. She was too scared to talk. Her mother stood next to her, wringing her hands. Amelia was dancing on the sidelines in her robe and slippers.

The homicide detectives flashed their badges. Their ID looked more fake than the cops' badges on TV.

The two homicide detectives were a before and after picture. Detective George Waxley wore a lumpy suit he could have borrowed from Stan next door. His tie was fat and striped. Waxley blinked a lot, as if his contacts didn't fit right. His dome was shiny bald and almost square, but he had a wreath of wispy hair from his ears down. Josie wanted to shave it off.

Waxley wore no wedding band.

Detective Michael Yawney had a better tailor and looked like Matt Dillon. He had Oakley sunglasses and a wedding ring. Naturally.

Why am I looking at wedding bands when I'm about to be arrested? Josie thought.

"We'd like to ask you a few questions," the handsome Detective Yawney said.

"About what?" Josie's mom stepped between them, fierce as a lioness guarding her cub. "If this is about the murders of Danessa and Serge, my daughter was here with me the entire evening."

Great, Josie thought. Mom was lying to the detectives in front of Amelia.

"How do you know we want to talk to your daughter about the murders?" Waxley the semibald cop said. Josie was even more scared now. That big square head held plenty of brains.

"Mom," Josie said, "why don't you help Amelia get dressed for school while I talk to the detectives?"

"Why don't you get dressed first so you aren't talking to strange men while you're wearing a T-shirt?" her mother said.

Josie realized the only thing she had on was a T-shirt that said, SUPPORT YOUR RIGHT TO ARM BEARS. Did that make her look violent—or just deranged?

"We'll have to check her room first," Detective Yawney said.

"What for?" Josie's mom said. Her mouth tightened into a belligerent line and her fists were clenched. Josie didn't know whether to hug her or haul her out of there.

"It's just a precaution," the detective said. "For possible weapons."

Amelia was staring openmouthed at her mother, as if she'd transformed herself into Thelma *and* Louise.

"This is an outrage," Jane said. She looked as if she was about to start swinging at the detectives.

"Mom, let them search the room. I'll put on some clothes and then we'll talk."

"You first," Detective Yawney said. Josie hoped the T-shirt kept her decent. If these guys ever left, she was going to switch to flannel nightgowns. No, pajamas with feet.

Yawney made her stand outside in the hall while he checked her bedroom. She could hear him opening her dresser drawers and the closet door.

"What do you want to wear?" he said.

"I'll come in and get it," she said.

"I'll hand it to you and you can change in the bathroom," he said.

Josie was suddenly, furiously angry. Who was this man invading her home, inspecting her bedroom, checking her dresser drawers? She'd done nothing wrong. She was a working mom.

Don't get angry, she thought. Your daughter is here. It won't help her and it won't help you.

"My jeans are on the chair by the bed," she said.

There was a pause. Was Yawney turning out the pockets? The detective handed Josie her jeans. They were wrinkled.

"My shoes are on the floor by the bed."

He handed those out next.

"I can't think of anything else," Josie said.

"A bra," her mother shouted, and Josie blushed scarlet.

"My blouse and bra are hanging on the bedroom doorknob," Josie said, then remembered what else was on that door. "No! Wait! I don't need it."

"Yes, you do," Jane shouted.

Detective Yawney handed Josie an embarrassingly padded bra and her white shirt from last night. He gave her the clothes without comment. Maybe he didn't see the dartboard.

"Bathroom clear," Detective Waxley said.

"You were in my bathroom?" Josie said.

"We have to check it out so you can get dressed in there," he said.

Josie hated that. The bathroom was her one refuge in the house. The lock on the door kept out Jane. Even her daughter wasn't allowed in. Amelia had her own bath down the hall.

Josie had turned the big old clawfoot tub into a luxurious retreat, with lavender-scented bubble bath, vanilla candles, an inflatable pillow and a reading rack. The bath's pink-and-black tile was so old it had been in and out of style a dozen times. The ceiling sloped down, so she had to duck to get into the tub. Josie didn't care. This was her private space.

Now the detective had pulled back her shower curtain, left his big footprint on her pink rug and looked in her medicine cabinet. Her room would never be the same. It had been invaded.

Josie closed and locked the bathroom door. Then she threw on the jeans and blouse she wore last night, which didn't look too fresh today. She could smell Detective Yawney's spicy aftershave where he'd touched her clothes. She promised herself she'd throw them out after he left.

Still, she felt more dignified with her clothes on. She slipped on her shoes, raked a comb through her hair, washed her face and ran to the living room. Her mother handed Josie a bright yellow mug of coffee.

"Thanks, Mom," Josie said. Tears wobbled on the edge of her voice. Suddenly she was scared.

"GBH," her mother said softly. Jane pointedly did not offer any coffee to the detectives. Josie appreciated her mother's loyalty, but she didn't think it was a good idea to offend the police.

"Would you like some coffee, detectives?" Josie said.

"No," they said, so quickly Josie wondered if Danessa and Serge had been poisoned.

Josie didn't drink her coffee. She just held the bright mug in her hands. She needed to feel something warm and comforting. Jane hovered anxiously nearby. She refused to leave Josie's side. Amelia was hanging around the kitchen door taking in every word while pretending to fix herself breakfast.

The detectives' questions were easy at first.

"How did you know Serge Orloff?" Waxley asked.

Josie thought carefully before she answered. She was not fooled by his cheap suit. It would not do to underestimate him.

"I didn't," she said. "I never met him. I didn't know where he lived."

"West County, it said on TV," her mother added helpfully.

"We'd prefer to conduct this interview, Mrs. Marcus, unless you'd rather we talked with Josie down at headquarters," the detective said.

Good thing the detective was bald already. Jane's glare would have scorched his dome clean.

"Mom, I'm fine," Josie said. "Will you take care of Amelia?"

Jane grabbed her granddaughter away from the storm troopers. "Come along, Amelia. Grandma will pack your lunch for school."

In the kitchen, Jane slammed the cabinet doors several times in protest. Then she must have realized she couldn't hear them talking if she made noise. After that, Jane fluttered silently in the background. Josie glanced back once at her daughter. Amelia was no longer bouncing with excitement. She looked big-eyed with fright.

I've brought this on my daughter with my stubbornness, Josie thought. Then she didn't have time to worry about Amelia or her mother. The easy questions were over. Now the detectives were bombarding her with questions that had to be answered carefully. She concentrated on each word.

"Tell us about the argument over your report." That was Detective Waxley, the sly, balding one.

Josie did. The police would move quickly on a high-profile investigation. They already had copies of the report. She figured they'd rousted her boss, Harry, and he'd told them about the fight. She might as well be straight with them.

"How long have you known the victim, Danessa Celedine?" the handsome Yawney said.

"Was this your first encounter with the victim or have you had prior dealings with her?" Yawney again.

"Where did you go when you left the Danessa store?" Waxley looked deceptively sympathetic, a kindly teacher asking after her progress.

"Give us a detailed account of your whereabouts during the time frame from when you left the store at Plaza Venetia yesterday until the victim's body was discovered," Detective Yawney said.

That was the tough one. Josie squeezed her coffee for

the last warmth, but there was no comfort. The mug was cool.

Should I tell them that I was at Plaza Venetia again last night? They're going to find out anyway, she decided. The chocolate lady probably saw me go into Danessa's store. And I bought the candy with a credit card. That would give the police the time I was there.

"I went out for milk about eight o'clock last night," she said.

"Mo-o-om," Amelia said, "where's the milk?"

"Have a Pop-Tart," Jane said in a stage whisper.

"But, Grandma, you always say I need to eat a healthy breakfast," Amelia said. "You tell me to start my day with oatmeal and milk."

"Go upstairs to Grandma's apartment and I'll fix it for you," Jane said. "I have milk."

"Didn't Mom buy milk last night?" Amelia said. "She said that's where she was going."

"Upstairs!" Jane hissed.

Amelia stomped up the steps, whining, "I'm trying to do the right thing and this is the thanks I get."

Josie stared straight ahead, trapped and panicked, wondering what to say next.

"You went out for milk," Detective Yawney prompted.

"But I didn't buy any," Josie said. "I was distracted and tired. Instead I drove around for about an hour and forty-five minutes. Then I found myself at Plaza Venetia. I treated myself to some chocolate at that little shop on the second floor—the Queen of Chocolate. I bought some for Amelia, and my mom. Then I went across to the Danessa store and got Mom an autographed photo. She's a big fan. She'd strangle me if I didn't come home with a photo of her idol."

Detective Yawney's perfectly arched left eyebrow jumped when she said that.

"Why didn't you get a photo while you were there as a mystery shopper?" he said.

"Because they were out of photos. I put that in my

report. I'd had a fight with my mom after dinner last night. The photo was a peace offering."

"You've had a lot of fights lately," Yawney said.

"It was a bad day," Josie said.

"What did you fight about with your mother?"

"My mom doesn't think being a mystery shopper is a good career for me. I went for a drive to cool off. I called her from the mall about ten o'clock last night to check on Amelia. I told my mom I'd lost track of the time and I was on my way home."

"What do you know about a red snakeskin belt?" Detective Waxley said.

"The twenty-seven-hundred-dollar one?" Josie said.

Waxley nodded. Now he wasn't blinking like a guy with bad contacts. His eyes bored into her and they were scary.

Why would the police care about that belt? Josie wondered. Had it been stolen? She tried to remember if it had been on display last night, but she couldn't.

"When I mystery-shopped the store yesterday morning, the snakeskin belt was on a Lucite display stand. I tried on the belt and asked the salesperson, Marina, some questions about it."

"Can you describe this Marina?"

Josie did.

"According to the people at your office, the victim said there was no one who looked like that working at any Danessa store."

"Believe me, I wouldn't make up a six-feet-two blonde with a Russian accent." Josie laughed. The cops did not. Her nervous laughter strangled in her throat and died. Josie shivered and clung to her cold coffee cup.

"Can we send a technician to take your fingerprints?" Detective Waxley asked.

"Sure," Josie said. "But if you're taking fingerprints at the Plaza Venetia store, you should know that it didn't look the way it did in my mystery-shopper report. I wrote that the store was a mess, and it was. Fingerprints were all over the place, especially the display stands. One even had pink bubble gum stuck on it. But when I went back at ten last night, the shop had been cleaned. All the stands had been wiped down."

Detective Waxley said nothing.

"I don't know if that makes a difference," Josie said. Her words trailed off lamely.

Shut up! Josie told herself. You're babbling. The three of them sat in a deafening silence, until the handsome detective spoke.

"One more thing," Detective Yawney said. "We'd like to photograph your dartboard."

Chapter 9

"Mommy, are you going to jail?"

Josie gathered her daughter into her arms, saw the cinnamon sprinkle of freckles on her nose and felt her heart break.

"No, no, no," she crooned as she rocked the sturdy little body. "Nothing like that. They wanted to ask me some questions because I talked to Danessa, the lady who died."

"But they said you had a fight with her," Amelia said. "And then she got murdered."

"So? I had a fight with your grandma, too, and she looks pretty healthy. I haven't killed her."

"So the police won't put you in jail?" Amelia would not be put off with Josie's jokes. She wanted a proper answer.

Jane charged into the conversation. "Don't even think such a thing, Amelia. Don't say it. Don't talk to anyone about the police being here. Don't tell your teachers, your friends at school or the neighbors. Don't tell anyone, understand?" Jane's arms were stiffly at her sides, her hands balled into angry fists.

Maybe I should have said I haven't killed Grandma *yet,* Josie thought. Poor Jane. You could count on her to come out fighting. It was her greatest virtue and her worst fault.

Now Amelia needed more serious soothing. Each

"don't" from her grandmother made her more anxious. Amelia's eyes were clouded with fear.

Josie held her daughter closer, smoothed her hair and smelled her little-girl fragrance. "Amelia," she said, "it's going to be all right. I did not hurt Danessa. I'm not saying that to make you feel better. This is a pinky swear."

Josie crooked her little finger. Amelia crooked hers. They shook solemnly. Pinky swears were sacred. You couldn't lie when you locked little fingers.

"I know you have a bunch of questions, but I don't want you late for school," Josie said. "We'll talk in the car, okay? Go get dressed."

Josie waited until Amelia was in her room with her radio turned up to a level that should have had Josie banging on the door. For once, she was grateful it was so loud.

Jane's hands were no longer balled into fists. Now she was wringing them again. "Josie, I'm sure Mrs. Mueller saw those police detectives. Her curtains are twitching. I'll call her right now and tell her the police came to you because you have information about an important case."

Jane could show a White House spin doctor how to put the best face on a disaster. By the time Jane finished her call, Mrs. Mueller would think Josie was the lead detective on the Danessa murder.

"Oh, Mom," Josie said. "Do you have to make a career of lying to the neighbors?"

"That's not a lie," Jane said, her bulldog jaw thrust forward. "You did have important information."

"Mom, why are you sucking up to that old gossip?" Josie said.

"I'm not sucking up," her mother said. "I'm trying to save your reputation."

"Right. That's why you told her I was a widow. I bet she's been down at the county license bureau, checking the marriage licenses."

"Won't do her any good," Jane said smugly. "I said

you got married on the beach in the Caribbean, but I never told her which island."

"Mom, who cares anymore if I was married or not?"

"I do," her mother said. "While you're gallivanting around the malls dressed like a tramp, I have to live in this neighborhood. I have to hold my head up at the grocery store, the ladies' sodality, and Wednesday-night bingo."

Josie felt a sudden stab of pity for Jane, who was so achingly conventional. Her mother really cared what Mrs. Mueller thought. She would be hurt if the old gossip said ugly things about her daughter. Josie figured she owed her mom that much. She would let Jane lie her way into respectability.

"Okay, Mom, tell the neighbors whatever you want. I've got to get ready for work."

"You need your breakfast today," Jane said. "I won't let you leave without eating it."

On Josie's kitchen table was a small yellow pot of tea and a plate of cinnamon toast. Josie was touched.

"Cinnamon toast! My absolute favorite," she said.

Two thick slices of white bread were covered with luscious mounds of butter-soaked cinnamon and sugar. Tea and cinnamon toast were Josie's I-don't-feel-well foods. Her mother had made them on those mornings when Josie had stayed home from school with measles or chicken pox. Nice old Mrs. Malloy would watch the ailing Josie, but her mother came home from the bank on her lunch hour and sat by Josie while she ate Campbell's chicken soup and peanut-butter crackers.

"Eat," Jane commanded.

Josie ate, crunching happily on the fragrant butter-drenched breakfast. She rarely had time to eat breakfast at home on a workday. For a moment, Josie was six years old and the only homicide detectives were on TV.

Jane waited until Josie finished her toast before she said, "You aren't wearing that slut costume today." Another command.

"No, Mom. I'm mystery-shopping Pleasin' Pizza restaurants. I get to dress like my normal self in jeans and a shirt. By the way, you wouldn't happen to have any cash, would you? I'm giving away cash prizes, and it would save me a trip to the ATM. I could use two hundred dollars.''

Jane looked stricken. "Two hundred dollars? I don't have that kind of money lying around."

Odd. Her mother used to keep at least two hundred bucks in the sugar bowl for emergencies. Well, it was none of Josie's business. She noticed her mother had a grease spot on the front of her blue pantsuit and she wasn't wearing lipstick. Jane was one of those women who considered herself naked without lipstick.

"Mom, is everything all right?" Josie said.

"Why wouldn't it be? Because I don't want to give you two hundred dollars for your stupid job? Because the police are questioning my daughter? Everything is just peachy."

Well, Josie thought, lipstick or no lipstick, Mom was her old self.

"GBH," Josie said. She gave her mother a well-deserved hug.

"I'm so worried about you," Jane said. "What have you gotten yourself into?"

"I'm fine, Mom," Josie said. "Don't worry so much. I've got to get the kid to school."

Ten minutes later Josie herded a washed, brushed and dressed Amelia into the car. If they hurried, they would make it. Stan the Man Next Door ambushed her in the driveway.

"Uh, your mom said we're going out Thursday night," he said.

"Right, Stan. What time?"

"How about if I pick you up for dinner at five?"

Five? That was early. But Josie figured the sooner it started, the sooner it would be over.

She winced when she saw what Stan was wearing to work: brown self-belted pants, a short-sleeved gray shirt, and a pocket protector. The only thing that could make him look nerdier would be black Buddy Holly glasses held together with tape.

Josie sighed. Stan was such a sweet, helpful guy. There wasn't a mean bone in his head. But *I can't believe I'm going out with a guy who wears a pocket protector. If he worried about his shirt pockets, God knows what kind of a sheath he would put on his*—.

"Mom, it's twenty till eight. I'm going to be late," Amelia said, saving her mother from completing that raunchy thought. *Josie would enter a convent before Stan entered her.*

"Sorry, Stan. Gotta run," she said.

"I need to talk to you about your compressor," he said.

"Later," she said and put the car in gear. Stan jumped out of the way.

"Mom, that's the second time this week you nearly ran over Stan," Amelia said. "Are you trying to tell him something?"

"Yeah, but he won't listen," Josie said.

"That's not funny, Mom," Amelia said seriously. "If you hit Stan, the police will be really suspicious."

Josie did not make any smart replies. Amelia suddenly seemed subdued and very small, dwarfed by her enormous green backpack. Some days, her daughter was a budding teenager, growing up too fast. On her ninth birthday, Amelia had announced that "Mommy" was for babies. Now that she was older, Amelia said, she would use "Mom."

But this morning, when Amelia had been really scared, she'd called Josie "Mommy."

I've done this to my daughter, Josie thought. *I've undermined her confidence and frightened her into being a little girl again. I imagined every possible fear, every variation on potential disasters, but I never thought I'd be a murder suspect.*

Josie saw herself talking to her daughter on a phone while she sat behind a Plexiglas screen on visiting day. She'd miss Amelia's prom, her graduation, her wedding.

Maybe they'd let Amelia stop by in her bridal gown to see her mother the jailbird on her wedding day. Josie quickly tried to erase those pictures.

"Amelia," she said, "please don't worry. I had nothing to do with Danessa."

"Then why did the police come to our house?" Amelia said.

"They're trying to find out what happened to her, so they can catch the bad person who did hurt her. I saw Danessa the day she died. The police wanted to talk to me about it. It's their job."

"Why did Grandma tell me not to say anything?" Amelia asked.

Interrogation by a nine-year-old was as tricky as talking to the police. Josie took a deep breath and plunged on. "Because not everyone is your friend, and they may take this harmless information and twist it around so it sounds bad."

Amelia thought about what Josie had said. "Like when Hannah saw me reading that book about Egypt and it had statues of goddesses and they didn't wear any clothes and Hannah said I was looking at pictures of naked people and I got called into Mrs. Apple's office?"

"Exactly." Josie was relieved. Amelia understood. Josie was more relieved when she saw the winding, tree-lined drive of the Barrington School. The interrogation was at an end.

"We're here with five minutes to spare," Josie said.

"Tomorrow is the big school book sale," Amelia said. It was Barrington's major fall fund-raiser.

"Don't worry. I've signed up to bring brownies and I'm working the booths from five to seven."

"You promise? You won't get stuck at work or something?"

"I promise." Josie read the desperation in her daughter's eyes. Amelia wanted her mother to be like all the other moms.

"I won't wear my tube top, either," Josie said, but Amelia didn't smile. She jumped out of the car. Josie thought her daughter moved slower than usual, weighed down by her backpack and her mother's problems.

Josie waved to Emma's mother as she pulled away from the curb and prayed that she looked like a soccer mom and not a murder suspect.

On the road, Josie suddenly realized she hadn't had any coffee. She'd held a cup, but she hadn't drunk any. She couldn't start mystery-shopping Pleasin' Pizzas until noon. Coffee, she thought, as she headed to Has Beans. A double espresso would get her going. The tea had been nice, but only coffee gave her the zip she needed. Oh, admit it, she told herself. It isn't caffeine that has your heart beating faster.

The coffeehouse's parking lot was empty. It was one of the weird moments that suddenly happened during the morning rush hour, when the customers would vanish, then return in droves a few minutes later.

"Josie!" Josh said. His goatee looked wicked. Josie wondered if the stories about what a guy could do with a soul patch were true.

"What do you want?" he asked.

She surprised herself by bursting into tears.

The next thing she knew, Josh was around the counter, holding her. She was crying on his shoulder. She felt like a fool, but it was a very nice shoulder. His shirt felt so soft.

"Hey, hey, what's with the tears?" Josh handed her a pile of napkins to blow her nose.

"Bad morning."

"How bad? Something wrong with the kid?"

"The police were at my house. They think I murdered Danessa Celedine." She told him the whole story.

"That's bad." Josh looked serious now. He sat her down on a couch, moved a pile of newspapers and looked directly into her eyes.

"Josie, did the cops Mirandize you?"

"You mean, did they read me my rights, like on TV: 'You have the right to remain silent—'?"

"Yes, exactly. Did they do that? It's very important," Josh said.

"No," she said.

"That's good. It means you may be a suspect, but you're not *the* suspect."

"How do you know?" Josie said.

"Let's say I used to push more interesting things than caffeine."

I really know how to pick 'em, Josie thought.

"I'm sorry, Josie," he said. "Two soy lattes and a decaf skim cappuccino just pulled into the parking lot. I have to run. The rush is on again."

Josh handed her a double espresso. "On the house. I wish I could stay with you. You shouldn't be alone right now. Is there someone you can talk to?"

"Yeah, my best friend, Alyce."

"Why don't you give her a call? Do you need a lawyer?"

"No, I don't think so. Not yet," Josie said.

"Don't talk to the cops again without one," he said. "Promise me that."

"I promise," she said, and he kissed her lightly on the lips, just before the door opened and caffeine-deprived customers poured into the shop. Josie felt a little electric zing. How could such a light kiss be so heavy with promise?

Josie sat on the lumpy coffeehouse couch, which felt like it was stuffed with broken crockery. She was slightly dazed. It was a morning of firsts: her first police interrogation, her first kiss from Josh, and thanks to her mother, her first date with a man who wore a pocket protector. Right now, the kiss from Josh overshadowed the murder. I really am shallow, she thought, as she pulled out her cell phone and speed-dialed Alyce Bohannon.

No, I'm not. I'm young and healthy, and I got kissed by a hunk who cares about me. Why did I tell him so much? Because he listened. When was the last time she'd cried on anyone's shoulder, male or female? She'd been carrying too many burdens for too long.

"You won't believe what's happening here," Josie said when Alyce answered.

"You won't believe what's happening here," Alyce said.

"You first," Josie said. She was suddenly shy about telling her friend that she'd been braced by two homicide cops and kissed by a man who might have been a drug dealer.

"You know that Danessa Celedine and Serge Orloff live—lived—on my street. The cops are all over their house," Alyce said breathlessly. "We expected that. But now the FBI is out here, interviewing everyone. Guys in moon suits are running around Danessa's lawn with Geiger counters."

"Geiger counters? Why?"

"I guess they're Geiger counters," Alyce said. "They're all bristly and scary looking, that's for sure. There are some people from an investigative arm of the Nuclear Regulatory Agency, about a million unmarked cars and some weird trucks."

"Good Lord," Josie said.

"ICE is here, too," Alyce said. "That's the U.S. Immigration and Customs Enforcement. This is really serious."

"Alyce, what's going on?"

"They're looking for"—Alyce's voice dropped to a whisper—"nuclear contaminants."

Josie was confused. "What's that got to do with Danessa? Did she sell purses that glowed in the dark?"

"It's not Danessa. It's Serge. The FBI thinks he was selling nuclear weapons materials."

"No!" Josie said.

"Yes! Sneaked them right out of Russia. Something called osmium-187."

"The FBI told you that?"

"The FBI isn't telling anyone anything, especially me. I heard it from my housekeeper, Mrs. Donatelli, who heard it from Danessa's housekeeper, Mrs. Perkins."

"What the heck is osmium-187?" Josie said.

"Mrs. Perkins says it's worth a fortune. She read an article in *Reader's Digest* or something about how all the Russian resources are being looted: nickel, copper, gold, art and nuclear materials. About ten years ago, someone got caught smuggling eight grams of osmium-187 out of Russia. It was worth half a million dollars back then. According to Mrs. Perkins, Serge got nearly five million bucks for the ten grams he had."

"Omigod," Josie said. "Do you think the housekeeper is right?"

"Housekeepers are always right," Alyce said. "Do you realize if the FBI finds radioactive contamination, they may have to raze our whole subdivision?"

"Oh my God." Josie said it much slower now.

Alyce didn't seem especially worried that her house might glow in the dark or be razed to rubble. Maybe she would enjoy the challenge of redecorating. What colors went with a nuclear winter?

"My husband is threatening a zillion lawsuits," Alyce said. "This subdivision is crawling with lawyers. Nobody knows who to sue yet, but somebody will pay and it won't be us."

"I can see why Serge would be murdered, but why kill Danessa?" Josie said. "She wasn't home. She was at her store. Has your housekeeper heard anything about that?"

"This is the best part," Alyce said. "Mrs. Perkins says she was fixing the investigators coffee in the kitchen, and she heard that the FBI thinks Danessa may have been bumped off because she knew too much about Serge's smuggling. Or because he was using her store to import his nuclear weapons materials. You know, hiding the contraband in the boxes of purses. Who takes a shipment of high-priced purses seriously?"

"Oh, good," Josie said. "That's terrific news. Because the cops think I killed her."

There was a long silence.

"Hello?" Josie said.

"I think you'd better come out here right now and explain yourself," Alyce said. "I'll make brunch."

Chapter 10

Someday Josie would understand this thing St. Louis suburban women had for brunch. The richer they were, the more elaborate the brunch.

Josie was sure if the end of the world was announced tomorrow, supermarkets would be stripped of eggs, coffee cake and fresh fruit, as suburban women fought to fix their final brunch.

Brunch had replaced chicken soup for comfort. It covered any social event from baby showers to funerals. When Josie told her best friend she was a murder suspect, Alyce's first reaction was to prepare brunch.

Josie didn't find salvation in scrambled eggs. What's the natural Maplewood response to personal disaster? she wondered. We're more city than suburb, and we're certainly not rich. In Maplewood, we'd get drunk.

Except in recent years, Maplewood had become surprisingly trendy. The new people would take Prozac. I'd still get drunk, Josie decided. My neighborhood got fashionable, but I didn't.

Josie felt a flicker of hope after her talk with Alyce. If Serge was selling nuclear weapons materials, Josie was off the hook. He was probably killed by a terrorist and Danessa was unlucky enough to die with him.

At the top of the hour, Josie skipped through the radio stations in her car, listening for the local news, hoping to hear something about Danessa and Serge.

Finally, an announcer said, "And on the Power Couple Murders, the medical examiner has released the cause of death. Serge Orloff died from an overdose of warfarin, commonly known as rat poison. Police found the poison in his palatial West County home."

That was the second time the media had called the house palatial, Josie thought. It did look big.

"His business partner and longtime companion, Danessa Celedine, was found strangled at her store in Plaza Venetia."

Josie nearly ran the car into a ditch. "Omigod, omigod, omigod," she said.

No wonder the handsome homicide cop had raised his eyebrow when Josie said her mother would strangle her if she didn't bring home a picture of Danessa.

"Omigod, omigod, omigod." She must have sounded guilty as hell. Or criminally stupid. Josie felt sick to her stomach again. She rolled down the car window, just in case.

No newscast mentioned that Serge was suspected of selling nuclear arms. That story should have been all over the headlines. Didn't the press know? Could the government hush it up for national security reasons?

Or did Alyce have it wrong? She was repeating something one housekeeper told another. Josie was sure the story grew more inaccurate with each telling. Maybe by the time it got to Alyce, crime-scene techs had morphed into government agents, plainclothes police detectives had become FBI agents and ordinary evidence vans were "weird" vehicles.

All my hope is gone, Josie thought. If Serge didn't sell nuclear materials, then the suspicion spotlight swings back to me. I'm a prime suspect.

Josie was so upset she had trouble navigating the twisty country roads close to Alyce's house. It was lonely out here, nothing but hills, woods and private drives. Barren rocks jutted out of the hillsides. Small animals ran in front of her car.

Her friend Alyce thought the lonesome landscape was a bucolic paradise. She was always telling Josie about the wildlife that shyly ventured into her yard. Alyce saw a doe and two "darling" fawns. The week before that, it was a fox with her kits. Josie never saw anything more exotic than squashed roadkill.

Alyce was right about one thing: Today there was a lot of official-looking activity. The Estates at Wood Winds was a gated community, but the guard usually waved Josie through. This time, he stopped her, asked to see her driver's license and called Alyce to confirm her visit.

One entire road was blocked off with yellow crime-scene tape, but it was at the crest of a wooded hill. Josie couldn't see anything beyond the police car posted by the tape. The road to Alyce's house was open. Josie pulled into the driveway of the Tudor mansion, which was between a minicastle and a semi-demi-Italian palace. She gave her three-knock signal on the side door and entered.

Josie was always momentarily stunned by the luxury of Alyce's house. Her friend had white silk couches—with a one-year-old baby—and not a sticky handprint on the cushions. There were fresh white roses in crystal vases, gorgeous rugs in muted grays and blues, sensuous piles of pillows. The tall windows were free of little finger smudges. No toys or games marred the perfection.

Alyce's voice floated downstairs. "Come on in, Josie. The food's in the kitchen. Serve yourself. I'm putting the baby down for his nap. It's the nanny's morning off."

Josie found fluffy scrambled eggs on a warmer, crisp bacon on a special drainer from Williams-Sonoma and coffee in a machine so complicated she'd need an engineering degree to operate it. Alyce had set out bowls of fresh fruit, including a huge mound of raspberries, which cost more than marijuana in Maplewood.

"The juice is in the fridge," Alyce called. "It's fresh squeezed."

Where was the refrigerator? Josie wondered. She stood in the kitchen and looked around, ashamed to ask.

Why hadn't she noticed before? Why was a fridge so hard to find?

At her house the refrigerator was a big white box with GE on the front. But Alyce's kitchen was paneled in linen-fold oak, like an English library. Josie didn't see any handles sticking out on the oak panels.

She found a handhold buried in a slab of oak and tried to open it. It swung out to reveal a well-stocked pantry. Josie broke a nail trying to open the next hunk of paneling. Nothing there. The third time, she found the fridge. She was suddenly hungry, and fixed herself a generous breakfast.

"Alyce, you're the perfect hostess," Josie called up the stairs. "You think of every comfort."

With that, three strapping young men came through the side door. Josie nearly dropped her fork. Wow, Alyce really did think of everything.

"We're here to fix the bathroom tile grout," the handsomest of the three said, dashing Josie's hopes. They all had wedding rings. Naturally.

After the men disappeared into a guestroom bath, Alyce came down the stairs. Josie didn't hear her. Alyce was doing that floating thing again. Josie wondered how she did that. Where did a woman learn to walk soundlessly, buy bacon drainers and find invisible refrigerators?

"Justin is asleep," Alyce said. "With any luck, he'll stay out for the next hour or so and we can talk." She put a spoonful of eggs on her plate and counted out ten raspberries, and Josie knew her friend was tormenting herself with another diet.

"The guard called when you arrived. Did you have trouble at the gate?" Alyce asked.

"Not really," Josie said. "But this is the most security I've ever seen here."

"It's exciting." Alyce's eyes were shining and her fair skin was pinker than usual. "I've had two men in suits come by to talk to me. They asked me all sorts of questions about Serge and Danessa."

"Like what?" Josie helped herself to more eggs and bacon. No point in throwing them out. She added some raspberries, too, to make her plate look healthier.

"Questions like, Did I ever see any unusual activity? Notice any strangers? Did any visitors seem foreign or out of the ordinary? Were there any cars or trucks late at night?"

No wonder Alyce was excited. "This is classic spy novel stuff," Josie said. "I'm surprised they didn't ask if you saw mysterious strangers hauling heavy boxes on moonless nights. What did you see?"

"Nothing exciting," Alyce said. "The story of my life. Just lots of TV and newspaper reporters getting sound bites from Serge or Danessa. We knew all the media cars and vans. Serge always had a pronouncement on something."

"Yeah, I got in a fight with Mom over the American medical system because of Serge," Josie said.

"I got in a fight with Jake over the American legal system because of Serge," Alyce said.

They both laughed. Josie was feeling better. Another spoonful of eggs should help, she decided. She cut herself a generous slab of homemade coffeecake so Alyce wouldn't feel unappreciated.

"Yum. This cake is good," Josie said. "What was the power couple like?"

"I met them at a few parties, mostly around the holidays. Danessa made a big fuss over Jake because he was an important lawyer, but she ignored me. I was just a housewife. No, wait. She didn't totally ignore me. Danessa made a bitchy remark about my dress at the Wood Winds Labor Day dance. She asked me if I'd made it myself. Jake yelled at me later for not spending enough money on my clothes. Said it made him look bad."

"What about Serge?" Josie said.

"He kissed my hand passionately."

"You're joking."

"I'm not kidding," Alyce said. "It was romantic. Sort of European. That's when I noticed how big his hand was. Serge really came on to me, even if my dress did look homemade. Jake didn't notice. I guess he didn't think another man could be interested in me. It's been a long time since a man looked at me that way."

Alyce sounded so wistful. Josie felt sad, even though her love life wasn't any better. She'd had one kiss in a coffeehouse and a date with a guy who wore a pocket protector.

Alyce gave a sweet smile. "Well, I can't complain. I'm luckier than most women. I never have to worry about money, I have my beautiful baby boy and I've got mystery shopping with you for excitement."

Alyce was the perfect partner when Josie had to shop a store more than once. Nobody ever noticed two housewives. Josie thought there was something sad about that, too. Sadder still, Alyce did it for free. It was her idea of fun.

"Do you think any women really fell into bed with Serge?" Josie said.

"All the time," Alyce said. "Amy the Slut bragged about her conquest of Serge at tennis."

"Before or after Danessa bitch-slapped her?"

"Both. Amy never shut up about going to bed with him. I think it was her revenge. She was angry at Danessa. The way Danessa went after her at the club had to be humiliating."

"What happened?" Josie said. "I've never heard the full story."

"Amy was holding court in the bar—big surprise— with some male admirers, but there were plenty of other witnesses. The club's Friday lobster supper always draws a crowd. One of the barflies came onto Amy, and she said something like, 'You'd better be good. I've just been with Serge. You have a lot to measure up to.' Everyone heard her. She gets loud when she's had a few. Drinks, I mean, not men.

"She didn't see that Danessa had walked into the bar. Danessa grabbed Amy by the hair, slapped her twice across the face, and threw her against the bar.

" 'You stupid slut,' Danessa said. 'You're just another public convenience, like a toilet.' "

"Ouch," Josie said.

" A lot of wronged wives thought it served Amy right. She couldn't miss the smiles on their faces."

"Did I ever meet Amy?" Josie said.

"She lives in the Italian palace up the road," Alyce said. "You met her at my New Year's Eve party. She wore those tight velvet pants and draped herself all over Noreen's husband."

"Oh, yeah. I think I surprised them together in the guest bathroom," Josie said.

"I think Amy accidentally on purpose forgot to lock the door. She lives for those little surprises. Amy would have loved to take a man away from the famous Danessa. The way I heard it, Serge was more than another pair of boots under Amy's bed. She had a bit of a thing for him. Can't blame her for that. He was so manly."

Alyce's voice seemed soft as a sigh with that last sentence. Did her friend have a thing for Serge? Josie looked at Alyce carefully. Nope. Those eyes were too innocent, Josie decided. Alyce had had a flirtation maybe, but not an affair. Serge had made her feel like a desirable woman, instead of an overweight wife. If that was Serge's secret technique, he must have been the West County Casanova.

"Amy's too easy," Josie said. "Did Serge have any real conquests?"

"Definitely," Alyce said. "That man had a roving eye. I'll tell you who I suspect, though I can't prove it. Kate, my neighbor to the east, turned red whenever Serge's name was mentioned after the subdivision's fall mixer. Her house is up for sale now. It's right next to Serge's.

"Poor Kate would be easy prey for Serge. Her surgeon husband is such a bastard. Mr. Catholic Family

Doctor. He bragged in some newspaper that he and his wife never use birth control. Easy for him. He goes off to the hospital seven days a week and leaves her stuck home with two sets of twins."

Josie was surprised by Alyce's bitterness.

"But that's enough about the goings-on here," Alyce said. "Tell me everything that's been happening to you."

Josie did.

"You need a lawyer," Alyce said when Josie finished.

"Can't afford one," Josie said.

"Jake will help," she said.

"I can't afford your husband."

"Look, he won't charge you. He does boring corporate stuff all day. He'd love to do something interesting."

"I'm fine for now," Josie said.

Josie took her plate to the sink. She didn't attempt to find the dishwasher. But she did feel better. Maybe there was something to that brunch business after all.

They heard Justin fussing on the baby monitor. Alyce floated upstairs to check on him. Josie followed. Justin was a beautiful little boy. He had his father's dark eyes and hair. It was still in soft ringlets.

"Jake wants me to get him a boy cut," Alyce said. "He says I've got him looking like a sissy girl. But Justin's hair is so pretty, I can't bring myself to cut it yet."

"He's definitely got his father's eyes and hair," Josie said. "No doubt who his daddy is."

Alyce seemed inordinately pleased by this compliment. "I thought so, too," she said.

"You're so lucky to have a nanny for Justin," Josie said. "I can't even afford day care. I'm dependent on Mom."

"You're the lucky one," Alyce said. "Your mom wouldn't try to steal your man."

Josie was silent while Alyce's words sank in. "You think Jake is having an affair with your nanny?"

"I found a used condom in her wastebasket."

"Maybe she snuck in her boyfriend," Josie said.

"She doesn't have a boyfriend."

"Oh," Josie said. "What are you going to do? Have you asked him about it?"

"I'm afraid to," Alyce said. "If I say something, my marriage could blow up in my face. I can't divorce Jake. I have a one-year-old. I have no money. My work skills are so outdated, they're useless. I used to be a decent systems analyst, but I haven't worked seriously on a computer for three years. I'd have to go back to school. I can't compete with younger, cheaper workers. Jake will take Justin and leave me with nothing. You don't know what it's like to have no money."

"Actually, I do," Josie said.

"Sorry, I wasn't thinking."

"Alyce, this is terrible. You must feel so trapped. Can you go back to school and brush up your skills?"

"Jake wouldn't let me. He wants me to be a full-time mom."

"What about marriage counseling?" Josie said.

"Jake says there's no problem, it's all in my head. There's nothing I can do." Alyce kissed her son and nuzzled his soft skin. There didn't seem to be anything else to say on the subject.

"I'd better get going if I want to make the Clarkson Pleasin' Pizza by noon," Josie said.

"I'll keep you posted on anything I hear through the housekeeper network," Alyce said. "They have the best information."

Maybe my situation isn't so bad after all, Josie thought, as she drove away. I may be a murder suspect, but I'm not serving a life sentence with an unfaithful man.

Chapter 11

"Yes, ma'am," the young server said. "That's a medium pepperoni Pleasin' Pizza with extra onions, a small salad with Italian dressing on the side and a large Pleasin' Cola, all to go."

"That's right," Josie said.

The kid's name tag said he was Matt. He blushed when he looked at Josie, and his ears turned red. They were rather large and stuck out from his buzz-cut head. A boy at Maplewood High with ears like that had been called Wing Nut—until he topped six four and joined the Marines.

Josie was sure Matt's big ears and large bony feet were a misery now, but once he grew into them, he'd be downright handsome. Hang in there for another year, Matt, she wanted to tell him. Your world will get better soon. If he remembered the magic words, it would improve right now.

"And won't you have an extra Pleasin' Cola?" Matt said.

Yes! Josie thought.

"Congratulations, Matt," Josie said. "I'm the Pleasin' Pizza mystery shopper, and you've won fifty dollars in our Fifty Is Nifty campaign for remembering to ask customers to buy another Pleasin' Cola."

Matt's eyes lit up like he'd won the lottery. His smile stretched across his face. His ears flapped. He was one happy kid.

"Sweet," he said, sounding like Amelia. "How do I get the money?"

"Hold out your hand," Josie said and planted five tens on his palm.

She wished she had a picture of Matt's grin. In fact, she'd put that in the comments section of her report. She'd suggest the company photograph some of the Fifty Is Nifty winners. The restaurants hired such cute kids for servers.

Josie loved this part of her job. If only her mother could see her now. Josie did more than criticize people. She praised hard workers who might be overlooked by management. She gave them pats on the back, and for this promotion, fifty bucks cash.

"Here's your pizza, salad and two Pleasin' Colas," Matt said. "I double-bagged the salad so the dressing container won't leak on your car seat if it tips."

Matt was the third Pleasin' Pizza server she'd given cash to today, after she stopped at the ATM. Once again Josie wondered why her mom didn't have any money in her sugar bowl. It wasn't like Jane. But lots of things weren't like her lately. Josie was surprised to see her mother's hair was unpermed. Jane's hairdresser usually kept it curled and sprayed into a tidy gray helmet. Her mother was always a neat dresser, but now Josie saw small spots on her clothes.

Was Jane depressed or worried about money? Josie thought her mother was fairly well fixed, thanks to Social Security and her bank pension. Maybe Jane had made some bad investments.

By the time Josie saw the red-checked awning of the Ballwin Pleasin' Pizza, she'd resolved to look into her mom's situation and make sure she was okay. If she needed help, Josie would see that she got it. Lord knows, her mother took care of her.

Josie knew when she walked up to the door of this latest Pleasin' Pizza that she wouldn't be giving out fifty dollars to anyone. The glass door was covered with fingerprints, an early warning sign that this restaurant wasn't carefully managed. Inside, the floor was littered with paper napkins. There was gum on the red-and-white tile. More black marks for Josie's report.

Josie stood at the PLEASE WAIT TO BE SEATED sign. The second hand on her watch swept around twice before the hostess seated her. The tabletop was wet and had a scattering of crumbs near the condiment basket.

Her waitress, a pert brunette, seemed to be mumbling to herself. Josie looked closer. She wasn't mumbling. She was on the phone. Josie checked the server's name tag: LEXIE. She had one of those dangly headsets.

"I don't know, Tori," Lexie the server said into her mouthpiece. "He's so not there when you talk to him. Just a minute."

"Can I get you anything?" she said to Josie.

The server said into her phone, "Tori, you'll have to hold. I can't make a decision about Mark right now. It's too important."

Lexie was not going through an awkward stage like Matt, the last Pleasin' Pizza server. She was cute and she knew it. Her red-checked uniform was too tight and too short, and she'd unbuttoned two top buttons instead of the regulation one. She flipped her long brown pony-tail from side to side.

"I'd like a medium sausage pizza with extra peppers," Josie said.

"Tori! Cut it out," Lexie said to her phone.

"What do you want again?" Lexie said to Josie.

"I want a medium sausage pizza with extra peppers," Josie said slowly. She was enjoying this. "I want a small salad with Italian dressing on the side and a large Pleasin' Cola, all to go."

"Okay," Lexie said. She was supposed to repeat the order, but she didn't.

"Tori!" she said into the phone. "Shut up! You're like so totally fucked."

Nice, Josie thought. She could add profanity to her report.

"Is that all?" Lexie said to Josie.

"Yes," Josie said. "That's enough."

Lexie flounced across the room, ponytail flipping, lips flapping on her phone call.

"Oh, Lexie," Josie said, calling her back.

"Hold on, Tori," Lexie said into her phone as she returned to Josie's table.

"There is something else?" she said to Josie. Lexie was not happy with the interruption.

"Yes," Josie said. "I forgot to give you this."

She handed Lexie the "I'm sorry" card. "I'm the Pleasin' Pizza mystery shopper. You forgot to ask me if I wanted another Pleasin' Cola. I'm sorry, but I can't give you fifty dollars for our Fifty Is Nifty promotion."

Josie wasn't sorry at all. She'd never met a server who deserved this more.

Lexie went into an instant pout. "This is like so totally unfair. I was going to ask you. You didn't give me a chance."

"I gave you lots of chances. You were on the phone to Tori. Better luck next time." Josie smiled insincerely.

Josie thought she heard Lexie mutter "bitch" as she stomped off to the kitchen. When Lexie returned with Josie's order, she threw it on the table. Outside the restaurant, Josie tossed it in the Dumpster. She suspected Lexie might have spit in her food.

Josie checked her watch. It was almost two o'clock. This was a good day after all. She got to reward the good servers and punish the bad. Her work was done and she had enough time to pick up Amelia at school. They'd split a medium pizza before she went to the school book sale. Josie would take another pizza to her mom and give the third to Stan the Man Next Door. He'd volunteered to look at her ailing air conditioner. Once again, Josie wished her mother hadn't interfered. Stan was a good neighbor and a good friend, but he was never going to be anything else. This Thursday night date would make things awkward.

Wait a minute . . . two o'clock. She'd better check the local news and see if there was anything on the Serge and Danessa murders.

Josie flipped on the radio and heard the announcer say, "—anonymous sources say murder victim Serge Orloff was selling nuclear weapons material, osmium-187, worth millions of dollars, and there is a possible terrorist link to his murder. These same sources say his longtime companion, Danessa Celedine, was killed because of her connection to Serge Orloff.

"Police refuse to confirm or deny the story, saying it is not in the public interest to comment at this time. And here's Jim with the stock market report."

Josie punched the buttons for a few other stations, but there was nothing more on the murders. She didn't care. What she'd heard on her radio was good news. Someone had leaked the Orloff nuclear arms story.

I'm safe, Josie thought. The police will have to start hunting down terrorists and leave me alone. I'll swing over to pick up Amelia, get dressed for the book sale and play a proper mom at the Barrington School. Amelia will quit worrying about her mother the future felon.

Josie's cell phone rang. It was her mother. Jane sounded old and quavery with worry. "Josie, those homicide detectives are here again. They want to talk to you."

"I have to pick up Amelia, Mom."

"I don't think you should keep them waiting, Josie. You should come home now. What will the neighbors say— police cars parked in front of our house again? This is twice in the same day." Jane's voice grew more vigorous at the mention of her neighbors. Josie felt a hot slash of irritation. She wanted to say she didn't give a rat's rear end about the neighbors, but she restrained herself.

"Josie Marcus, you will come home right now, and you get those detectives out of my house." It was the same voice Jane had used when Josie stayed out past curfew at age fifteen. She didn't sound old or frail now.

"Okay, Mom," Josie said. "Would you pick up Amelia at school, please? And relax. You've been watching too many cop shows. The police won't hound a suburban mom. I haven't done anything."

"Josie, I don't like this," Jane said. "I'm really worried. They're sitting in your living room right now, and they don't look happy. Maybe you should get a lawyer."

Josie nearly dropped the phone in surprise. Maplewoodians of her mother's generation thought shrinks were for crazy people and lawyers were for guilty ones. She remembered her promise to Josh to get a lawyer, but her mother's words hardened something in her heart.

"Mom, I can't afford a lawyer. I don't need one. I haven't done anything wrong. Please pick up Amelia. I'll come straight home."

"I will get her. I just hope her mother won't be in jail by the time I get that child home." Josie had barely shut her cell phone when it rang again.

"It's me. Alyce. I've got the scoop de la scoop."

"Shoot," Josie said. Her friend sounded really excited. Josie could see her, slate-blue eyes sparkling, blond hair nearly floating off her head. She must have more news about Serge the terrorist victim.

"It's from Danessa's housekeeper, so I know it's good," Alyce said. "You'll never guess what Danessa was strangled with."

"What?" Josie said. What did terrorists use? A scarf hand-woven by native virgins? A string of bullets? A garrote?

"A red snakeskin belt," Alyce said. "It cost twenty-seven hundred dollars. Can you believe it? Snakeskin. It couldn't be more appropriate. Sweets for the sweet. Snakes for the snakes."

That wretched snakeskin belt, Josie thought. Is that why the detectives asked her about it before? She'd deliberately made the saleswoman dismantle that display so she could try it on. Now she was going to regret that petty power play.

She heard a loud buzzing in her ears. Her voice came out in a croak.

"Alyce," Josie said, "my fingerprints are all over that belt."

Chapter 12

"Don't go home," Alyce said. "Don't go near those cops, Josie."

"I can't hide," Josie said. "Then I'll really look guilty. Anyway, where would I go?"

"You can stay with me," Alyce said. "I'll protect you."

"Some protection. Your place is swarming with cops."

"You're right," Alyce said. "I wasn't thinking. Let me get you a lawyer. I'll make a few phone calls. It will take me about fifteen minutes. Go sit in a coffee shop until I find someone. Then you can go together to talk with the police. It's too dangerous alone. Promise me."

Promise me, Josh had said, *you won't talk to the police again without a lawyer.* Josie had promised as he kissed her and went off to his coffee customers. Now she was breaking her promise to him.

So what? she thought defiantly. Why should I promise anyone anything? Josh is a fantasy man. There's nothing real about him or his promises.

"Josie, are you there?" Alyce said.

"Alyce, I don't need a lawyer. I don't live in your world," Josie said. "Rich people have lawyers. Poor people don't. The cops wouldn't think twice if you had one. They'd expect it. But they'll wonder why Josie from Maplewood is lawyering up."

"Please," Alyce said, "listen to me." Her friend was begging. Was she crying, too? "You think I'm a sheltered little suburbanite, but I do know something about the law. Don't do this."

"The police aren't going after me, Alyce. I'm Miss White Bread."

"So was Martha Stewart."

"I'm a mom," Josie said.

"Exactly," Alyce said. "You have a daughter to consider. What if you're arrested? How will Amelia take that?"

Josie saw Amelia's frightened little face, the sweet sprinkle of freckles standing out on her pale skin like tiny drops of cinnamon. If I go to jail, Amelia will be brought up by my mother. Jane will take my daughter out of Barrington. She'll make her eat soy burgers. Amelia will never go on another guerrilla gorilla expedition again.

"That's why I have to fight this my way," Josie said. "I've always told Amelia she has nothing to fear if she tells the truth."

"If Amelia accidentally broke a lamp, she wouldn't be punished for telling the truth," Alyce said. "But this isn't the same. Get real, Josie. The truth won't set you free. It will put you in jail."

"I've got to go now," Josie said.

"Why are you being so damn stubborn?" Alyce said. Now Josie was sure she was crying. "You owe me that much. Tell me. I'm your friend."

"It bites my butt that I'll have to pay some lawyer two hundred an hour to tell me to shut up when I haven't done anything wrong," Josie said. "I don't have the money for that."

"You won't have to pay two hundred an hour," Alyce said. "Jake will help you."

"Worse. I'll be beholden to your husband."

"Josie, this is what friends do. They help one another. If you're worried about the money, I can lend it to you. You can pay me back at ten dollars a week."

"I don't want your money," Josie said. "I told you when you married Jake and moved to the Estates at

Wood Winds, if we were going to stay friends we'd have to be equals. That means we go Dutch at lunch and you don't buy me expensive presents because I can't afford them."

"I agreed because of your crazy pride," Alyce said. "But money means nothing to me."

"It means everything to me," Josie said. "When you don't have it, you know how important it is. I have a reasonable explanation for why my fingerprints are on that belt. All I have to do is tell the police. I don't need a legal babysitter."

"The police have an equally reasonable explanation," Alyce said. "They think you killed Danessa."

"No, they don't. They haven't Mirandized me," Josie said.

"Yet," Alyce said.

"Thanks for being worried about me," Josie said, "but I'll be fine."

"Is there anything I can do to change your mind?"

"Nope," Josie said.

"Promise me you'll call when the police leave," Alyce said.

Josie could keep that promise. She drove down her street as if she were seeing the redbrick houses for the first time. Her mother's white Buick was gone. Good. That meant Jane was picking up Amelia at school. Her neighbor Stan was not home, but Mrs. Mueller was. Her lace curtains were twitching. Josie was tempted to flip the old biddy the bird, but she refrained for her mother's sake. She did wave at the Mueller windows and the curtains stopped twitching.

Parked in front of Josie's house was a plain gray car that could only be an unmarked police vehicle.

Josie's home was a narrow two-family flat with two windows upstairs, one down. Josie had lived there most of her life: upstairs with her mother until she went to college, downstairs after Amelia was born.

At age nine, she'd pulled weeds in the yard for a dollar a bucket. At sixteen, she'd run over the peony bush when she was learning to drive. She'd been photographed on the porch with Les Steinberg, her high school prom date. Les was so young and embarrassed in his rented tux, a red carnation pinned crookedly to the lapel. Josie had felt sophisticated in red lipstick and a black dress.

Her mother's geraniums bloomed in pots on the porch. The concrete statue of the Blessed Virgin was whitewashed and planted with yellow-orange mums for fall. Josie hated their odd acrid smell. Jane may have let her own appearance slide, but the house was painted, planted and properly mowed for the neighbors.

Josie stumbled on the uneven concrete sidewalk, and her gut tightened. She hadn't felt this scared in more than nine years. The last time was when she'd told her mother she was pregnant, she wasn't marrying the baby's father and she was dropping out of college to be a mystery shopper.

"You've ruined my life and yours," her mother had wailed, as if Josie was dead instead of knocked up.

That crisis seemed mild now. Her mother, after the first shock, stood by her daughter. When Josie had carried Amelia home from the hospital, her personal disaster had turned into a triumph.

But Josie didn't think she'd have a happy ending waiting at the end of this walk. Two homicide detectives were sitting in her living room.

I've been a stubborn fool. I should have called a lawyer, she thought. But she couldn't bring herself to spend nearly a week's pay so a pin-striped suit could sit beside her.

I'm smart enough to watch what I say. I do that all day at my job. How many tense situations in the stores have I talked my way out of? Then an old saw of her grandmother's drifted into her mind: If you are your own lawyer, you have a fool for a client.

Josie shook off her misgivings and opened her front door. The slanting afternoon sun was cruel. She saw that the entrance hall needed a coat of paint. The beige carpet was worn. Amelia had dropped a sweatshirt and her pink inline skates by the door. She could hear the air conditioner wheezing and rattling. The air was warm and humid.

The detectives were sitting on Josie's couch, side by side, with the air of small boys who'd been up to something. Everything in the room seemed slightly off kilter. She wondered if they'd done an illegal search.

Josie offered them coffee. They said no thanks.

"We just want to ask you a few questions," the handsome Detective Yawney said. The balding, square-headed Detective Waxley said nothing, but he watched Josie until she felt like a bug under a microscope.

"We'd like to begin by advising you of your rights," Detective Yawney said, and the bottom fell out of Josie's stomach.

You're not a suspect until they Mirandize you, Josh had told her.

"Am—am I a suspect?" Josie said.

"It's just a formality," Waxley said. His baby-bald head gleamed innocently.

His partner began the familiar chant that she'd heard so often on TV. Josie's mind scrambled desperately to make a decision. Should she call a lawyer? Was this really only a formality? Why did Detective Yawney remind her of the guy who sold her that overpriced dining room set for only forty-eight easy payments?

If I wait for a lawyer, I'll be late for the Barrington book sale. My mother will have to work my shift. She'll wear one of her polyester pantsuits and Amelia will hear the giggles and snotty little remarks.

"I don't need a lawyer," she said firmly.

It seemed to Josie that the detectives stayed for years. They were there so long, she examined her living room down to the last detail. She'd never realized how small, boxy and badly proportioned it was.

The ceiling was too high. The molding was too dark. The tiny stained-glass window by the fireplace had a crack in the green pane. A cobweb went from the lamp to the wall. And the walls. They seemed to move in on her.

"Tell us about the snakeskin belt," Detective Yawney said.

His eyes crinkled when he smiled, but Josie didn't trust that smile. She tried to explain the display, a red belt artistically arranged like a striking snake. Her words poured out, awkward and unconvincing even to her. Not so much talk, she reminded herself. There. She could handle this. That's what any lawyer would tell her: Keep her answers short and honest.

"Wasn't Danessa known for selling purses?" Detective Waxley asked, as if fashion was a mystery to him. It probably was. His white shirt was gray from too many washings. The stitching along the pocket had puckered. He could use a pocket protector, Josie thought, and nearly giggled. She caught herself and gave a short, serious answer.

"Yes."

"Then why didn't you ask to see a purse?" Waxley said.

"The snakeskin belt display looked like the most difficult to dismantle," Josie said. "The saleswoman had ticked me off and I wanted to make her work a little."

That sounded impossibly petty, but she thought it had the ring of truth.

"Did your job assignment specifically direct you to choose a belt rather than a purse?" Detective Waxley asked.

"No. It could be any product sold in the store."

"Why that particular belt?" he said. "Do you wear twenty-seven-hundred-dollar belts? Are you familiar with how they should look and feel?"

Of course Josie wasn't. The detectives could look around the room and know that.

She'd bought the sagging couch for three hundred dollars at a garage sale. The tables and lamps were new from Target. She doubted if all the furniture in her flat came to twenty-seven hundred dollars, and that included the fourteen-hundred-dollar dining room set.

"I'm familiar with high-end goods from mystery shopping," she said.

"We found your fingerprints on the belt," Detective Yawney said. There were no smile crinkles now. Josie saw that he'd missed a small, dark patch of beard near his left ear.

"I told you. I tried it on. My fingerprints would be on it."

"Trying it on would be a good excuse to get your fingerprints on the belt," he said.

"And you think I'd do that? You think I'm that clever?"

"Well, let's think about that." Detective Yawney's handsome mouth took on an ugly twist. "You tell lies for a living. You wear disguises. For most people, mystery shopping is a part-time job that brings in a few thousand a year. But you earn a living at it."

Not a good one, Josie wanted to say, looking at her shabby living room. But she was too frightened to speak. Detective Yawney knew way too much about her.

The homicide cop was still talking. "So, yes, you're clever. Maybe this time you were too clever. Didn't you tell us that the store was cleaned up when you came back at ten at night? Why didn't the staff wipe your fingerprints off the belt?"

I've trapped myself, Josie thought. I volunteered too much information.

"Why don't you ask them?" she said.

"We did. The salesperson, Olga, said she wiped down everything on direct orders from Danessa. Including the snakeskin belt."

"Of course she'd say that," Josie said. "She's not going to tell you she did a sloppy job and skipped the belt."

"Did you touch other things when you mystery-shopped?" Detective Waxley said. His mild eyes blinked rapidly.

Did I? Josie wondered, wildly searching her memory. Wait. Yes! "I bought three eyeglass holders. I stood at the counter while the salesperson rang up my purchase, so there might be some fingerprints there. When I came back at night, I took two autographed photos from the basket on the counter."

"We didn't find your fingerprints anywhere else in the store," Detective Waxley said. "Just on the belt."

"Tell us about that snakeskin belt," Detective Yawney said again. Josie tried to remember what she'd said the first time, but her words seemed to run away and hide.

The detectives asked Josie the same questions over and over until the walls came together and the air left the room.

Finally, they asked a new question: "Would you consent to a polygraph test?"

Oh, God, Josie thought. They think I'm lying.

Chapter 13

"When?" Josie said.

That one word dropped down with the finality of a guillotine blade, cutting off all hope. The police wanted her to take a lie detector test. They didn't believe her. The walls in her drab living room leaned inward. She felt like she was in a cell already—lightless, airless, doomed.

"When do you want me to take the test?" Josie's voice shriveled to a whisper.

You had the right to remain silent, she thought. But you had to talk. You've talked your way into prison because you didn't want to spend two hundred dollars. That's the old Maplewood way: Squeeze a penny till it screams for mercy, then lose thousands because you're too cheap to spend it. How long will it take you to make two hundred dollars stamping out license plates in prison?

"We can go right now," Detective Yawney said.

How could Josie have thought anyone so cruel was handsome?

"We can have you back home in about three hours," he said.

Josie sneaked a glance at her watch and was surprised to see it was only three thirty. She'd be back by six thirty. But she had to be at the Barrington School at five.

"I can't take a lie detector test right now. My daughter—"

"Is with your mother," Yawney said.

Those words terrified Josie more than the lie detector

test. She couldn't fail Amelia. She had to put on her Rich Suburban Lady outfit and pretend to be a normal mother helping out at the school book sale. She couldn't embarrass Amelia by being hauled off to police headquarters for a lie detector test.

Josie looked around wildly for something to hit Yawney with. She would take the two detectives by surprise. They'd never expect it. She'd knock out Yawney and Waxley with the green table lamp—that color was a mistake anyway—and make a run for the Barrington School.

After she served her time in the book room, the cops could take her away for assaulting the homicide detectives.

Josie pushed away that crazy plan and began to plead. Her daughter's future depended on her argument. "Detective Yawney, do you have children?"

Yawney shifted in his chair but didn't answer.

Gotcha! Josie thought. He has kids and he feels guilty, like all working parents.

"My girl asks very little of me," Josie said. "But Amelia needs me to be at the Barrington School at five o'clock to work the book sale with the other mothers. If I'm not there, she'll be embarrassed. She'll be singled out. You must know what that's like for a child. She's already different. She doesn't have a father and she lives in a flat in Maplewood instead of a mansion in Ladue.

"I have to be there for her. The school expects parents to participate in fund-raising activities. The kids suffer socially if we don't. The school doesn't do it on purpose. It just happens.

"My volunteer shift is over at seven. You can go with me. You can stand next to me at the sale table. I'll give you coffee. You can even buy books. Twenty percent of the proceeds go to the school. Afterward, I'll have Mom pick up Amelia and you can take me to the lie detector test. Please, please don't do this to her. She's only nine years old."

Josie's voice broke as she finished her speech. She

was shaking. Detective Yawney said nothing. Some small silent signal seemed to pass between him and Waxley, a nod or maybe a blink.

Then Yawney said, "Be at the police headquarters at eight o'clock tomorrow morning. You can sign your statement while you're at it." He gave her a room number and directions.

After they left, Josie put the pizza for Stan on his porch swing, along with a note thanking him for offering to look at her air conditioner. By the time she was back home, Amelia and her mother were in the kitchen, putting away boxes and cartons.

Jane looked hot and irritated. "The traffic on Manchester was awful and we had to stop to get you milk, bread and cereal," she said. "Amelia said you were out of food."

"Thanks, Mom." Josie kissed her mother's cheek and said, "Amelia, run along and change. We have to go to school. I have pizza for dinner."

"Pepperoni with extra onions?" Amelia said.

"Another meal with no nutrition?" her mother said.

"I got a salad," Josie said.

"Iceberg lettuce, no doubt. It's mostly water, you know." Jane checked to see that Amelia was in her room, then dropped her voice to a whisper. "What did the cops want?" She sounded like Ma Barker.

"Just a couple of questions," Josie lied. "I have to be there at eight tomorrow morning to sign my statement. Could you take Amelia to school?"

"I could, since I have nothing better to do than play chauffeur for you. But if my granddaughter were in a Catholic school, I wouldn't have to. She could walk."

"Mom, I don't think Catholic school would be good for Amelia. She's kind of a free spirit."

"That's the same argument I heard from your father. It's why I sent you to public school instead of getting you a good Catholic education. And look how you turned out."

Josie heard the rest of that sentence, even though her

mother didn't say it: pregnant, unmarried and a college dropout.

"I don't think I turned out badly," Josie said. You have the right to remain silent, she thought. That works for mothers as well as homicide detectives. Jane has had a bad day. It must have been an awful shock when those two detectives turned up on her doorstep again. She had to be crabby. Besides, she did your shopping. Typical Mom. All the time she grumped at you, she was also helping you out.

"Thanks for the groceries," Josie said. "How much do I owe you?"

"Forty-one dollars and fifty-eight cents," Jane said.

Josie dutifully counted out the cash. "I have to get dressed. Thanks, Mom. You're always there when I need you."

She gave her mother a hug, but Jane remained stiff and unyielding. She went upstairs to her flat, slamming the door behind her.

Josie had half an hour to put on her Rich Suburban Lady outfit. It was her dullest disguise—navy blue Ralph Lauren blazer, white silk turtleneck, camel pants and flat shoes. She brushed her hair into a severe style and put on the bare minimum makeup.

She felt like an imposter in those clothes, but Josie could see the relief in her daughter's eyes when she came into the kitchen. Josie would look like all the other mothers. She would not embarrass her daughter. Amelia would never say that, but Josie had seen—and heard—what happened to the children whose mothers were different.

Vaniqua, an African American scholarship student, had to listen to little remarks about her mother's "ethnicity" because of her flowing purple caftans and head wraps. Josie admired the woman's bold style. But Vaniqua—and the rest of the Barrington School—were strict preppies, dull and disapproving as Puritans in their dress.

In the car, Josie studied her daughter for signs that

she was upset or worried. Amelia didn't seem to know that the police had been to their home again. She talked about boys on the trip to school. From what Josie could figure out, all the girls had boyfriends in class, but the boys didn't know it.

"Jennifer broke up with Matt," Amelia announced.

"How did Matt take it?" Josie said.

Amelia shrugged. "Jennifer didn't actually tell him. She just doesn't like him anymore."

Josie bit her lip to keep from smiling. She hoped her daughter had invisible boyfriends for a long time.

As they pulled into the school parking lot, Amelia spotted her best friend's SUV. "There's Emma. Can I go in with her, Mom?"

"Sure," Josie said. "But don't wander off. I want to see you."

Josie could smell the old money as she walked through the school doors, a distillation of leather, cigar smoke and dust. The place was decorated with gently worn Oriental rugs, portraits of rich old white guys, trophies, class photos and slippery leather wing chairs.

I bet I'm the only mom here who ever had a polygraph, she thought. But some of the fathers might have. At least two Barrington dads had been indicted in brokerage scandals.

Josie signed in at the volunteers' desk and presented her brownies, bought at the bakery and transferred to a paper plate covered with foil to look homemade. Mrs. Jacobs, who had blue hair and a majestic bosom, gave Josie her assignment.

"You will work the Nature section in the book room. All the sections are marked. There's nibbles on the table by the back door. Help yourself. The children will be in the gym and the playroom and volunteers will keep them busy in supervised play. Did you bring Amelia?"

"She's with her best friend, Emma," Josie said.

"Super," Mrs. Jacobs said and turned to the next volunteer.

The hyperskinny Barrington women were wearing

their Rich Suburban Lady outfits, too, but their clothes
didn't seem like disguises. Josie wondered why. Her silk
turtleneck was slightly irregular, but the dropped stitches
didn't show under her resale-shop blazer. Maybe it was
the pants. No matter how much she paid, she couldn't
get her pants to fit like theirs.

Josie said hello to Emma's mother, then stopped at
the food table and put a single cheese cracker and two
celery sticks on her plate. She wanted to pile on the
food. She was ravenous. By the time she'd made sure
Amelia was fed and dressed this evening, she hadn't had
time to eat. But a Barrington mom did not stuff her face.

Josie wished her friend Alyce was here tonight. Her
one-year-old son had been enrolled at birth, like his father, but Alyce wouldn't have to volunteer for a few
years yet. Josie did see two of Alyce's neighbors. Saint
Kate, as everyone called her behind her back, was a
sweet-natured doctor's wife with prominent teeth and a
powerful urge to do good works.

"Our own Eleanor Roosevelt," sniped Amy the Slut.

Amy claimed to have slept with every husband in the
Wood Winds subdivision. She looked wicked in skintight
black D&G, four-inch fuck-me heels, and the infamous
twenty-seven-hundred-dollar snakeskin belt from Danessa.
This one was black. Josie felt sick when she saw it coiled
around Amy's waist. The snake looked at home there.

Did Amy make the saleswoman dismantle the display,
too? Did the police talk to her? Josie wondered how
Amy made out with Detective Yawney, then decided
that was a bad choice of words.

Josie smiled her way through more Barrington moms.
Mrs. Harrow Forbes III (Mrs. Trey to her friends) was
setting out the punch no one ever drank. Her daughter-
in-law, Mrs. Harrow Forbes IV (known as Ivy for her
husband's Roman numerals), was presiding over the
Home and Garden section at the table next to Josie. She
was pushing something called *The Proper Way to Hire,
Fire and Supervise Your Household Staff.*

"This little manual is super," Ivy said. "Good help is so hard to find."

I can't believe she actually said that, Josie thought.

"Oh, I can find plenty of help," Elizabeth, another Barrington mom, said. "They just aren't any good. My current housekeeper can't tell a do-rag from a dust rag."

She laughed charmingly at her own racist remark.

"What about you, Josie?" Ivy said. "Do you have trouble getting good help?"

Josie studied Ivy's bland, blond face for signs of malice, but didn't see any. The silly twit thought everyone had household staff.

"My cleaning lady is so lazy," Josie said. "I ask her to do things, but she always has an excuse why she can't. I'm lucky she runs the vacuum cleaner and dusts. I can't fire her. She's a single mom."

Both Barrington mothers nodded their sympathy.

I'd love to fire me, Josie thought. I sure can't get me to clean the place.

"You'd only find someone worse," Ivy said. "At least you can get her to vacuum and dust."

Elizabeth and Ivy happily discussed the servant problem for another half hour. Then Elizabeth bought three hundred dollars' worth of books, spending for the school in the best Barrington tradition.

Josie calculated she'd have to spend fifty bucks minimum to get out without embarrassing Amelia. She'd encourage her daughter to buy lots of chapter books so it would look like more. Josie had her eye on *Easy Home Decorating Solutions Under $100.*

It was nearly eight o'clock by the time Josie and Amelia left school with their load of books. Amelia bought *Artemis Fowl*, proud to be moving from the big-print books to more grown-up ones. She read to Josie by the dash light as they drove home.

After she got her daughter in bed, Josie put a slab of pizza in the microwave and opened the fridge. The fixings for margaritas were staring her in the face. She deserved one after this day. Josie fixed herself a pitcher while she ran a hot bubble bath. She lit all the candles in the bath, then poured herself a cold margarita, the edge of the glass rimmed with salt.

Once in the tub, she realized she'd forgotten the re-heated pizza. Oh, well. She'd eat it after her bath.

Josie didn't feel so nervous about her polygraph after the first drink, so she had another. Then she didn't feel nervous at all. She remembered that margaritas were responsible for bringing Amelia into the world and had another to celebrate.

"To my daughter, Amelia, the best mistake I ever made," she said and raised her glass in a toast.

Josie woke up at five a.m. in a tub of cold water, horribly hungover.

Chapter 14

"You know why you are here, don't you?" the polygraph examiner said.

Josie nodded and her head nearly fell off and rolled across the floor.

She was holding on to the doorframe of the polygraph room to keep from falling forward. A pile driver was pounding her brain flat. Her stomach lurched and sloshed.

This hangover was worse than morning sickness. Josie craved coffee but couldn't keep it down. She'd managed to swallow some white soda and a saltine. The cracker was like chewing sawdust. When she found last night's leathery pizza in the microwave, oozing orange grease, she'd almost lost it.

Did she really down a whole pitcher of margaritas? That first drink had been so relaxing. But Josie wasn't used to alcohol. She hadn't done any serious drinking in nearly a decade, since she found out she was pregnant with Amelia.

Now she wanted to crawl into a nice soft bed, lie down and die. Instead, she had to take the lie detector test. Driving to the Venetia Park police headquarters in morning rush-hour traffic was an ordeal. Josie jumped at every honk and winced at every brake screech.

Thanks to the tax money from Plaza Venetia, the suburban community was rich enough to have its own Colonial police station, landscaped by the Venetia Park garden club with authentic early American roses. Josie

was surprised the club hadn't put in stocks and a dunk-
ing stool to complete the Colonial motif.

There was nothing antique about the polygraph room.
It was soundproofed, dim and cool, with lights in the
hall to warn passersby to maintain silence when a session
was in progress.

The examiner gave his name, but it slid out of her
brain. He was one of those chubby pink men who
seemed jolly—unless you crossed him. He had a Santa
smile and cop's eyes.

Josie felt like Frankenstein's monster when the examiner hooked up all the wires and gadgets. There were
two bands around her chest, a blood-pressure cuff on
her arm, and some weird things on her fingertips.

"These sensors will measure three things," the examiner said. "Your heart rate, breathing pattern and the
sweat coming off your fingertips."

She was drenched in sweat. Flop sweat, alcohol poisoning, sheer terror—she had no idea what kind it was,
but there were gallons of it. Could she get electrocuted
by the salty water pouring off her skin onto the wires?

Josie hoped the machine didn't measure odors. Her
fear was an oily, pungent stink.

The examiner kept up a chipper little patter. Josie had
trouble taking in everything he said. He asked her a
zillion questions about her health and medications: Was
she on lithium, Prozac, Valium or Xanax? Did she have
a heart condition? Did she have a cold or a respiratory
illness? Had she ever had a stroke or a history of epi-
lepsy? Was she pregnant?

No, no and no.

"Are you in pain?" the examiner asked.

Oh, boy, am I, Josie thought. Last night I felt no pain
in Margaritaville. But this morning I'm in a world of
hurt.

The examiner was still talking. "By pain I mean, for
instance, a toothache, a headache or a recent injury."

Does a hangover count? Right. Be sure and tell the
examiner you got drunk and passed out last night. That

will really help your case. The police will say I murdered Danessa in an alcoholic blackout.

Why was he even asking? Couldn't the examiner see her pale skin and straggly hair? She looked like she'd crawled out of a train wreck. Or did everyone look like her when facing the polygraph Grand Inquisitor?

"I'm fine," Josie lied.

"You'll know the questions before the actual test," the examiner said cheerfully. "In fact, I've written them out. You read them over and think about them. Take your time. I have to make a phone call. I'll be back."

He put the clipboard in front of Josie, and she saw a healthy clump of whitish hair in his ears, like a ghostly shrub. Josie wondered if it could be successfully transplanted to his pink scalp. No, it was too wild and wiry. It would look like crabgrass in a zoysia lawn.

A lightning strike of pain hit her head, and Josie tried to gather her scattered thoughts. What was wrong with her? Why was she worried about the guy's ears? She needed to concentrate on this test.

She studied the clipboard with the questions. Some were no-brainers, even today, when she didn't have any functioning gray cells: "Is your name Josie Marcus? Were you born in St. Louis?"

Others were fairly straightforward: "Did you touch a red snakeskin belt worth twenty-seven hundred dollars?"

Some frightened her just reading them: "Did you kill Danessa Celedine? Did you strangle Danessa Celedine with the belt?"

What if she answered honestly but the machine thought she was lying? Her stomach did a barrel roll.

Josie looked up. There was a window-sized mirror with an odd silvery glaze on the wall across from her chair. A two-way mirror. She saw a lot of them in the discount stores that she mystery-shopped.

That jolly old liar. The examiner wasn't making a phone call. He was watching her while she read the questionnaire. She was sure Detectives Yawney and Waxley were back there, too. Josie wondered if her reaction to the clipboard questionnaire was the real test. She was tempted to stick out her tongue at the mirror, but in her current state it might flop out and not go back in.

She tried to read the questions again, but another lightning bolt of pain burned her brain. Josie put her head down on the desk. Should she tell the examiner she was too sick to take the test? Then she'd have to come back here again. She'd probably be sick and sweaty even without a hangover. She wanted to get the test over with.

The examiner came back in the room, smiling and rubbing his hands. "Any questions about the questions? Anything you don't understand about the test? I want to make sure that you understand everything I'll be asking you."

"I understand," Josie said.

"Good. Let me do a little pretest question, just to show you how it works. I want you to lie to me."

"What?" Josie's pounding brain had trouble taking in his words. "You want me to lie on purpose?"

"Riiiight!" The examiner was unbearably chipper. If Josie murdered anyone, it would be this man, right now, for willful and persistent cheerfulness. "Just answer yes or no, but make it a deliberate lie.

"Is your name Josie Marcus?" he asked.

"No," Josie said. She couldn't see the results on the examiner's computer screen, but she heard a printer clack and whir. The examiner handed her a chart with a huge spike sticking up from an almost flat line. Damn! she thought. The thing really leaps up when I lie.

The sweat poured off her in waterfalls now. The hair at her neck was wet. Her hands were slippery. Her head was going to split open any second.

They're going to catch me, she thought. I can't escape. *But I haven't done anything wrong.* She almost shouted it out loud. She had to keep reminding herself.

Josie forgot that hangovers made her feel like a Kafka creature, overwhelmed by doom and guilt. She was a bad mom, a bad daughter, a slacker and a sinner.

"Uh, Josie—I can call you Josie, right?" The examiner

gave his guileless smile, but he couldn't make those hard eyes twinkle.

"I wanted to ask you some pre-interview questions. We want to make sure you don't give us any false positives for information that has nothing to do with this case. We want to eliminate these now so we don't get a false positive when the test starts. I don't have the polygraph going. These questions and answers won't be on your polygraph test.

"Have you ever murdered anyone besides Danessa Celedine?"

A trick question. "I didn't murder Ms. Celedine or anyone else. Ever," Josie said.

"Do you know for sure that you have stolen anything valued in excess of one hundred dollars?"

"No," Josie said. "I mean yes. I mean I haven't stolen anything valuable. Sometimes when I sign credit-card receipts, the pens wind up in my purse. But I don't take them on purpose and they're mostly giveaways anyway."

"Have you ever shoplifted anything?"

"No." Josie could answer that one with confidence. It was a mystery shopper's biggest temptation, and the fastest way to end a career. She'd never taken so much as a candy bar.

"Have you ever brandished a weapon or otherwise threatened a person with bodily harm?"

"No," Josie said firmly.

"Have you ever committed any vandalism or other acts of revenge, no matter how minor?"

"No, never."

"Ever set any fires?"

Josie started to smile. "The only fire I ever set was at Mrs. Mueller's house. She's our nosy neighbor. She snitched me out to Mom. Said I was smoking behind the garage when I was fifteen. I found some really nasty dog doo, put it in a paper bag and set the bag on fire on her front porch. Then I rang her doorbell. When Mrs. Mueller saw the smoldering fire, she put her foot right into the big smelly pile. I got grounded for a month with no TV or phone, but it was worth it."

Josie thought the examiner's smile might have reached his eyes that time.

It was ten o'clock before they were ready to start the actual lie detector test. Josie had been sitting there for two hours, sick, scared and sweating like a road worker in August. She knew she wasn't thinking well. Even the easy polygraph questions were difficult to answer.

"Is your name Josie Marcus?" the examiner asked.

She nodded yes. Her head felt like a bowling ball.

"Please answer yes or no."

"Yes," Josie said.

"Is your hair brown?"

Was it? Lately, she'd been getting some gray. Josie used a L'Oreal rinse. But her hair was brown, even if it was touched up, wasn't it? Why hadn't she thought of that when she'd looked over the questions? Because she couldn't think.

She looked at her brown hair in the two-way mirror and said, "Yes." She was screwing this up. She knew it. Josie's palms were slick with sweat.

"Were you at Plaza Venetia on Wednesday, September sixteenth?"

"Yes."

"Did you see Danessa Celedine in the store on that day?"

"No."

"Did you see a salesperson named Marina?"

"Yes."

"Did you touch a red snakeskin belt worth twenty-seven hundred dollars?"

"Yes."

Here it comes, Josie thought. Here comes the question that decides everything. She remembered it from the list. Her stomach clenched.

"Did you kill Danessa Celedine?" the examiner asked.

"NO!" Josie shouted. Her head throbbed.

"Did you strangle Danessa Celedine with the belt?"

"No." She felt calmer this time.

"Do you know for sure who killed Danessa Celedine?"

"No."

"Did you have Danessa Celedine killed?"

"No." Josie almost laughed. She couldn't afford a lawyer, much less a hit man.

"Have you been completely truthful with the detectives as to your knowledge of how Danessa Celedine died?"

"Yes," Josie said. It was over. She sighed with relief.

"Thank you, Josie. I'd like to ask you those questions again."

The examiner asked them twice more. Each time he came to the crucial questions, Josie's heart pounded and her stomach squeezed into a tight ball.

After the third time, the examiner said, "That's it, Josie. Thank you." His smile was stillborn. His eyes were steel.

Josie knew she'd failed the polygraph.

She didn't know what signal the examiner gave to the two-way mirror, but Detectives Yawney and Waxley walked into the polygraph room together. Once again, they looked like a before-and-after photo: The balding Waxley was rumpled as an unmade bed. The handsome Yawney was model-sleek.

They sat down beside her, one on each side of her chair. The examiner stayed at his desk, blocking any run she might make for the door. She was trapped.

"You failed your polygraph," Detective Yawney said. His jaw was square and manly. He could be an actor playing a homicide detective. Josie wished he was. She wished none of this was real.

"We'd like to read you your rights again and have you sign this Miranda statement. You have the right to remain—"

Josie didn't let him finish. "I want my lawyer," she said.

Chapter 15

Josie decided if she ever met the devil, he'd look like Michael Yawney. The detective was darkly elegant. His powers of persuasion were impressive. But what made the man so dangerous was that he appeared to agree with her while twisting her words.

Detective Waxley sat silently at his side, an untidy imp.

"Of course you want a lawyer, Josie," Detective Yawney said. "That's your right. We know what happened to Danessa wasn't planned. If you talk to us now, without a lawyer, we can get you help."

Detective Waxley nodded.

"I want my lawyer," Josie said.

"It's easy to understand what happened. Danessa tried to take away your job. She was going to sue you." Detective Yawney's dark eyes were sincere and sympathetic. "Talk to us now, Josie, and I'll—"

Josie cut him off. "I want my lawyer."

"Once you get a lawyer, we can't help you anymore, Josie." He seemed sad now.

"I want my lawyer." Josie raised her voice until it was almost a scream. "Get me a lawyer now or I'll say you refused to despite the Miranda warning."

"Okay, Josie. You can call your lawyer."

That's when Josie realized she didn't have one.

She speed-dialed Alyce on her cellphone and prayed

her friend would be home. For the only time that day, something good happened: Alyce answered her phone.

"Thank God you're there. It's Josie. I need a lawyer. Right now."

"Josie, where are you?"

"At the Venetia Park police station. I flunked the lie detector test."

"Omigod. What happened? Never mind. Don't say another word to me or the police. I'll get you a lawyer right away, I promise. Stay right there. Well, of course you'll stay there. Hold on. I'll help you."

Alyce hung up. Josie could see her friend, blond hair flapping as she ran through the house gathering her purse and coat and giving instructions to her nanny.

There was nothing to do but wait, think and worry. In the dim room, soulless computer lights blinked like fiends' eyes. Small demons beat her skull with hammers and ran through her stomach with hot iron shoes. Josie's guilt tormented her with terrible visions of the future. She saw Amelia weeping as her mother was led off to jail. She saw cruel children at the Barrington School taunting her daughter. She saw Amelia growing up angry and alienated until she joined her mother in jail.

And Josie's poor mother. Jane would never hold her head up again in Maplewood. Mrs. Mueller's curtains would go into a twitching frenzy. Josie had brought this on the people she loved most.

It was nearly one o'clock when Josie heard voices outside the room and a woman in a navy pin-striped pantsuit strode through the door.

Josie's jaw dropped. It was Alyce, except this woman looked nothing like her fluffy friend. Alyce's floating hair was pulled into a severe chignon. She carried a black Dunhill briefcase. Her crisp white shirt was impeccable. Supermom had morphed into the Warrior Woman Lawyer. Josie had no idea Alyce could be so commanding.

"I'd like to talk to my client a moment," Alyce said.

Client? Josie thought.

"Certainly," Detective Yawney said. He and Detective Waxley started to leave the polygraph room.

"I'd like to talk to my client in a room that doesn't have a two-way mirror," Alyce said.

"I don't know if we—" Yawney said.

"You do," Alyce said in a take-no-prisoners voice. Josie had heard her use that voice only once before, when a pediatrician's assistant said the doctor couldn't see a coughing baby Justin until next Wednesday. An appointment suddenly opened at three that same afternoon.

"That room we passed when I came here will do fine," Alyce said. "I didn't see any other exits or windows in there. You can wait outside the door."

They were ushered into a small, windowless room painted institutional green. The two women sat at a scratched table bolted to the floor. After the door shut, Josie said in a frantic whisper, "Alyce, what are you doing here?"

"Representing you. All the lawyers I know, including my husband, are at some big conference for two days. You'll have to make do with me."

"But you told the police you're an attorney. Isn't that illegal?" Josie said.

"I didn't say I was a lawyer. I said you were my client. They just assumed I was a lawyer. Don't worry. I helped put Jake through law school. I took notes for his classes when he slept late. Crim Law was at seven thirty a.m., and he missed it two out of three days a week. I took the final exam for Jake, too. It was a huge class and I slipped in the back unnoticed. I got an A. Also, I watch a lot of crime movies."

"I don't—"

"My price is right. I won't charge you. I did good in there, Josie, didn't I? You would never guess I was a housewife."

Josie smiled for the first time all day. "You did terrific. You were tough."

"I'm serving on six volunteer boards. Two homicide detectives are nothing."

"Where'd you get that bit about the two-way mirror?" Josie said.

"I saw it in a movie. Any dedicated shopper knows a two-way mirror when she sees one. Listen, Josie, we can't waste time. You've got to follow my lead. Don't volunteer anything. Don't talk unless I say so. If I cut you off, stop immediately, even if you're in the middle of a sentence. Got that?"

"Yes," Josie said.

"Why do you think you flunked the test?" Alyce said.

"Because I was scared and hungover," Josie said.

"Did you tell the examiner you were hungover?"

"No," Josie said.

"That was a mistake, but we won't go into that now. After they read you your rights today did you say anything?"

"No," Josie said.

"Good."

"But they read me my rights last night, too. I don't know if that counts for today or not."

"Me, either," Alyce said. "The Miranda class was at three thirty and Jake never missed it. Well, we'll say they don't count today. Most lawyering is bluffing.

"Did you say anything during the pretest? Jake has a lot of corporate clients, and they make their employees take these lie detector tests. The actual polygraph is beside the point. They nail you with the pretest admissions. For instance, a company may ask you to take a lie detector test about drug use on the job. In the pretest they'll say, 'Now, so we don't get a false positive on the actual test, have you ever used any drugs outside the office?'

"You say, 'I smoke a little weed on the weekends.' Bingo, they've got you. You didn't use drugs at work, but they can say you admitted that you use illegal drugs. Did you tell the examiner anything during the pretest?"

"Just that I set fire to a pile of doggy doo on Mrs. Mueller's porch when I was fifteen," Josie said.

Alyce did not laugh, and this worried Josie.

"Okay, we're forewarned," Alyce said. "You tried on

that snakeskin belt at the store, right? Is that how you got your fingerprints on it?"

"Yes," Josie said.

"Then we're ready. Let's go."

Alyce knocked on the door, and the two detectives took them to a coffinlike box of a room with a brushed-steel table. Josie and Alyce sat on one side of the table, the two detectives on the other.

"You failed your polygraph test, Ms. Marcus," Detective Yawney said. She was no longer Josie. All trace of his devilish charm was gone.

Josie opened her mouth to speak. Alyce stamped hard on her foot, which distracted Josie from the pain in her head.

"Polygraph test results are not admissible in court," Alyce said. "There's a reason for that. We can take our own polygraph if you want when my client is feeling better."

"If she was sick, why didn't she say something? It's one of the questions our examiner asks."

"I—" Josie said. Alyce stamped on her foot again.

"My client was afraid it would prejudice you against her. Now, if that's all you have—"

"By her own admission, your client has a history of revenge and violent acts," Detective Yawney said. "She admits setting a fire when she became angry at a neighbor."

"She was fifteen. Setting fire to a bag of dog waste is a common teenage prank. Did the neighbor report this alleged fire to the authorities?"

"Juvenile records are sealed," Detective Yawney said.

"I know that," Alyce said. "But you didn't answer my question."

"No," Yawney said.

Alyce was good, Josie thought. Why was she wasting her time on charity boards? She should be arguing before the Supreme Court. But Josie knew the answer. It was the same reason she was traipsing through malls. Because she liked it.

"The mall security cameras had her going into the

Danessa store at nine fifty-two and coming out at nine fifty-seven," Detective Yawney said.

This time Josie didn't say a word.

"What about the cameras in the Danessa store?" Alyce said.

"Uh, they didn't have any film," the handsome detective said. "But a cell phone call at ten oh two places your client in the vicinity of Plaza Venetia."

"My client has already admitted being at Plaza Venetia that evening," Alyce said. "The cell phone call shows Ms. Marcus is telling the truth. She told you how her fingerprints got on that belt, detective. Were her prints only on the clasp, or were they in a position consistent with manual strangulation?"

"You know we can't tell you that," Detective Yawney said.

"That's what I thought. They were on the clasp," Alyce said. "The FBI tells me that Serge Orloff was selling nuclear arms to terrorists. They think one of his clients may have killed him and Danessa."

Thank goodness for the housekeeper mafia, Josie thought.

"You know my client isn't in the running for this murder, detectives. Are you going to charge her?" Alyce asked.

"Not at this time, Counselor. But tell her not to leave town."

"She understands. I hope you understand the legal consequences for damaging the reputation of a blameless working mother. Come along, Ms. Marcus. Good day, officers."

Josie followed her friend out. In the parking lot, she threw her arms around Alyce. "You were magnificent. You should go to law school. You'd make a terrific attorney."

"This isn't about me," Alyce said. "I've got the police off your back for the moment. Now we need to decide what to do next. Why don't you buy me lunch at Spencer's Grill?"

Tactful Alyce, Josie thought. Spencer's Grill is one place I can afford to take her.

The classic diner was on the Old Route 66, in downtown Kirkwood. Its fantastic neon thirties clock sign was a local landmark. Inside, the Grill's main room had six booths and a counter. The day's special was from another era: Salisbury steak, green beans and cottage cheese.

"I can see Jimmy Stewart eating here. And Judy Garland," Josie said.

"Doesn't say much for the food," Alyce said. "They're all dead."

Josie started giggling. Alyce did, too, and then they couldn't stop until the waitress showed up at their table with her order pad.

"Glad someone is having fun today. What can I get you ladies?"

Josie realized she was starving. She'd drained her water glass like she'd hiked the Sahara. She ordered a cheeseburger, fries, a Coke and coffee. The Coke came in a red plastic glass big enough to hold a dozen roses. Alyce had coffee only. She was still dieting.

"I really want to thank you," Josie said. "Where did you learn to talk back like that?"

"I told you. I'm on all these charity boards. I was one of the few women on this board with a bunch of doctors. I was supposed to be the citizens' advocate. One board member lived in my subdivision. He proposed me because he thought I was a mouse.

"It was a two-year term. The first year the doctors bullied me. My stomach clenched whenever I went to the meetings."

Josie's burger and fries arrived and her stomach did a happy little *sproing*. The waitress filled her cup. Josie nearly swooned at the smell of coffee. She was going to live after all.

"The second year I got some backbone," Alyce said. "After all, I was supposed to be representing the patients as an average person. The first time I spoke up, the doctors looked as if the potted plant had talked. They tried to browbeat me, but I didn't back down. After that, it was easy. The docs couldn't shoot me. I figured the worst that could happen was they'd throw me off the board—and that was fine with me. I quit being so afraid and started getting invited to serve on more boards. On another, we had to oust the board president. After you shout down twenty people, two detectives are easy."

Josie didn't think there was anything easy about Yawney and Waxley, but she was too busy wolfing down her food to say so. The patient waitress kept their coffee cups full.

"People make fun of clubwomen like me," Alyce said. "But it's good training. We know how to handle ourselves."

Poor Alyce, Josie thought. She could stand up to anyone except her husband. But Alyce had already explained why she wasn't afraid of the others—they had no power over her. Jake controlled their son and their money.

"This is my board suit." Alyce patted her pinstripes. "What do you think?"

"Very serious," Josie said.

"The briefcase is an old one of Jake's. Since we're being serious, what are we going to do about you?"

"I have to find out who killed Danessa," Josie said.

Alyce laughed. "Great idea. Why not fix the economy and bring peace to the Mideast while you're at it?"

"Look, I know if it's terrorists the feds will find Serge's killer," Josie said. "But I don't think that's who killed Danessa, or she would have died with Serge. She was strangled with her own belt, in her own store, by someone she let get close enough to put it around her neck. That's personal. It happened in my territory—in a mall and in a shop. Nobody understands stores and shopping better than I do. I've got the police beat on that count."

Josie bit into a crisp, salty fry, and the conversation

stopped. She pushed her plate toward Alyce. "Try these," she said. "They're a religious experience."

"Maybe one," Alyce said.

The fries went faster than iPods at Christmas. When there was nothing but salt crystals left on her plate, Josie said, "Danessa had a knack for making enemies, but she also knew how to play to the press. Since she was the darling of the media, they never reported her rages. She must have fired or threatened employees or customers. Once she was crossed, Danessa couldn't control that temper. I saw her in full rage. It was scary. Believe me, when she finished screaming, you wanted to kill her."

"Makes sense," Alyce said. "So what's your plan?"

"Visit all the Danessa stores. Try to find Marina and talk to Olga."

Alyce sloshed coffee into her saucer. "Are you nuts? You want to go back to Plaza Venetia?"

"It's the only way," Josie said. "Besides, it's like your charity boards. The worst they can do is throw me out."

"I'd better go with you," Alyce said. "You may need a lawyer. I'll pick you up at eight thirty tomorrow morning."

"Make it nine-thirty. I have to take Amelia to school. Omigod! What time is it?" She looked at her watch. "Two twenty-five! I can't believe it. I've got to call Mom."

Josie dug in her purse for her cell phone. She must have turned it off at the police station. She had fourteen calls from her mother and six from her boss. She called Jane first.

"Josie, where are you?" her mother said. "What good are all those fancy functions on that overpriced cell phone if you don't turn it on? I've been trying to reach you all day. Something bad has happened."

Fear gripped Josie's heart. "What's wrong, Mom? Is Amelia okay? Are you all right?"

"It's that terrible person you work for. Harry. He says you have to call right now. He was so rude."

"I'll call him, Mom, and kick his fat fanny. I'm on my

way to pick up Amelia. Don't worry. Everything is fine."
She clicked off her phone.

"What is it?" Alyce said.

"My boss, Harry. He's making trouble for Mom. I
better call him now."

"Your mouthpiece is standing by," Alyce said. Before
Josie could punch in Harry's number, her cell phone rang.

"Where have you been?" her boss said. His voice was
oozing trouble. "The cops were here again. They said
you flunked your lie detector test and you were at the
mall when Danessa was killed."

"Can they tell you that?" Josie asked.

"They just did," he said.

"Lie detector tests are not admissible in court,"
Josie said.

"Neither is Section 131-B," Harry said. "You lied
about that. I checked with the company lawyers. I am
hereby placing you on unpaid administrative leave. If
and when your name is cleared, I'll rehire you."

"But—"

Alyce grabbed the phone from Josie. "This is Alyce
Bohannon, counsel for Josie Marcus. I heard you yelling
at my client. Are you her supervisor? Good. I've been
in touch with the FBI. They believe Serge and Danessa
were killed by terrorists. You will not place her on unpaid leave. You will put her on paid leave. Paid leave.
Do you understand? If and when she is arrested, which
the police tell me will not happen, we will reconsider her
employment status. In the meantime, you are looking at
one fat lawsuit."

Josie could hear Harry yelling. "Paid leave," he
screamed. "No way. I'm not paying her to do nothing.
She can work if she wants to be paid."

"Fine," Alyce said.

Josie heaved a sigh of relief.

"She'll work the dregs, I tell you," Harry shouted.
"The dregs."

"If she's working for you, she's used to that," Alyce
said, and snapped the phone shut.

Chapter 16

The Danessa store at Plaza Venetia was in mourning.

The Lucite stands were draped in sheer black silk, like widows' veils. The purses in warm winter reds and gaudy summer-sale shades were gone. Everything displayed was dead black.

"Should I be wearing this red suit?" Josie had on her resale-shop Escada with the gold braid, the one that made her feel like a doorman.

"Why not?" Alyce said. "I'm wearing green, and that woman at the counter looks like the Great Pumpkin in orange. She's even heavier than I am. It's a store, not a funeral home."

But it felt like a wake.

The shop was overflowing with flowers from Danessa worshipers. There was everything from a single grocery-store rose in green paper to bouquets suitable for a mob funeral. Flower arrangements spilled out the door and were lined up in front of the store, along with teddy bears, Russian dolls and a pink Danessa purse filled with violets. Josie recognized the color as last season's.

"This is creepy," Josie said. "The last time I was here, Danessa was dead in the back room."

"At least there aren't any snakeskin belts out," Alyce said.

Black-clad customers carrying Danessa purses stood in little groups. Josie could hear scraps of conversation:

"—donated ten thousand dollars. Danessa was so generous."

"She and Serge showed up in matching full-length sable coats. Fur is terribly politically incorrect, but they looked like movie stars. Serge said that in his country fur—"

"—won't be the same without her."

What won't be the same, Josie wondered: the city, the charity scene, or the Danessa stores?

All three, she decided.

The basket of autographed Danessa photos had been replaced by a single black-draped portrait flanked by bouquets of lilies. Danessa looked shining, surreal, untouchable. It was as if the screaming harridan who'd rushed into Harry's office never existed. Danessa was becoming an icon, the retail Princess Di.

The store was packed, but no one was buying. Hordes of curiosity seekers came to see the murder scene. They were fatter than the elegant mourning customers, and favored pastel polyester pantsuits and flea-market Fendi.

"Is that price tag a mistake, hon, or is this piddly little purse really three thousand dollars?" A plump grandmother in lavender dangled something the size of a teabag.

The razor-thin mourning customers reacted with scandalized silence.

Josie thought the woman had good sense—and good taste. Like many Danessa products, the three-grand purse was not first quality. The stitches on the strap were crooked.

A sleek little sales associate cut the lavender woman dead and hurried toward Josie and Alyce.

"Looks like we passed inspection," Josie said.

"My name is Olga. May I help you?" Josie remembered the saleswoman, but Olga seemed to have forgotten her. Retail amnesia was a common disease. Olga was still small and neat, but today she didn't look like a self-satisfied cat. Close up, the saleswoman seemed frantic.

Her spiky hair looked like she'd been trying to tear it out. White showed all around her eyes, like a frightened animal. In the crowded store she was rapidly losing her catlike self-possession.

"Yes," Josie said. "Last time I was here, I was waited on by a saleswoman named Marina. Is she here today?"

Olga seemed to go rigid. "No Marina works here," she said. She would not look Josie in the eye.

"I'm sure she waited on me, too," Alyce said.

The saleswoman stared at Alyce. "You look familiar. You have been here before. Perhaps I waited on you."

"Oh, no," Alyce said. "You don't look anything like Marina. She was tall and blond."

"We have had no tall blondes here, except Danessa. If the store became busy, Danessa would personally wait on customers. That's who you saw."

"Oh, we both know who Danessa was," Josie said. "Everyone does. Marina had an accent like yours. It's very attractive. Russian, right?"

Olga looked wildly around the room, then said, "May I get you something? If not, I must go. We are short of hands. That is correct to say, yes?"

"Yes. You are shorthanded. But you've been helpful. I'd like to come back when it isn't so crowded and do some serious shopping. You said your name is Olga?"

"Olga Rachmaninoff, like the composer." She fled into the crowd like a cat who'd been stepped on.

"Well, that was interesting," Josie said, as they headed toward Alyce's luxurious SUV. She sank into the soft leather seats. "Olga was lying her little head off. She knows Marina."

"Certainly does," Alyce said. "What do you want to do next?"

"Can I talk to Danessa's housekeeper?" Josie said.

"Mrs. Perkins? You can, but she won't talk to you. Oh, she'll be polite, but she won't tell you anything. When the FBI interviewed her, she bored them silly with her household routine. The feds asked her what Serge and Danessa were like, and she said he ate four eggs, pork chops and bacon for breakfast and Danessa wanted her sheets changed twice a day."

"Why wouldn't Mrs. Perkins cooperate with the police?" Josie said.

"With Serge and Danessa dead, she's out of a job. Housekeepers who tell secrets don't work again. Mrs. Perkins knows we're all watching her. On the other hand, she may talk to you as a favor to me. It's very delicate. Mrs. P. has to be approached carefully. Let me ask my housekeeper, Mrs. Donatelli, the best way to talk to her. What do you want to do in the meantime?"

"Let's visit the other Danessa stores and see if we can find Marina," Josie said. "Is that too much driving for you?"

"My time is yours, until two o'clock."

They headed west on Highway 40 to the new rich subdivisions. There'd been a cold snap last night, and the oaks and maples lining the highway were a riot of red, yellow and orange.

"Fall is my favorite time of year," Josie said. "I couldn't live in a climate like Florida, where you don't have four seasons."

"It's beautiful," Alyce said. "But it makes me feel sad. The seasons mark the passage of time, and I wonder what kind of future I have."

"A good one, from the way you performed at the police station."

"That was a fluke," Alyce said. "I feel old, fat and trapped."

Josie wanted to tell her friend how smart and strong she was, how she could succeed at anything if she'd believe in herself. But Josie had heard that same lecture too often. She knew it would do no good. Besides, who am I to judge a woman who has a gorgeous house and a rich husband? What do I have that she doesn't?

Your freedom, whispered a little voice. Unless the cops arrest you.

"I rushed out of Spencer's Grill to pick up Amelia yesterday," Josie said. "I didn't thank you properly for saving my job."

"Don't thank me until you see what Harry is giving you," Alyce said. "You may be cursing my name."

"This is such a mess," Josie said. "It's bad enough I've sucked Mom into this. When I was growing up, she worked hard for me. Now that she's retired from the bank, she deserves to have fun. It's not her job to raise my child. I feel so guilty. Then yesterday I roped you into this."

"Josie," Alyce said, "your mom loves you. You're my best friend. We want to help you. Quit feeling guilty. You're a mom. You're supposed to make other people feel guilty."

Josie laughed. But Alyce's gracious speech didn't make her feel better. She didn't like owing people.

"Why did the police come down so hard on me yesterday?" Josie said. "So what if I flunked that lie detector test? Those tests aren't admissible and they aren't reliable."

"The cops did it because they could," Alyce said. "My husband Jake goes on about this all the time. His firm sees it with white-collar crimes, too. This is far worse. It's a high-profile double murder. The police are under tremendous pressure. They'll use any means to go after a suspect. Don't take this wrong, Josie, but you're not protected like the people at Wood Winds. That's why I wanted you to get a lawyer, someone from Jake's crowd."

Alyce seemed embarrassed to have mentioned money, even indirectly. She abruptly switched the subject. "Do you ever find these malls depressing? It's the same stores, the same people, the same canned air and music."

"Oh, no," Josie said. "Everyone thinks that. But malls are like Levittown, that subdivision where all the houses were alike. Scholars went back later and found that people had stamped their own personalities on the houses. The homes had become different.

"Malls are that way, too. Some get better, some get worse with age. Malls can make dumb decisions. One nicely moneyed mall put in a shop that sold gang clothes and ran off their high-priced tenants. Some malls make smart moves, like Plaza Frontenac. They added those upscale movie theaters that serve espresso. Brilliant. It revived that shopping center.

"The Mall at Covington is an interesting case. Mid-westerners think valet parking is a waste of time and money, and they don't like the car parkers playing with their radio buttons. Many Midwest malls have only a token valet service. But a bunch of transplanted New Yorkers live out by Covington. New Yorkers think valet parking is classy. So Covington had to expand its valet service."

Inside the Mall at Covington, the Danessa store looked exactly like the one at Plaza Venetia. It was packed with curiosity seekers, a scattering of mourning customers, and enough flowers for a greenhouse. The cloying scent of hothouse blooms and high-priced perfume made Josie dizzy.

An elegant saleswoman named Charlotte told them, "We've never had any Marina work here."

"Excuse me, miss, do you have this in yellow?" a woman said. "Or brown?"

"I have to go," Charlotte said, rushing off to locate the handbag.

"I think she's telling the truth," Josie said. She was examining a black Danessa clutch. One of the pavé diamonds on the clasp was covered with glue, a careless little detail.

"Me, too," Alyce said. "Let's get out of here. It reminds me of my grandmother's wake. All it needs is an open casket by the cash register."

They reached the green lawns and carefully tended flower beds of the Shoppes at Greenhills twenty minutes later.

"This place looks like Forest Lawn," Alyce said.

"You've got funerals on the brain," Josie said.

"Gee, I wonder why?" Alyce said.

This Danessa store had the most extravagant displays of grief. Josie and Alyce picked their way through piles of teddy bears, homemade cards, a WE LOVE YOU FOR-EVER, DANESSA banner, and mounds of mums, roses and stargazer lilies. The funeral-flower scent sucked the life from the room. The elegant mourning customers and the chubby curiosity seekers mingled uneasily, carefully avoiding one another.

"Hi, my name is Barbara. How may I help you?" This saleswoman was a brisk redhead of about thirty.

"I'm looking for an evening purse in gold," Alyce said.

Josie stared at her, but said nothing. This wasn't part of the plan. Alyce had never shown any interest in little frivolities. Her friend was full of surprises lately.

Barbara brought out satin-lined boxes of tiny purses. Josie hated evening purses. Carrying one made her feel like she was in drag. Alyce picked through the pretty trifles, snapped several open and shut and settled on a delicate gold-filigree number for a thousand bucks.

When Barbara went into the back room for more wrapping paper, Josie said, "What's got into you, spending a grand on a useless purse? I've never seen you pay more than five hundred dollars for a dress."

"Last night Jake said I dressed like a country bumpkin at his law firm functions. Those were his exact words. He said my clothes didn't cost enough and I made him look bad. I have to go to the firm's winter dinner-dance. Well, that's one problem in our marriage I can fix. Our credit-card bills are going to look like the national debt."

Oh, oh, Josie thought. Grudge spending—the wronged wife's revenge.

"Also, I thought the salesperson might talk to us more if I bought something," Alyce said.

Barbara returned with a credit card receipt and a pile of filmy black paper printed with silver *D*'s. She began tenderly wrapping the tiny purse.

"I guess you've sold a lot with all these people here," Josie said.

"This is my only sale today," Barbara said. "Nobody is buying. They're all lookie-loos."

"Last time I was here, I was waited on by Marina," Josie said. "Tall blonde with a Russian accent. Does she still work here?"

"She never did," Barbara said, and two bitter lines appeared around her mouth. "Marina is Serge's sister. I can see why you'd think she was staff. She walks around like she owns the place."

Alyce isn't the only one who wants revenge today, Josie thought.

Then it hit her: Marina was real. I'm not crazy. I didn't make her up. Charlotte has just confirmed that Marina was in this store.

"Actually, she waited on me," Josie said. "She was rude and I didn't buy anything, but she did show me—" She started to say "a snakeskin belt" then changed it to "some things."

"You definitely got Marina." Barbara's eyes lit up with anger. "She's always horning in on our sales. 'I am a natural at selling,' she says in that stagy accent. She comes by to 'help' us." Barbara made quote marks with her fingers. "Mostly she interferes with our sales and jams the cash register. She wanted part of my commission. I nearly quit over that one. Danessa gave her the commission, but to her credit she didn't take it out of my money."

"How is Marina taking Serge and Danessa's deaths?"

"I have no idea," Barbara said. "I haven't seen her in a month. If I'm really lucky, I'll never see her again."

Josie raised an eyebrow.

"I must sound terrible, but it's one of the curses of retail—putting up with the owner's relatives—or in this case, the owner's boyfriend's relatives."

"I'm sorry," Josie said.

That small show of sympathy started the words pouring from Barbara. Josie could only guess what set her off: the hot, crowded store, the sales dry spell, the weird tributes from grief-stricken people who never knew Danessa.

"You don't know what it's been like working here," Barbara said. "Danessa's moods, the craziness with Marina, the arguments. Marina, Danessa and Serge were always fighting. They'd yell and throw things in the stockroom. I had to stand out here on the floor and smile and pretend I didn't hear the shouts and thumps in the back room."

"I'm not surprised," Josie said. "Sales is an emotional business. What did they fight about?"

"I'm not sure," Barbara said. "When Marina got really upset, she'd lapse into Russian, which Serge and Danessa understood, but I didn't. The last time she was here, I heard her fighting with Serge in the stockroom, but I didn't understand a word.

"I guess you think I'm being disloyal." Barbara's pale skin was flushed with anger, or maybe embarrassment. "But I can't take it anymore. I'm quitting. Today is my last day. I have a job at the Galleria. Danessa's death was the last straw. We had people with Geiger counters or something, testing all three stores for radiation."

"Did they find anything?" Josie asked.

"Of course not," Barbara said. "They would have closed us down if they did. But ever since Danessa's murder, I'm scared to work here. I won't go in that stockroom alone after dark. I keep wondering which of us is going to die next."

Chapter 17

"What a drama queen," Alyce said. "Did she really say, 'I keep wondering which of us is going to die next'?"

Josie and her friend were strolling toward their parking spot at the Shoppes at Greenhills. The mall's lawn and flower beds seemed peaceful and protected as an English estate. They seemed to say that murder happened to less-privileged people.

"You're too rough on her," Josie said. "Barbara's boss was found dead in a stockroom. Sure, it happened at the other store, but it would freak me out. Did you get a look at some of Barbara's customers? Ghouls bringing flowers and touching the dead woman's purses. I swear some of those people had extra-long eyeteeth."

"The store should have closed for a mourning period," Alyce said. "It's attracting the wrong people. The right ones won't come back."

"I'm surprised the PR woman didn't step in and insist that the stores be closed for a few days," Josie said.

"You mean Stephanie? She's too young to have any power," Alyce said. "I'd like to know what she's doing in that job."

Alyce's blond hair and moss green dress floated on the cool fall air. A hint of gold glinted at her ears. She was a stately woman. How could her husband say she looked like a bumpkin? What was Jake really saying? You've gained weight after the baby and you're no longer a hot babe?

"Hey, this was a good trip," Josie said. "I'm happy with what we learned. There really is a Marina."

"Those people had to be crazy," Alyce said. "Marina, Danessa and Serge all yelling at one another and throwing things in the stockroom."

As she got worked up, Alyce's stroll turned into a quick, impatient stride. It was easy for her. She was wearing flats. Josie fought to keep up in her rich lady heels. Her pinched feet hurt.

"That's retail," Josie said. She felt like a terrier running alongside a car. "Especially the small family-owned stores. At least Danessa and Serge kept their fights confined to the back room. I've been in shops where the owners have screaming battles in front of the customers over what dress to display. I've seen partners literally faint from rage. Sometimes the staff calls in sick to avoid the family fights.

"If there were knockdown drag-outs going on in the back room at Danessa, I'd say it's typical of a certain kind of retail operation—even restrained."

"Amazing," Alyce said. "Just when you think everyone is on Prozac."

Josie climbed into the monster SUV and kicked off her needle-nosed shoes. Ahh. Comfort at last.

"Why didn't you ask that saleswoman if she told the police Marina was Serge's sister?" Alyce said as she backed out of the parking spot.

"I wanted to," Josie said, "but it would have ruined my cover as a rich suburban lady. We're not supposed to know about the police. I'll tell Detective Yawney if he calls me again."

"You can count on that," Alyce said. "But what do you have? The first name—Barbara—of a woman who doesn't work for Danessa anymore. We don't even know where her new job is."

"The police are smart enough to track her down at the Galleria," Josie said.

She leaned back on the pillow-soft headrest and felt suddenly exhausted. She had slept little last night. She'd lied to her mother and daughter yesterday, saying she'd signed a routine statement for the police. She suspected Jane didn't believe her, and the shadows were back in Amelia's eyes. Josie's lies were like boulders on her back. She had to find a way to carry this burden or it would crush her.

Alyce's cell phone rang. "Mrs. Donatelli!" Alyce said, and mouthed, "My housekeeper.

"She'll see us? When? Now? Super. We can be there in ten minutes.

"Got her!" Alyce snapped the phone shut in triumph. "Mrs. Perkins, Danessa's housekeeper, wants to talk with you right now. It's eleven thirty. Is that okay?"

"It's terrific." Josie struggled to put aside her weariness. This was important.

"Mrs. Perkins will talk to you on one condition," Alyce said. "She wants the lowdown on how to be a mystery shopper. I think she wants to quit the housekeeping business. Your meeting is secret and has to stay that way. She'll tell you what you want to know if you'll tell her all about your job."

Josie groaned and looked down at her mall-tortured toes. "Is she in for a rude awakening."

The SUV pulled into the long drive at Danessa's. There was still yellow crime-scene tape and a police car guarding the main house. They took the side road back by the pool, as Mrs. Perkins had instructed. She lived in a rose-covered cottage that was bigger than Josie's house.

Mrs. Perkins was a short, sturdy woman with blue-gray hair and smile crinkles. Josie was sure Sherlock Holmes's Mrs. Hudson would look like her. Mrs. Perkins smelled of cinnamon and apples. She took Josie into a sunny yellow kitchen and sat her down at a blue table.

"I'll just take a book and read by the pool, Mrs. Perkins," Alyce said.

"Good idea, my dear. May I bring you some tea and an apple tart?"

"That will be lovely, thank you," Alyce said.

"Cream or ice cream?"

"Neither, thank you, Mrs. Perkins. I'm on a diet."

Mrs. Perkins clucked her disapproval. She was a born fusser and seemed to enjoy setting a pretty tray for Alyce with a Blue Willow cup and a generous slice of apple tart. She kept the teapot at her place and poured for Josie.

Mrs. Perkins took her tea and tart with heavy cream. Josie followed her example. At the first bite, Josie wondered how Danessa had stayed so slim. She'd be built as generously as Mrs. Perkins if she ate like this every day.

"I want the rules straight before we begin," Mrs. Perkins said, with a look that must have terrified many a maid. "Everything I say stays here. You will not tell the police or your friend outside. I can't have loose lips flapping."

"I understand," Josie said. "But the silence must be mutual. I can't be giving away my trade secrets."

Mrs. Perkins looked pleased with her bargain. "Precisely," she said, with great satisfaction. "What do you want to know?"

"You had a chance to observe Danessa like no one else. The media painted her as the next Martha Stewart. Was she really a shrewd businesswoman?"

"Danessa couldn't balance a checkbook," Mrs. Perkins said, and took a hefty forkful of apple tart. "I know, because I saw her throw one across her office here when she couldn't get the numbers right. The real money and the business know-how came from Serge. He was her silent partner."

"Serge? Silent?" Josie said.

"You'd never guess it the way he talked to reporters. But he kept quiet when it was important. Danessa was the beautiful front for the business. He was the money and the brains."

"Where did Serge get the money?" Josie said. "This apple tart is wonderful." Josie was afraid her compliment would distract Mrs. Perkins, but she took it as her due.

"He came over from Russia with tons of it. At least, that's my understanding."

"Do you think he was smuggling nuclear materials?" Josie said.

Mrs. Perkins looked indignant. "I never saw anything of the kind. That's what I told those government gentlemen. I would consider it my patriotic duty to tell them if I saw foreign spies sneaking around here. I wouldn't put up with it for a minute."

Josie thought she'd feel a lot safer if Mrs. Perkins was working for the CIA.

"The FBI hasn't found anything," Mrs. Perkins said. "All those men in moon suits haven't either, though they tore up the house and yard something terrible. I don't know how I'm going to get it back in order."

Josie wanted to make sure she understood. "They didn't find any radioactivity?"

"Not a trace," Mrs. Perkins said. "They had government agencies I've never heard of running around with things I've never seen before."

Interesting. Josie had her first juicy bit of information.

"How did Danessa and Serge get along?" she said.

"Like cats and dogs," Mrs. Perkins said. "Both had tempers. I wouldn't have been surprised if they killed each other. They fought all the time. I used to look at those newspaper photos of them gazing into each other's eyes and laugh. Their romance was all for show. But I'll say this—their fights never left this house."

Except when they took them to work, Josie thought.

"What did they fight about?"

"He used to switch to Russian when he thought I was around," Mrs. Perkins said. "But there were plenty of times when he didn't know I was there. Serge was pressuring Danessa to marry him. He was having problems staying in this country and he needed an American wife. Danessa didn't want to marry him. Serge was afraid he'd be deported."

"Surely he wouldn't have a problem finding an American woman to marry him," Josie said. "Serge was handsome, famous and rich."

"Immigration does not look kindly on marriages of convenience." Mrs. Perkins poured more tea and dished out another helping of apple tart. Josie didn't want to stop her talking, so she let it stay on her plate.

"Serge thought Danessa owed him marriage after the millions he poured into her stores," Mrs. Perkins said. "She might have gone through with it. But then she caught him in bed with a neighbor lady."

"Amy?" Josie said. "Or Kate?"

"Both," the housekeeper said.

Josie spilled the sugar. She figured Amy the Slut would do almost anything, but she didn't see Saint Kate going in for threesomes.

Mrs. Perkins laughed. "Oh, not both at once, but both in the same week. There were other women, but he snuck around with those two the most. Danessa had almost forgiven Serge for Amy, because, well, everybody sleeps with Amy. But then she caught him with Kate."

Mrs. Perkins seemed to be enjoying her delicious scandal. Her eyes were bright and her cheeks were red. She leaned in over the tea things and lowered her voice. "Kate's husband is a surgeon at St. Helen's Hospital. He leaves at four thirty every morning. Serge would be in Kate's bed by five. Danessa slept right through his absences. She was a sound sleeper and they didn't share the same bed. Serge had Amy in the afternoon when Danessa was at the stores.

"Danessa caught Serge with Amy first. He swore it was over and he'd be faithful forever. Six days later, Danessa had a touch of the flu. She got up early one morning to use the bathroom and saw him sneaking across the yard to Kate's.

"Danessa threw him out of the house, but he wormed his way back. She needed his money until this big Creshan deal went through. Then I think she wanted to dump him. She refused to marry him, even to save his immigration status."

"Do you think Danessa poisoned him?" Josie said.

The housekeeper laughed. "She should have, but Serge took that rat poison himself. He needed a blood thinner, Coumadin, and he was too cheap to pay for it. His doctor said Serge was a candidate for stroke. Serge said the price of that medicine was what would give him a stroke. He thought American prescriptions were too high."

"I remember when he said that," Josie said. "My mother read it to me in the paper."

"Coumadin is warfarin, the same ingredient in rat poison. That's how the rats die. They bleed to death, you know." Mrs. Perkins had the same delightfully shocked look as when she discussed Serge's double infidelity.

"That's how he died. He hit his head and bled to death. You won't see that in the papers. I heard the FBI talking in this very kitchen. The poison killed him—but he bled to death on the living room floor. Just like the rats." She nearly smacked her lips in satisfaction.

"Serge thought he'd save money, so he took rat poison," Mrs. Perkins said. "He carefully calibrated his weight compared to that of a rat, and mixed the poison in his orange juice. When someone wanted to get rid of that big rat, Serge, she simply increased his dose. Easy. Simple. Safe."

"Except for him," Josie said. "He was a multimillionaire. Couldn't he afford the medicine?"

"My dear, you have no idea how cheap the rich can be," Mrs. Perkins said. "One of my past employers was going on vacation. He had half a ham in his icebox. He charged me for it. I'd worked for him fifteen years, and he made me pay seven dollars for a used ham. Serge was that kind of millionaire. He was killed by someone who knew his cheap habit and upped the dose."

That made Danessa the chief suspect, except she was dead and the police weren't acting like she'd killed her lover. Josie bet Danessa wasn't the only woman who was mad at Serge, if he was hopping in and out of beds like a Russian rabbit.

"Who do you think killed Serge, if it wasn't Danessa?"

"One of his women," Mrs. Perkins said. "I didn't tell the police that, because I may want to get another position in this area."

"I understand. Who killed Danessa? Do you think it was the same person?"

"I do not." Mrs. Perkins was emphatic. "They had enough enemies for two people. I think one of her employees murdered her. Danessa was mean. She made that hotel lady, Leona Helmsley, look like Employer of the Year. She knew better than to mess with me. Good housekeepers are too hard to find. But she'd take it out on the store staff. Danessa would show up at the shop and start ordering people around. She cut people's pay and kept the stores short-staffed. She liked to brag about it. She didn't care if a sales clerk quit. There was always another.

"When your mystery-shopper report came out, she went crazy. I thought it was her own fault. She didn't hire a cleaning staff. She made her employees clean the store. It was a mistake. When the sales staff got busy, they didn't have time to wipe down those Lucite stands, and they show every fingerprint. I could have told her that.

"Also, most of the staff didn't know it, but they would be losing their health insurance when the new company took over. That was the one benefit they got working there, but Creshan never gave their employees insurance. Olga tumbled to that."

"You mean the saleswoman at the Plaza Venetia store—small, dark, spiky hair?" Josie said.

"That's her. She's their top sales associate. She was a good friend, too. She spent the night here sometimes. Olga loved this house, maybe even more than Serge and Danessa."

"Was Olga one of Serge's lovers?" Josie asked.

"No." Mrs. Perkins stopped to consider the idea. "I really think she was just a friend. Serge seemed to find her company restful for that reason.

"Olga called Danessa at home two days before she died. Olga was so mad, she was screaming and calling Danessa a bitch. That's what she said to me, 'Mrs. Perkins, is that lying bitch in?' She threatened to punch Danessa. Olga has a heart condition. She needs her health insurance."

"How do you know that?" Josie said.

"I accidentally left the phone off the hook after I fetched Danessa."

Josie looked at Mrs. Perkins's bland face. She was a sensational liar.

"I did tell the police about Olga," Mrs. Perkins said. "It was my duty."

Thank God, Josie thought. It was probably the only thing keeping me out of jail. Olga had a good reason for leaving my fingerprints on that blasted snakeskin belt.

"Did you know anyone called Marina—a tall blonde with a Russian accent?" Josie said. "Was she Serge's sister?"

"Marina called herself his sister, but I saw them kissing once, and I had my doubts," Mrs. Perkins said. Again, she looked agreeably shocked. "If Marina was a sister, it was a strange relationship. She came around the house, but not often. Danessa barely tolerated her. They didn't speak English around me."

Josie was reeling. Serge had a possible incestuous relationship?

"Anything else I can tell you?" Mrs. Perkins said.

"That was quite enough," Josie said. She wanted a shower.

"How about more tea and a little more tart?" Mrs. Perkins helped herself to another generous slice and more cream.

Josie's last helping had disappeared, and she wasn't sure how. "No, thank you. This was delicious."

"Well, then." Mrs. Perkins folded her hands. "Now you can help me. You know all the best places for bargains. You can tell me the best outlet malls."

"Actually, outlet malls may not be the best places for

bargains, " Josie said. "In many cases, you're not getting terrific discounts. You're getting things made especially for the outlets. Ever hear of cutups?"

Mrs. Perkins shook her head no.

"The clothing makers take last year's fabric and make it into this year's styles," Josie said. "Some outlet-mall clothes have things wrong with them. I bought a gorgeous white designer suit at an outlet mall. When I got it home, I saw that the lining had been patched. Because the jacket was white, the patch showed. I couldn't wear it."

"You don't say," Mrs. Perkins said.

"I do," Josie said. "Do you have any store credit cards?"

"Never use them," Mrs. Perkins said.

"Many stores will give you ten percent off the day you open a new charge account with them. Just remember to pay your whole bill when it arrives. The interest rates will kill you."

Mrs. Perkins nodded solemnly, as if she was receiving the word on two stone tablets.

"You may get better buys at department stores and big clothing chains than the outlets. Many department stores start discounting their merchandise after two months or so. Some of the big clothing chains start sooner, at one month. The first markdown is usually twenty to thirty percent. If you're hard to fit—"

"I am an ample woman," Mrs. Perkins said.

"Then you'll want to take the first discount. If you like to gamble, wait another month. The clothes will be marked half off. The third markdown, often two to three weeks later, is a whopping seventy percent, but by then you have little choice."

"That is extraordinary. I'd never guess." Mrs. Perkins looked pleased. "Do you get to mystery-shop the department stores?"

"Oh, yes," Josie said. "Also boutiques, discount stores, restaurants, casinos and tourist attractions. I shop the big apartment complexes to make sure they are rented properly."

"My word." Mrs. Perkins lowered her voice again. "Now, will you tell me what you make?"

"I will, but that's my deepest secret." Josie took a deep breath and told.

Mrs. Perkins looked shocked. "That's all you make—for all that work? For tramping to the ends of the earth? That's terrible. I may as well stick to housekeeping, though it's hard on my knees. I can name my price as a housekeeper. But not if they know I've been talking to you."

Josie held up the cream pitcher. "I solemnly swear on this mother's milk that I will never reveal your secrets if you will never reveal mine."

Mrs. Perkins patted the fat pitcher and said, "Amen."

Chapter 18

"You swore on a pitcher of whole cream?" Alyce said.

"Hey, a cow is a mother, too," Josie said.

Alyce began making gasping sounds, then pulled the SUV over to the side of the road.

"Are you okay?" Josie said, alarmed.

"No, I'm laughing so hard I'm going to run us into a ditch." Alyce's face was red and tears ran down her cheeks.

"It's not that funny," Josie said. "None of it is. This is serious business. I flunked that lie detector test, remember? The cops are after me."

Alyce wiped her eyes and tried to wipe the smile off her face. "Okay, then, let's go about this in an organized way. I'll be chair of the Save Josie Committee. We can hold our first meeting on Highway 40, while I drive you back to your house. What's our agenda?"

"To find out who killed Danessa," Josie said. "It's the only way to get the cops off my back. If terrorists murdered her, we're out of luck. But I don't think so. Serge and Danessa's deaths seem too personal and too fitting."

"What do you mean?" Alyce said. "What's fitting about poisoning and strangling?"

"Danessa acted like a snake with her employees and died by a snakeskin belt," Josie said. "Serge was a rat with women and died a rodent's death. I could see terrorists blowing him up, feeding him a cyanide capsule, or machine-gunning him. But rat poison and strangling are personal. If you ask me, one of his lovers offed him.''

"Hmm. Did Mrs. Perkins tell you who those are?'' Alyce said as she eased the powerful SUV in front of a semi and put her foot down on the gas. The furious truck driver blasted his air horn and speeded up. Josie saw the grill in Alyce's rearview mirror.

"Yes, but I'm sworn to secrecy.'' Josie wondered if the secret would die with her, right on Highway 40.

"Then let me guess. We start with Amy the Slut,'' Alyce said. She smoothly outdistanced the truck.

"Do you really think Amy is a killer?'' Josie wasn't surprised that Alyce had correctly guessed the name. Not with Amy's reputation.

"Normally, I'd say she's too lazy,'' Alyce said. "If Amy can't buy a killer in Neiman's Christmas catalog, she doesn't want one. But Danessa really humiliated her in front of our crowd. Besides, she slept with Serge and she knows all the gossip. We need to start with her. We could have a girl-talk lunch.''

"Would she talk in front of me?'' Josie said. "She hardly knows me.''

"Honey, with the news stories about the murder, she'll probably take out a billboard,'' Alyce said. "Amy loves to brag about her conquests.''

"Is Amy married?''

"Of course, she's married,'' Alyce said.

"Where's her husband?'' Josie said. "Doesn't he care about her affairs?''

Alyce shrugged. "He may get other things out of the marriage.''

"Did he marry Amy for her money?''

Alyce laughed. "Amy's family lost their money years ago. There are rumors her husband is still in the closet. Happens a lot in the old families. The son has to marry and produce an heir, no matter what his inclinations, if he wants to inherit the family millions. The wife gets his money and social position.

"Amy had done her duty. She has a little boy in the first grade. The family name is secure. Now she can amuse herself in one of three ways: religion, alcohol, or affairs. I haven't seen Amy in church in some time."

For the first time, Josie felt sorry for Amy the Slut.

"Have I shocked you?" Alyce said.

"I think so," Josie said.

"Good," Alyce said. "You usually make me feel like the naive one. People with money have too much at stake to worry about a little infidelity."

Josie wondered if her friend was talking about Amy or her own husband. Josie had caught hints that Jake might have strayed while Alyce was pregnant. And now there was the nanny. Well, that was Alyce's business. If and when she wanted to talk about it, Josie would listen.

"I'll set up a lunch with Amy," Alyce said. "What else do you want to do?"

"Can we talk to Olga again?" Josie said.

"The Danessa saleswoman? Why?"

"I'm convinced she lied. She's hiding something."

"She's from Russia," Alyce said. "She's probably terrified of the immigration authorities. Do you think she'll tell you anything?"

"She might. If I offered her money. I have two hundred dollars stashed away. I know that's nothing for you, Alyce, but if someone is making minimum wage, it's a week's pay. I've looked up Olga's address on the Internet. She lives in South St. Louis. We can talk to her at home. I called the store and found out tomorrow is her day off."

"Did she agree to see you?"

"Of course not," Josie said. "I want to surprise her at home. Nine o'clock is pretty early on a day off. We'll get her in her robe and bunny slippers."

Alyce shrugged. "I think it's a waste, but have it your way. I'll pick you up at eight thirty tomorrow. When's D-Day?"

Josie looked puzzled.

"Date Day. When is your date with Stan the man?"

Josie groaned. "Don't remind me. It's Thursday night. Thanks to my mother, my love life has hit a new low."

"What about that hot guy at Has Beans?"

"Definitely a spark there," Josie said, "but we can't get anything going. Every time we start a serious conversation, he has to make coffee."

"Then ask him out for a drink."

"Me?" Josie said. Her voice was a squeak.

"Of course you. What do you think this is, 1950?"

"I wish it was," Josie said. "Rules were simpler when Mom was young. Women just waited by the telephone for the right guy to call."

"I doubt that," Alyce said. "Women have always gone after the men they wanted. You're too young to be sitting home alone, or going on dates with duds. Promise me you'll give that coffeehouse hottie a call."

"Well—" Josie said.

"Do you want me to go with you tomorrow?"

Josie heard the threat in Alyce's voice. "Okay, I'll do it," she said. "In fact, why don't you drop me off at Has Beans now and I'll walk home? I can use the exercise after two apple tarts."

"Good girl," Alyce said.

The worst Josh can say is no, Josie told herself. It won't kill me.

But it would hurt, a little voice whispered.

Josie squared her shoulders, opened the door to the shop and was hit with the smell of strong coffee.

Her heart gave a little leap. Damn, Josh looked good. Long, lean body, good shoulders, tight ass. She liked the way he moved—swift, sure, economical. This man didn't dither.

"Josie!" he said, and smiled a crooked grin. His right eyebrow went up. Josie was a sucker for moving eyebrows.

"Hi," she said.

"You haven't been in for two days. Everything okay?"

He noticed, she thought.

"Not exactly," she said.

"Let me fix you some coffee and we can talk," he said. "At least until the next thirsty horde arrives. Sit down."

Josie sat down on the hard, lumpy couch, happy to be waited on by a handsome man. Josh brought over a double espresso and two chocolate-chip biscotti. Josie took a delicate nibble, then polished off both biscotti.

There was only one customer in the store, a skinny guy in a jeans jacket sitting at the computer.

"So tell me what happened," Josh said, and Josie did, beginning with the lie detector test.

When she finished, he said, "You're okay, Josie. They're playing head games. That's all it was. The police don't really think you're guilty, or you'd be in jail. Sounds like you've got a good lawyer."

"The best," Josie said. That I can afford right now, she thought, mentally crossing her fingers.

"So who do you think offed St. Louis's royal couple?" Josh said.

"One of Serge's jealous girlfriends. She'd have a good reason to kill Serge and Danessa both. But the FBI says he was selling nuclear weapons materials, something called osmium-187."

Josh gave a braying laugh, and the skinny guy at the computer turned and stared.

"I heard that on the news and nearly fell over laughing," Josh said.

"Did I say something funny?" Josie asked.

"Osmium-187 is an Internet legend. It's a scam. I can't believe that story is still around. Reporters are so lazy. They keep repeating this same news item about a smuggler being arrested for taking osmium-187 out of Russia. They say the stuff was worth major money. They never check that story. Everyone in the sci-fi world knows it's bogus."

"What do you mean?" Josie said.

Josh went back for more coffee and biscotti, while Josie waited impatiently. Finally he sat down beside her. "Osmium-187 isn't used in nuclear weapons. It's not radioactive. It's absolutely harmless.

"Years ago, it was used in pen points and light fila-ments. If it was really half a million dollars a gram, you couldn't afford a lightbulb. But there's this story going around the Net that in 1993 some Moscow official was caught trying to smuggle out eight grams of osmium-187 worth five hundred thousand dollars. Here, I'll show you. Give me a minute."

Josh went back behind the counter and pressed a red button on the espresso machine. It gave a loud buzz. The skinny guy at the coffeehouse computer jumped.

Josh hurried over to him. "Excuse me," Josh said. "That buzz was our in-house virus detector. We have a Sector 4 virus that could do major damage. I need to remove it immediately or the whole system will crash and infect everything, including your Hotmail account."

"Uh, okay, sure. Thanks, dude." The guy tossed his coffee cup in the trash and headed out the door.

"I didn't mean to chase off a customer," Josie said.

"He needed to go," Josh said. "He's been here since nine this morning, hogging that computer and sucking on one cup of coffee."

Josh typed in "Osmium-187" and showed her a long list of stories, all debunking its nuclear capabilities.

"I don't get it," Josie said. "What does it mean?"

"Don't you see?" Josh said. "If Serge was really sell-ing osmium-187, then he was scamming someone. The easiest con game in the world right now is to say you're a Russian pushing nuclear weapons materials from the old Soviet Union. People will believe you. They think everyone with a Russian accent made it out with two or three leaky old nuclear bombs in their luggage.

"There are guys selling bags of worthless rocks, claim-ing they have weapons-grade uranium. Others are selling osmium-187 to gullible warmongers."

"Why do they fall for a scam that you can find on the Net?" Josie said.

"Why do people fall for the pigeon drop, the oldest scam in the world?" Josh said. He was cute when he was sincere. "Because they want an unbelievable deal.

Serge was a smooth talker. He probably fed them some line and they bought it."

"Serge's housekeeper says the FBI and a bunch of other agencies were testing his house for radioactivity and didn't find a thing. So either the tip that he was dealing nuclear weapons materials wasn't true or he was passing off worthless osmium-187."

"If you scam some terrorists, who do they complain to—the Better Business Bureau?" Josh said. "You take their money in Iraq or Istanbul, change your name and run for the good old USA with your loot."

"And get away scot-free," Josie said. "Unless you're addicted to sounding off in the newspapers and someone sees your picture."

"Right," Josh said. "Serge shot his mouth off for the media. Sooner or later, the people he scammed were going to find him."

"There's the perfect motive for murder," Josie said. "Serge was killed by someone he swindled in a nuclear arms deal."

Josh looked deep into Josie's eyes. "Exactly. You figured it out. You're smart. You're beautiful. You're sensitive. There's something I've been trying to get up the nerve to ask you for a long time."

"Yes?" Josie fluttered her eyelashes the way women did in the chick movies. Josh was going to ask her out.

"Would you read the manuscript of my novel?" he said.

"Uh." Josie felt like she'd been punched in the gut. Did she look like a literary agent?

"I know you're surprised," Josh said. He was talking very quickly, the way Amelia did when she tried to persuade her mother it was okay to let her stay up late on a school night.

"You probably don't read science fiction. But my novel is so good it transcends the genre. I can bring it tomorrow and give it to you when you come in for your coffee."

"I need a drink," Josie said flatly. "Why don't you meet me for a beer Sunday at the Schlafly Bottleworks?"

Josh raised one eyebrow. "I didn't know you were a beer drinker."

"Hey, I'm a St. Louis girl. Beer is in my blood. But not over the accepted legal limit, of course."

Josh laughed. "Meet you there at two?"

"Deal," Josie said.

Josh leaned toward her to seal it with a kiss when the doorbell chimed.

"Hey, anybody here?" the skinny guy called. "Is the computer fixed yet?"

Josie floated out of the coffeehouse, down the street to her flat and into her car. It was only when she was halfway to Amelia's school that she came back down to earth.

Josh had given her new information on osmium-187. He'd also strengthened the case for terrorists as the killers.

But if terrorists poisoned Serge when they found out he'd sold them worthless nuclear materials, why kill Danessa? Was she an innocent bystander who died because she lived with Serge?

Or was Danessa part of the bogus nuclear weapons scam, hiding the worthless osmium-187 in shipments of purses? Did she know what was going on? Or did she find out?

Is that what caused those bitter arguments with Serge and Marina in the stockroom? How did the mysterious Marina fit in this? Where was the Russian Amazon?

And what about Olga? The saleswoman had been snooping in the store and found out her health insurance was about to be canceled. Did she find out something even more disturbing?

If Olga was a top saleswoman, why did she stay with Danessa? Someone with her ability and high-end client list could have easily found a job with an employer who treated her better. Was it easier for Olga to collect those blackmail payments if she stayed at the store?

Josie thought Olga was a liar. She was also the only person who knew the truth about Danessa.

Chapter 19

South St. Louis had many charming apartment houses, but this wasn't one of them.

Olga lived in a yellow-brick box built in the sixties. The brick had turned a dirty tan, like a dog that needed a bath. A screen hung loose on one window and dingy curtains flapped on the sill, the flag of surrender in uncertain neighborhoods.

There were eight units in Olga's apartment house. All the doors were painted a sad green, except one, which was nailed over with plywood and spray-painted BOB'S BOARD UP. Josie wondered what disaster it covered. A break-in? A fire? Or did the police have to force their way inside?

"Nice neighborhood," Alyce said. She looked frightened. This wasn't her world. People here joined gangs, not committees.

Josie shrugged. She'd had to shop worse neighborhoods. She'd deliberately dressed to attract no attention. She wore old jeans, a faded T-shirt and cheap tennis shoes no one wanted to steal.

Josie walked confidently across the dead lawn with a don't-mess-with-me strut. Alyce picked her way delicately on slick-bottomed Italian leather shoes. Her understated blue linen dress belonged at a Junior League lunch. Her creamy skin and white-blond hair came only with money. Alyce's golden life gave her a glow that made her a mark here. She looked like a society lady in a slum. And she was, Josie thought.

"I just have to ask Olga a couple of questions and we're out of here," Josie said. "She lives in Unit Seven."

The bell dangled from the wall by naked wires. Josie figured it wasn't working. She pounded on the green door. No answer.

"Olga!" Josie kept pounding.

A dog barked two doors down, but there was no other response. No curtains twitched. The Mrs. Muellers, the guardians of neighborhood propriety, had left long ago—or been mugged out of existence. The apartments on either side were sightless and silent. The only sound was the furious dog, throwing itself against a locked door.

"Maybe you have the wrong apartment number," Alyce said.

"Nope. It says 'O. Rachmaninoff' over the bell," Josie said. The letters were printed in an odd square script on a white card thumbtacked to the wood.

"Olga, open up," Josie said. "It's important."

"Great. Now she'll think you're from immigration," Alyce said.

Josie tried the door handle. Locked. "In the movies, it always swings open," she said.

"Well, this one didn't," Alyce said. "Let's go. This place creeps me out."

"One last thing. Let me go around back and check her kitchen window," Josie said. "Maybe I can see inside. Olga could be hiding in a back room."

"She could also be calling the police," Alyce said. "You can trespass if you want, but I am not going in that horrible backyard."

"Fine, stay on the porch," Josie said. "You can be a real pain sometimes, you know?"

Alyce said nothing. She stood there with her arms folded, looking scared and out of place.

Josie went around the side of the building. To get to the backyard, she had to pick her way through a narrow gangway piled with junk. Josie stepped over a rusty bike, bent rakes, broken clay pots, rotting boards, and busted garden hoses. She could see the fleas hopping on an old mattress and prayed none of them jumped on her as she brushed past it.

Rats, snakes and spiders are in here for sure, Josie thought. She stepped carefully, listening for hissing and scurrying, hoping she didn't feel the feathery brush of a black widow or a brown recluse.

She heard a low growl and picked up a bent aluminum clothes prop in case she had to chase away the dog.

Josie, carrying the clothes prop like a spear, came out of the gangway into a dry, dead little yard surrounded by a chain-link fence. From the size of the dog piles, the creature throwing itself against that door was at least seven feet tall. Josie walked carefully and wished she had something bigger than a bent pole.

Olga's back window was shut. It was a narrow slit about a foot above Josie's head. She went back into the gangway, found a cinder block, put it under the window and stood on it.

Josie heard an odd buzzing noise. She looked in at the kitchen. It was a seventies' nightmare in harvest gold and avocado green.

Olga's floor may be uglier than mine, Josie thought. She has avocado green tile with some sort of weird red-black splash pattern—

Omigod. It's blood. Olga was lying on the floor and there was blood all over. Her eyes were wide open, her head resting against a kitchen-table leg. Josie thought she saw Olga's black spiky hair, but then it moved. Josie pounded on the window, and the hair rose up and flew away.

It wasn't hair.

It was flies. Hundreds of black flies, crawling over what was left of the little saleswoman's head. They set up an infernal buzzing. Josie thought if she went to hell, she'd hear that sound.

Olga was wearing her work outfit, the sleek black

pantsuit. It looked stiff with blood. Olga's pale skin was an odd greenish white. One small hand reached out, grasping at nothing. Josie thought she'd never seen anything so heartbreaking.

She fell backward off the cinder block. She didn't bother brushing off the mud and grass on her jeans. Josie sprinted through the gangway like an Olympic hurdler, nimbly leaping rakes, hoses and boards.

Alyce was still on the porch, arms folded, face in a frown. "Josie, what's wrong?"

"Olga's dead." Josie realized she was carrying the aluminum pole.

"Are you sure?" Alyce said. "Maybe she's hurt."

"Her head's almost gone," Josie said. "I think she was shot. I know you don't survive an injury like that."

"Let's get out of here." Alyce grabbed her hand. "What if the killer is still around?"

"He's long gone," Josie said. "The blood looks dried. We've got to call the police."

"You can't call them," Alyce said. "What are you going to say? 'Hi, I'm Josie Marcus. You already think I killed Danessa Celedine and I flunked a lie detector test. Now I accidentally found her head salesperson— the one who didn't wipe my fingerprints off the fatal snakeskin belt—and guess what? She's dead, too. I didn't kill her. I'm telling the truth.' "

Josie stared at her friend. "That's quite a speech, Counselor."

"I'm not debating with you," Alyce said. "We need to move, right now." She started across the dry brown lawn. This time there were no delicate steps. Alyce planted her feet firmly and marched.

"We can't leave her in that kitchen," Josie said. "She's crawling with flies."

"We'll call the police as soon as we're out of here."

Suddenly that seemed like a good idea. Josie sprinted across the dried-up lawn after Alyce.

"I'll unlock the door, but you have to let go of that clothes prop to get in the car," Alyce said.

Josie looked down at the dirty, bent pole and saw her handprint on it.

"My prints," Josie said.

"Actually, I'm a princess," Alyce said.

"My fingerprints are all over everything," Josie said. "Do you have a rag? I need to wipe them off."

Alyce handed her an old cloth diaper. Josie ran for the front door. She wiped down the door. In the back, she cleaned the window and the sill. She could hear the frantic buzzing of the trapped flies as she worked. She refused to look in the window again.

When she had wiped down everything she had touched, Josie carried the concrete block back to the trash in the gangway, then wiped it, too, even though she was pretty sure cinder blocks didn't take fingerprints. The aluminum pole was still leaning against the SUV. Josie threw it in the back and said, "Drive on."

"Why did you bring that?" Alyce said.

"Because I don't want to waste more time wiping it down," Josie said. "We need to find a pay phone."

"I have my cell," Alyce said.

"And I have mine," Josie said. "But those calls can be traced back to us."

"Oh," Alyce said. "You're good at this."

"Please don't tell my mother," Josie said.

They drove for ten minutes looking for a working pay phone. Most had been either vandalized or removed to prevent drug deals.

"Do you think anyone saw us?" Alyce said as they scanned the streets for a functioning pay phone.

"I hope not," Josie said. "But we were pretty obvious. We drove up in a big fancy SUV that doesn't belong in this neighborhood. A tall blonde in a designer dress and her short brunette sidekick beat on the door, shouted at each other and then drove off."

"Maybe they won't believe what they saw," Alyce said.

"There's a lot of crack around here," Josie said. "We could be a hallucination."

"I almost hope I am caught," Alyce said. "Jake won't think I'm so boring if he has to bail me out for murder."

"Jake doesn't think that," Josie said. She saw a single tear slide down her friend's cheek and realized she didn't know what Jake thought.

"Look, Alyce, I wouldn't worry. This isn't an area where people get involved with the police."

"Look! Outside that convenience store—a pay phone," Alyce said and pulled a U-turn across three lanes of traffic. Horns blared and single digits saluted them.

"Way to go," Josie said. "You'll be a city girl yet."

"No, I won't. I don't like this neighborhood, or the three men hanging around the door."

Three dark-skinned teenagers slouched against the smudged door of the convenience store, smoking cigarettes and drinking malt liquor. They were five feet from the pay phone, which stood in a pool of trash.

"Those are bored kids, not thugs. I can tell the difference," Josie said.

"I'm still going with you." Alyce pulled her pepper spray out of her purse. Josie walked through drifts of plastic bags, empty cups, and used condoms. The blacktop was sticky with what she hoped was spilled soda. The pay phone was covered with phone numbers, gang symbols and slogans: TIFFNY IS A HO. If this were New York, Josie thought, it would probably be in some museum as urban art.

"I'm going to burn these shoes when I get home," Alyce said. She looked disgusted and Josie couldn't blame her. They were a long way from West County, or even Maplewood. But Alyce followed Josie to the pay phone, pepper spray in hand. Josie expected catcalls, but the three young men drifted away, silent as ghosts.

Josie called Information and asked for the main police nonemergency number.

"Why not call 911?" Alyce said.

"Because those calls are traced," Josie said. "Someone here might remember us. I don't think calls to the main number are."

"You really do have a knack for this," Alyce said.

"I just hope my daughter didn't inherit that gene," Josie said, as she punched in the number.

"Hello?" Josie said, in a bad Russian accent. "Police-ski?"

Alyce stared at her.

Josie made her voice shrill and cracked, like an old woman's. "My neighbor Olga is not answerink her door. She iss home. Nice young woman. Works at that Danessa shopski where the boss lady vas killed. That's right. Danessa. But she's dead. I'm worryink about Olga. We are supposed to meet this mornink. Her car vas here, but she vas not answerink of the door.

"No, I cannot giff you my name. I giff you her name instead, Olga Rachmaninoff. Unit Seven. I am afraid for her. She vas a young lady livink alone. I knock and I knock and she does not answer. She vas supposed to be there for me. You vill check it out, yes?"

Josie hung up.

"How did I sound?"

"Like Natasha in those old Rocky and Bullwinkle cartoons," Alyce said.

Josie started laughing. Then she remembered the boarded-up door in that sad little apartment house. The police would have to break down another one. They would set loose a horde of blood-fed flies. They would find that small white hand, clutching at eternity.

That's when Josie started to cry.

Chapter 20

Josie cried all the way back to Maplewood.

"Josie, please, stop," Alyce said. "I know it has to be upsetting to find a body, but you didn't know this woman. You only talked to Olga twice. You didn't like her. You said she was a liar."

"I know," Josie said, sniffling into a wad of tissues.

"Then why are you crying?" Alyce said.

"It's the hand," Josie said.

"What hand?" Alyce said.

"Her hand." Josie saw Olga's small helpless hand reaching for the comfort she would never find. She started crying again.

"Would you like to stop for coffee at Has Beans?" Alyce said in her "mother has a treat for you" voice.

Josie stopped weeping long enough to say, "Oh, God, no. Josh can't see me like this."

Alyce took in Josie's red nose, puffy eyes, and dirt-streaked clothes. "You're right. Let's get you home. Listen, Josie, once you're inside, throw those clothes in the wash. You never know if the police can find traces of the crime scene on your jeans or shoes."

"You've got a real knack for this," Josie said, and attempted a smile.

Alyce didn't laugh.

Josie looked at her friend. Her creamy skin was paler than usual. Her white-blond hair hung in strings around her neck. Alyce has shared dozens of shopping adventures with me, Josie thought. But this one wasn't amusing. Alyce was not meant to find dead bodies and make phone calls at thug-ridden convenience stores. She lived in a beautifully controlled environment. Even her problems could be controlled by lawyers, doctors and well-paid servants. I belong to a wilder world Alyce has always found attractive—until today. She may be my faithful friend, but she still looks relieved to be dumping me off at my house.

"Are you going to be okay?" Alyce said. "Do you want me to come in with you? You don't have to go to work today, do you?"

"I'm fine," Josie said. "I don't start shopping Down and Dirty Discounts until tomorrow. Want to go with me?"

"Uh, sorry, I'm busy tomorrow," Alyce said, a little too quickly. "Are you going to get some rest today?"

"I'm more worried about you, Alyce," Josie said.

"You think this was too much for the sheltered little suburbanite?" Alyce said.

"I don't think anyone should have to find a dead body before lunch."

"I'm tougher than I look," Alyce said. "And I want to help you. I'll call Amy the Slut and set up that lunch as soon as I can."

Josie gave her friend a hug, waved good-bye and started up the sidewalk. After Olga's dingy little apartment, her home looked like a palace. She saw Mrs. Mueller's curtains move, and waved to her, too. For once, she didn't mind Mrs. Mueller. If Olga had had a Mrs. Mueller on her street she might still be alive.

Once inside, Josie heard her mother's TV blaring. An announcer urged, "You have twenty minutes left to buy this. . . ." Jane had the Home Shopping Network on again. Josie slipped into her apartment and dead-bolted the front door. Her mother didn't have that key.

Josie ran to the basement, stripped off her tennis shoes and clothes and dumped everything in the washing machine. She added soap and bleach and waited for the machine to start chugging.

Upstairs again, she took a long, hot shower and washed her hair. Josie only cried once, when she remembered the surreal moment when Olga's hair flew away.

Josie wrapped her wet hair in a towel, put on clean clothes and ran back downstairs. Her wash was done, damp and quiet in the machine. She poured in more soap and bleach, then washed her clothes and shoes a second time. She was taking no chances.

Back in her kitchen, Josie was surprised to see it was only eleven o'clock. She made coffee and fixed herself toast. She couldn't put strawberry jam on the toast after the dark red spatters she'd seen at Olga's. She couldn't get the dry toast down, either. It was like swallowing wallboard. Josie decided she wasn't hungry.

The hot coffee gave her strength. She took a sip, loaded it with sugar, then sat at the kitchen table and thought about the dead Danessa and Olga. She didn't like either woman, but now she was tied to them forever.

A week ago, Danessa had been a remote figure in the newspapers. Now she threatened everyone Josie loved. A week ago, she'd never heard of Olga. Now the little saleswoman would haunt her dreams until Josie died.

How had Josie's life gotten so out of control? She was supposed to have her own house and husband in the Estates at Wood Winds.

It had started with a pitcher of margaritas more than a decade ago.

Josie was twenty-one, a junior in college. She was working on her degree in marketing, but she was really in college to meet the man of her mother's dreams. Jane wanted Josie to get married, live in the best burbs and join the country club.

"It's just as easy to love a rich man as a poor one," her mother had said.

Josie never stopped to think if that was the life she wanted. She had loved a rich man, but she didn't love the way he'd made his money.

"You need to marry a good provider," her mother had said again and again. He'd provided adventure and excitement. No man had ever made Josie feel that way again.

She was still staring at her cold, sugary coffee when the phone rang.

"Josie, it's Alyce. How are you doing?"

"I'm fine," Josie said and realized she probably was.

"Can you meet me at the Woman's Exchange? Amy says the only time she can have lunch with us is today."

Josie nearly choked. "You're meeting her in a tea room? They don't even serve wine. And they do good works."

"That's why I want to go there," Alyce said. "It may be the only way to keep her in line. Amy can be a trial. Are you up for it?"

"Sure."

"Good. See you in half an hour."

Josie threw on another Rich Suburban Lady outfit, the camel pants with a beige twinset. She felt like she was auditioning for the role of June Cleaver. She considered a string of pearls but decided she'd toned herself down enough.

Josie never knew what it was about the Woman's Exchange that set her off. Something about its politely hushed perfection made her feel like an interloper. The staff was considerate. Their special salad and lemon meringue pie were delicious. But when she walked through the door, her hem fell out, her stockings ran, buttons popped off her clothes, and JOSIE FROM MAPLEWOOD flashed in neon on her forehead.

For Alyce, the Woman's Exchange was a second home. Today, standing beside her cool blond friend, Josie thought she could almost pass as one of them. Besides, Amy was such a scandal, no one would notice Josie in her boring beige. She wanted it that way.

Amy sauntered in beside Alyce, wearing a black dress that was too short, too tight and way too stylish for that crowd. Disapproving eyebrows went up like flags. Alyce seemed older and slower as she settled herself at the table. Josie had to admit that next to the hormonal Amy, her friend did look like a frump.

Amy dropped into her chair and ordered a double martini. Her voice was just a shade too loud, and Josie guessed it wasn't her first drink.

"I'm sorry," the soft-voiced waitress said. "But we don't serve alcohol."

"Shit," Amy said. "I was afraid of this. I'll have a lemonade."

When her lemonade arrived, Amy took a deep drink, then slipped a slim silver flask from her purse and topped off her glass with a generous dollop of a clear liquid. Vodka, Josie guessed.

After a good-sized gulp, Amy was eager to give too much information about Serge, including the fact that the deceased was "hung like a Clydesdale" and loved it "doggy style."

Josie could hear forks dropping all over the room. She wondered if any of these conversations ever got back to Amy's husband.

"Serge was quite the hound," Amy said. She took a deep drink of her doctored lemonade and smirked. "I think he had half the women in our subdivision."

"It could be a motive for his death. Did you tell the police?" Alyce asked.

"Of course. I had a long"—she drew out that word so even the dimmest diner knew what she meant—"and thorough interrogation by Officer Friendly. Detective Yawney is one of the city's finest." Amy winked.

Josie was fascinated. She didn't know any women who bragged about their affairs like boys in a locker room. Alyce was right. Amy would proclaim her fling with Serge on a billboard.

"Wasn't Detective Yawney's partner at the interview?" Alyce asked. Josie let her friend ask most of the questions. This was her world and she knew how to talk to Amy.

"The first time," Amy said. "But Yawney gave me his

card and said to call him if I thought of anything else. I thought of a lot of things."

Another wicked wink.

"You slept with him?" Josie knew she sounded hopelessly middle-class.

"No sleeping went on in that bed." Amy touched her pointed chin with a French-manicured fingernail.

"You're a suspect in a murder case," Josie said.

"I had an ironclad alibi," Amy said. She ran her hands through her long silky hair with actressy gestures. She was the star of her own little play. "I was at the Wood Winds Mothers Club meeting doing good works." Amy's tone was mocking. "We were planning the charity winter gala. It went on until eleven that night—long after Serge and Danessa were both dead."

"Did you know any of Serge's other lovers?" Josie said. She was trying to keep her promise to Mrs. Perkins and hint around about Kate at the same time. "Were there any surprises?"

"Well, well. I didn't think anyone but me knew that Saint Kate had fallen off her pedestal." Amy delighted in Kate's supposed sin. She did have enough grace to drop her voice so that no one at the nearby tables could hear.

Alyce nearly spilled her iced tea. She definitely didn't know about Kate.

Amy threw back the rest of her lemonade and said, "Saint Kate thought she was better than the rest of us. But she tumbled into bed when Serge crooked his little finger. That was a dangerous game for her. Serge knew I was only interested in recreational sex. I think it's good for the complexion. But poor Kate took it seriously. She convinced herself she loved Serge. Women like that always do. It makes them feel moral when they're cheating on their husbands. And Kate was cheating on Dr. Bigtime I-Don't-Believe-in-Abortion-or-Divorce Catholic. Personally, I think he made those statements because he works at a Catholic hospital. They're bound to help his career. The two sets of twins won't hurt, either."

Amy crossed her legs, revealing even more thigh, and waved the server over for another lemonade. "Kate cried buckets when Serge died. You'd think she was the widow."

The malicious gleam in her eye wasn't entirely due to the booze. Amy hated Kate. Could the golden, glamorous Amy be jealous of homely, lank-haired Kate?

Amy's drink arrived. She took a long gulp, then poured in a healthy slug from the flask. The woman drank like a sailor on leave. So far, Josie didn't see the signs in her face, but she wondered how long before booze blossoms ruined her delicate skin.

"You know Kate's house went up for sale right after Serge died?" Amy said. "I mean the next day. Kate and her husband will take a big loss. You can't sell a place when the feds are crawling all over claiming this subdivision glows in the dark. And if you've ever been in Kate's house, it's going to take a special buyer. Not many medieval monks can afford ten-bedroom mansions."

Alyce laughed. Josie, who hadn't seen the inside of Kate's house, didn't get the joke.

"Anyway, I do have one bit of news for you lady sleuths." Amy drained her new drink and ordered another. She was drawing the moment out, making her audience wait.

The delay made Josie crazy. She drummed the tabletop. Alyce tore a muffin apart and piled the shreds into a pyramid on her bread plate.

The new lemonade arrived. Amy slowly sipped it down, then carefully unscrewed the cap on her flask, and topped off her drink. At last, she finished. Amy delicately wiped her lips, took a healthy swig and said, "I saw Kate burying something by her FOR SALE sign in the front yard the night after Serge died. I think she was crying. It was after midnight. The FBI and the moon suits had all gone home.

"I watched her dig for a while with a garden spade. Then she buried something. I don't know what it was, but it was small and wrapped in a blanket."

Chapter 21

Something small wrapped in a blanket.

Amy's words gave Josie the shivers. "Do you think it was a baby?" Josie pushed her salad aside. She felt too heartsick to eat any more.

"I don't know what it was," Amy said, sipping her lemonade and gleefully observing the havoc her bombshell had caused. "It was a moonless night. But it was the right size. I know Saint Kate couldn't get it taken care of early on. Not in St. Louis. This city is a big small town. Someone would tell her loving husband."

Josie saw the scene. A baby, born dead or worse—murdered at birth—buried on a moonless night. Kate wept lonely tears as she lowered her nameless child into an unmarked grave. The baby had outlived his father by only one day.

"It's horrible," Alyce said, and finished her iced tea in one gulp.

Amy shrugged. "What's a mother to do?" she said. "Saint Kate was trapped. Her husband could chase nurses all over the hospital and he'd be a stud. She wasn't so lucky. Apparently she couldn't pass that baby off as her husband's. They'd been on the outs for some time. We aren't as broad-minded as we like to think we are. Suburban society will permit a girl like me to have a little fun"—she licked her lemonade glass salaciously—"but they have different expectations for good girls like Kate. She'd be branded with a big scarlet A."

"Oh, I don't know," Alyce said softly. "I heard Danessa wasn't very permissive. Wasn't there a scene with her at the country club?"

"That self-righteous bitch," Amy said. Her skin wasn't flushed with alcohol now, but anger. She stood up. "Well, ladies, it's been fun, but I have to go. Things to do, people to eat."

Amy laughed raucously and teetered out on her black stiletto heels, hips swinging provocatively. Her salad was untouched. She'd had a liquid lunch.

"You know her," Josie said. "Do you think Amy is telling the truth about Kate?"

"The only thing Amy likes better than sleeping with other women's husbands is trashing other women's reputations," Alyce said. "I enjoyed turning the tables on her for once."

Alyce said it with such bitterness, Josie wondered if Amy had been between the sheets with Jake. Was Alyce's barb about Danessa a payback? Amy must still burn with her public humiliation at the country club. She'd left suddenly after Alyce mentioned it. Did any of the politely eavesdropping women in the restaurant witness Danessa's attack on Amy?

"When you think about it," Josie said, "Amy's story doesn't make much sense. Why wouldn't Kate bury it in the backyard? The ones in your subdivision have high fences."

"Because her backyard is paved in granite blocks," Alyce said.

"Sounds cozy," Josie said.

"You have to see it to believe it."

"Do you really think Kate could have a baby and no one would notice she was pregnant?" Josie asked.

"I know this sounds mean, but no one notices anything about Kate but those teeth and that hair. I want to kidnap her and take her to a good salon. She has beautiful eyes and a terrific figure, but nobody sees it. Half the time she's wearing these flappy things that make her look like a scarecrow in a windstorm. So, yes, she could hide triplets under her clothes. From what I've heard about her husband, he wouldn't bother to look."

"Maybe she wasn't burying a baby," Josie said. "Maybe she was burying something that belonged to Serge—some papers, some of that fake nuclear weapons material, maybe some keepsake from their affair."

"It's possible," Alyce said. "But when you bury it in the dead of night, you sure don't want people to know what it is."

"Do you think Amy told the police that Kate may have buried something?" Josie said.

"I doubt it. We would have seen the crime-scene people digging up Kate's yard," Alyce said. "Amy's not a tattletale—she's a gossip. By her rules, ratting Kate out to the cops wouldn't be playing fair."

"So how do we get Kate to tell us what she buried?" Josie said.

"It won't be easy," Alyce said. "I've been on committees with her. She's a weeper. Kate bursts into tears to avoid anything unpleasant. We'll have to surprise her into talking. Once the waterworks start, you won't get much out of her."

"Let me do the questioning," Josie said. "You have to live in this neighborhood. Just get me into Kate's house."

"That's easy. We'll collect for my library charity," Alyce said. "But I'm going with you. I wouldn't miss this for the world—even if I'm barred from the women's club for life."

Kate lived next door to Serge and Danessa in a gray stone French château with a moat and swans. Three hundred years ago, the inhabitants would have been dragged from the house and guillotined.

As they drove up the hill to Kate's château, Josie looked at the FOR SALE sign and shuddered. She tried to see if there was a small mound near it, but there was no indication that anything had been buried in the beautifully manicured lawn.

"Kate's home," Alyce said. "That's her Cadillac Escalade."

"Which way does Amy live from here?" Josie said.

"Just over the hill," Alyce said. "Why?"

"Drive up to Amy's house," Josie said. "I want to see something."

Amy lived in a golden stone Italian palace. "Good Lord," Josie said. "It's immense. Look at the loggia and the courtyard with a fountain."

"I think Amy was a Borgia in a past life," Alyce said. "That's one reason why I've declined her dinner invitations."

"Is she home?" Josie said.

"No, she parks her Jaguar out front."

"Then park in front of Amy's place, will you?" Josie said.

Alyce pulled over. Josie rolled down the window and peered out. Amy's palace was surrounded on three sides by those tall, gloomy evergreens that showed up in so many Italian paintings. What did it cost to bring them in?

"Now drive around the side of Amy's house," Josie said.

"What do you see?" Alyce said.

"It's what I don't see," Josie said. "There's no way Amy saw Kate bury something by the For Sale sign if she looked out her windows. The front of the house faces away from Kate's. She'd have to look out the side. Kate's FOR SALE sign is screened by those tall evergreens. Kate's house is surrounded by a six-foot yew hedge. You only see the FOR SALE sign if you are coming up the hill toward Kate's house."

"I'm not sure what you're saying," Alyce said.

"If Amy saw Kate burying anything, she had to be in Kate's yard. That means she was either in Kate's yard helping her bury whatever it was or hiding out and stalking her. I don't believe she would help Kate do anything. Amy has a real hate-on for that woman. I saw it in her face at lunch. Even all that alcohol couldn't wash it away."

"So what's it mean?" Alyce said.

"I don't know yet."

"Then let's find out," Alyce said. "Batten down the hatches. Things are going to get soggy."

Josie was glad she had on her Suburban Lady outfit. When Kate answered the door, she was wearing almost the same thing. No flappy clothes today. But she didn't have anything to hide anymore. She looked like she'd either been crying or had a cold. Her eyes and nose were red. She carried a box of extra-soft tissues.

"I'm collecting donations for my inner-city library association," Alyce said. "Anything you can give us—books, textbooks, paperbacks or money—would be welcome."

"Oh, good," Kate said. "I have boxes of books. We're moving, you know. Come in. If you can take them off my hands, I'd be ever so grateful."

Kate sounded as if Alyce really was doing her a favor by taking the books. Alyce was right. Kate was not a pretty woman. Josie tried not to stare at her lank hair and prominent teeth. But there was something about her that was so sweet, Josie had to like her.

Alyce and Josie followed Kate into a vast entry hall. Their footsteps echoed on the stone floors. The walls were stone, too, and colder than a bill collector's heart. Even the fireplace and the tapestries on the walls didn't warm up the house. Josie expected beheadings on the back deck, jousting in the courtyard and prisoners groaning in the basement.

The library's bookshelves were twelve feet high. Stone statues of medieval saints with their eyes turned heavenward stood on pedestals. There was also a black-framed tomb rubbing of a knight, armored hands resting on his sword.

"That's an old rubbing," Kate said proudly, "before the British outlawed them."

Josie imagined the dead knight in her own living

room. He might scare Amelia into picking up her in-line skates.

An army of packers was wrapping books in white paper. "My husband's first editions," Kate said. "He has an extensive collection of medical textbooks. I can give you some children's books that my four boys have outgrown and boxes of popular novels, mostly romances and mysteries."

Love and death, Josie thought.

"Super," Alyce said. "Show me where they are and I'll start loading them."

"Oh, no," Kate said. "I'll have Marino carry them out."

She gave instructions to a short, muscular man. It took the man half an hour to haul the boxes out to Alyce's SUV. While he worked, Alyce and Kate sipped iced tea, ate dainty cookies and made small talk about committees until Josie was ready to climb the stone walls.

Josie wanted to ask Kate what was buried in her yard. But she knew Alyce was right. They had to lull Kate into talking about soothing subjects, then spring the tough one on her. While they talked, Kate never sneezed or blew her nose. Josie didn't think she had a cold. Kate was in deep mourning, for either her lost man or her lost child.

When the last box of books was loaded, Kate looked pointedly at her gold-and-diamond watch and said, "Anything else? I have to leave soon. I have an appointment."

Alyce gave a barely perceptible nod. It was time.

"Just one question," Josie said. "What did you bury by the FOR SALE sign?"

The blood drained from Kate's long face. Her lips drew back over her horse teeth, making them seem cruelly large. Her beautiful brown eyes were stricken.

"Please, please," she said, clinging desperately to Josie's arm. "You can't tell my husband. Bob doesn't know about him. I buried him at night so Bob would never find out. You can't tell him. You can't."

"I can," Josie said, "if you don't tell us what happened."

Kate started gulping air. "I didn't want to do it. I didn't. But I needed help so bad. I heard he was the only one who could do it."

Do what? Josie wondered. But now the words were spilling out of Kate.

"I paid cash to get him so my husband wouldn't see it on my charge card. I can't have Bob find out. We're Catholic, but he doesn't go in for things like that."

"Adultery?" Josie said, then wished she hadn't. Kate turned bright red, but didn't deny it.

"It's worse than that," Kate said. "I buried a statue of Saint Joseph by the FOR SALE sign."

She paused dramatically, as if she'd confessed to the crime of the decade.

Josie started to laugh. Burying Saint Joseph was a harmless city tradition for house sellers.

Kate didn't think it was funny. She burst into furious tears. Alyce gave Josie a "now you've done it" look.

"You don't know what Bob's like," Kate wept. "He's a doctor. A man of science. He hates superstition. He thinks burying statues is for the poor and ignorant."

Josie couldn't help it. Her eyes shifted to the bloodless stone saints lining the library.

"Those are different," Kate said quickly. "Those are works of art. My husband would be violently opposed to burying a plastic statue. He says it's lower class."

Josie got the feeling that was a greater sin than adultery.

"Bob is a good man," Kate said, "but relations between us are strained right now. I wouldn't do anything to make them worse. If he finds out, he'll be furious. It could be the end for us.

"I knew this house would be hard to sell. Our real estate agent said so. We had a murder next door and the police are still all over the subdivision. But everyone, even people who aren't Catholic, say Saint Joseph works. You're supposed to bury his statue upside down by the FOR SALE sign, and he'll sell the house for you. Bob and I had been talking about moving for some time. After Serge died, I couldn't bear to live here another moment."

Kate was crying and hugging the tissue box. She stopped to blow her nose noisily.

"You fell in love with him," Josie said gently. She didn't want to judge this woman. She wasn't a paragon of virtue herself.

Kate hung her head and sniffled.

"I won't tell your husband," Josie said. "I understand. It's lonely here, rattling around in this big empty house while Bob's at the hospital with all those glamorous nurses and women doctors."

Kate gave a small nod. "Bob was having an affair with an ER nurse. Someone was kind enough to tell me, but I knew already. My husband was never home. That's not an excuse, I know, for what I did. But I was lonely, like you said. The only people I talked to all day were my twins and my committee chair.

"Then I met Serge. I never intended our love to happen, but he was so masterful, so sensitive. He listened to me. He loved me."

Josie could feel the woman's loneliness clinging to her like a shroud. Kate prettied up her affair with florid phrases from the romance novels she loved to read. Marino had taken boxes of them to Alyce's SUV. He'd also moved heaps of murder mysteries. Josie wondered if Kate had absorbed their lessons as well.

Kate's crying had slowed, and she started talking again. "Serge said that Danessa didn't love him. She refused to marry him. Serge needed the love of a good woman. He wanted a wife and mother. He asked me to divorce Bob and marry him. I don't feel the same way about divorce that my husband does. Serge and I would have been happy, I know it. He would have been faithful to me. Serge was not the sort of man who was happy living in sin."

Especially not with immigration breathing down his neck, Josie thought.

"Then Serge was murdered. After that, I couldn't stand to be in this house any longer. I saw Serge everywhere. If I don't leave here soon, I'll go crazy.

"I told my husband I knew about his affair at the hospital. Bob said he was sorry he'd hurt me. He was tired of sneaking around. His romance with the nurse was over. He wanted a fresh start. Bob had a good offer from a big hospital in Dallas. We put this house up for sale the next day. Every time I looked out my window, I saw Serge running toward me in the morning mist, waiting to take me in his arms. I wanted to be a good wife to Bob, but I was haunted by my lost love.

"So I bought that statue of Saint Joseph. I knew my husband would hate it, absolutely hate it, but I needed all the help I could get. I kept it hidden in my underwear drawer, wrapped in one of the boys' old blue blankets. I waited until Bob was asleep, then sneaked out of the house. I buried the statue of Saint Joseph at midnight. I thought I was hidden by the hedge and no one would see me. I was wrong. I've betrayed my husband twice, once with Serge and now with Saint Joseph."

She buried her head in her hands. Alyce rolled her eyes. Josie bit her lip. The stone saints looked heavenward.

Kate, who was neither stone nor a saint, wept uncontrollably.

Chapter 22

"Grandma bought a toe ring last night," Amelia said.

"Right," Josie said. "And I had six Chippendales dancing in my living room."

"Mooooom," Amelia said. She hated when Josie was sarcastic. "I'm serious. We were watching the Home Shopping Network and the man said time was running out to call in for the special offer of a gold-filled toe ring with a matching ankle bracelet for only twenty-nine ninety. Gold-filled is good, right? It means filled with gold."

Josie sidestepped that shopping lesson for the more serious issue. "Are you sure? Grandma hates toe rings. She says they're tacky. She wouldn't let me wear one in high school. I know she wasn't buying it for you."

"I don't think she was buying it for anyone," Amelia said. "It was a good price, so she got it."

That didn't make sense. Maybe her mother bought the toe ring as a gag gift. Except Jane didn't go in for thirty-dollar jokes. She had a little money now, thanks to her pension and Social Security, but she'd spent her life scrimping and saving. Thirty dollars was serious money. She wouldn't throw it away.

Maybe Mom had secretly wanted a toe ring all her life and finally indulged. Josie had a sudden vision of her mother wearing leopard thong underwear and toe rings under her staid pantsuits and sensible flats.

Josie smiled for the first time that day.

"Well, it's your grandma's money," she said. "She worked hard for it. If she wants a toe ring, more power to her."

"Can I have an ankle bracelet if I buy it with my own money?" Amelia said.

"Absolutely not," Josie said. "You are not wearing an ankle bracelet. You are nine years old."

"But Zoe wears one."

Precocious Zoe also wore padded bras, stick-on nails, eyeliner—and probably a diaphragm. She was the bane of Josie's existence.

"I don't care what Zoe wears," Josie said. "You're not getting an ankle bracelet."

"Why not? I'll pay for it."

"Because I'm the mom and you're the kid," Josie said.

"It's not fair." Amelia stuck out her lower lip like a Ubangi princess in an old *National Geographic.*

"Life isn't fair," Josie said. "When you get your own house, you can do it your way."

Three mom clichés in three sentences. Josie was mortified. She sneaked a look at her daughter. Amelia took the pompous parental remarks in stride. Josie was glad they were in the car. Amelia talked more there. At home, she'd started lapsing into long silences, which Josie feared were a prelude to permanent teenage sullenness.

Her daughter was getting a new voice. Amelia wasn't really a teenager yet, but she didn't sound like a little girl anymore. She wanted her own way all the time. This afternoon, when Josie picked her up at the Barrington School, the first thing Amelia did was take over the radio. She was also getting very opinionated.

I wonder where she gets that from? Josie thought and smiled for the second time.

She glanced at the dashboard clock. It was 3:02. Josie switched to a local news station.

"Mooom, what are you doing?" Amelia said.

"I have to listen to the newscast. Then you can switch back to your station."

"We'll be home by then." Amelia stuck out her lip again.

"—that makes the third murder this month," the news announcer finished.

Murder? Josie hoped she hadn't missed Olga's story while she was bickering with Amelia for the radio.

"Another suspicious death in the Danessa Celedine case today," the announcer said. "A sales associate at the Plaza Venetia store was found shot to death in her South Side home. The victim's name has been withheld pending notification of next of kin. Police will not say if the victim's death is related to the recent murders of the entrepreneur and her longtime companion, Serge Orloff."

They won't say. But they know, Josie thought.

The announcer said, "In Washington, Missouri senator—"

"Okay, you can switch it back, Amelia."

"Did you want the story about the lady who was shot to death?" Amelia said.

"Yes," Josie said, as she negotiated a tricky left turn into traffic.

"Did you know she was going to be dead?"

Josie nearly ran off the road. "What? No, of course not. Listen, would you like a Granny Smith pie for dessert tonight?"

"With ice cream?" Amelia said.

"Absolutely," Josie said.

"Yeah! And macaroni for dinner?"

"That, too."

"No salad?" Amelia raised one eyebrow. This was the ultimate demand.

"None. But you'll have to eat some broccoli."

"Yay! I hate salad."

Apple pie and macaroni and cheese was Amelia's favorite dinner. After a day when Josie had discovered a dead body, had lunch with a suburban siren and nearly accused an innocent woman of murdering her baby, she needed to do something wholesome. The kid didn't care if her pie had a prefab crust. Josie felt like a magazine mom when she had one of her semi-homemade pies in the oven.

Pounding the top crust with a rolling pin helped her think. She really needed to figure out the Serge and Danessa murders. She couldn't see any connection between the three victims. Olga's death could be a break-in in a bad neighborhood, but Josie didn't think so. It was too much of a coincidence. It was too soon after the other two deaths.

If Olga had been blackmailing Serge or Danessa, they both had a reason to kill the snoopy saleswoman. But they'd already been murdered when Olga was killed. Someone else had to be involved. Was that person involved in the fake nuclear weapons scam, or was there some other reason?

Who? And why?

Josie had no idea. Unless—wait a minute. Josie still believed Serge's death was personal, not a professional hit. What if Serge and Danessa had been killed by one of his jealous lovers, and Olga had figured out who the murderer was? Smart Olga. Serge had a taste for rich women. Olga must have thought she could bleed the killer forever.

Josie ran the tart Granny Smith apples through the Cuisinart, then set out the other ingredients: lemon juice, cinnamon, nutmeg, brown sugar, white sugar—

Oops. The sugar canister was empty. Amelia probably used the last of it on her cereal. Josie checked the sugar bowl. Also empty. She'd loaded her coffee with sugar after she came home from Olga's. I can't believe this, Josie thought. I actually need to borrow a cup of sugar.

She went up the steps to her mother's flat and knocked on the door.

"Moooom?" She sounded like Amelia.

No answer. Jane wasn't home. Josie stood on tiptoe and felt along the top of the molding for the key. She didn't feel guilty going inside. Jane was always breaking into her place.

"Mom?" Josie said as she stood inside the door. Her

mother's home was unnaturally quiet. The TV was off. The green couch sagged against the wall, the slipcovers gone dingy at the arms. The rug was worn, too. One lamp had a tear in the shade.

When did Mom start letting the place go? Josie wondered. She'd always been a good housekeeper.

"Mom?" Josie called again.

There was no sign of her mother.

Josie marched boldly to the kitchen, sniffed, and wrinkled her nose. The trash needed to be taken out. Unwashed dishes were piled in the sink. The floor could use a good mopping. Josie's shoes stuck to the tile. This was so unlike her mother.

I should have checked on her more, Josie thought. Jane was always popping into Josie's home, but Josie rarely made the trip upstairs. I was so busy keeping Mom out of my life, I never bothered looking at hers. Mom needs help. I'll come up and clean the house for her.

Josie looked around the untidy kitchen and wondered if Jane was aging suddenly, or if her mother just needed a little help. Either way, Josie had a date with a mop and a broom.

On the old Formica kitchen counter was the same cheery red canister set that had been there since Josie was a kid. The sugar canister felt light and slightly sticky. Josie opened it. Empty. She looked in the kitchen cabinets. There was no sugar—and hardly any food.

Jane usually kept enough canned goods to ward off a famine. Josie didn't like this.

She opened the old-fashioned walk-in pantry. Jane always kept it stocked with sale staples, including flour, sugar and enough salt to preserve downtown Maplewood. Josie sighed with relief when she saw its crowded shelves.

She looked again. That wasn't food.

There were hundreds of cardboard boxes. Some were the size of a shoebox. Others were bigger than an end table. All were from the Home Shopping Network. Most had never been opened.

What on earth was going on?

Josie ran to the hall closet and yanked the door open. The closet was crammed with unopened packages. More boxes bulged out of the linen closet. The closet still smelled of lavender, but it didn't hold a single sheet or towel.

In her mother's bedroom Josie was relieved to see the crisp ruffled spread and pink china lamps. She smelled Jane's familiar Chanel cologne. The closet doors were discreetly closed. Josie prayed she'd find her mother's clothes on their padded hangers.

They were gone. All of them. Josie stared at hordes of boxes from the Home Shopping Network, stacked higher than her head. How many thousands of dollars were sitting in that cardboard, unopened, unused and unwanted?

How long had this been going on?

Bits of conversation came back. She heard Amelia saying, "We watched the Home Shopping Network at Grandma's."

Jane telling her, "I could buy it cheaper on the Home Shopping Network."

Amelia saying, "Grandma bought a toe ring last night."

Josie had thought that was funny. She wasn't laughing now as she looked at the towering boxes. She ran back into the kitchen. On the counter was a new knife set— from the Home Shopping Network, no doubt. At least Jane used that purchase.

Josie pulled the biggest knife from the set, grabbed a box from the pantry, and slashed it open. Inside was an olive-oil lip-finishing stick for $22.50 plus $4.95 shipping and handling. Josie didn't even know what a lip-finishing stick was.

Another box held a blond doll, all ruffles and curls, with a fancy $159 price tag. Josie's mother had never bought Amelia a doll that expensive. This beauty sat unopened in the closet.

The biggest box had a Body by Jake Ab Scissor with

a Cut the Fat Program ($229.95). Jane had never worked out in her life.

There were tons of toe rings, earrings and ankle bracelets with hearts, daisies and fake gems.

Josie remembered the sad story of those two elderly brothers who lived in an apartment piled with newspapers. Was her mother turning into them? Why didn't I notice all these package deliveries? Did Mom schedule them when she knew I'd be working?

Now there was an irony, Josie thought. I shop for a living. Mom lives to shop.

This was sick. But it was her mother's money. If Jane wanted to spend it on the Home Shopping Network that was her business.

No, it wasn't. This was a disease, like gambling or drinking. My mother is a shopaholic.

It was almost funny. Except it wasn't. Jane's once immaculate apartment had been neglected. So had her appearance. From the looks of her hair, Jane had stopped her weekly trips to the beauty parlor.

Come to think of it, the only places her mother went these days were to the doctor and to Sunday Mass. Jane used to have a long list of activities: dancing, card games, bingo, or "going bumming," as she called it, with her friends. Jane hadn't mentioned such things for weeks. Her phone used to ring constantly with invitations. Now Jane's phone was silent. Josie checked the answering machine. No blinking message light.

Jane had shut herself away with her television, buying gadgets she didn't need and would never use.

Oh, my God, Josie thought. My mom needs help. I used her as a free babysitter but never bothered checking on her.

When did this start? When did it get out of hand? How could I know so little about my own mother?

Josie could not answer any of those questions.

Chapter 23

"Josie, I want to talk to you."

Her mom was standing in Josie's bedroom door, in violation of their privacy agreement.

And I want to talk to you, Josie thought. Why are you hoarding boxes from the Home Shopping Network? What's happened to you, Mom? Have you looked in the mirror recently?

Jane's pink tailored pantsuit was a pretty color with her gray hair, but it had a spot of spaghetti sauce on the collar. Her hair had turned dingy. She was wearing the pink plastic earrings she'd bought at Marshalls.

Mom, you have boxes of gold and silver jewelry you've never opened. Why are you wearing plastic earrings?

"Mom—" Josie started to say.

"Don't interrupt me," Jane said. "I want to talk to you about your date with Stan tonight."

I'll tackle Mom tomorrow, Josie decided. One crisis at a time.

"I know you think Stan is dull," Jane said. "Well, think about where that man who was so exciting got you. Stan is a good provider."

Josie sighed. All through college, Jane had pushed her into dating budding lawyers, doctors and business tycoons because they were good providers. The men bored her, but who else was there? She didn't want to marry some Maplewood truck driver.

Josie had dated dozens of young tycoons who talked about "challenges," "issues-based questions" and "implementing maximum productivity." They sounded like her father, Robert. At least, the few times she'd talked with him. Robert lived in Chicago with his new wife and family. She hadn't seen him in five years.

"Mom, Stan is a friend. That's all he'll ever be."

"Friendship is an excellent basis for marriage, Josie," her mother said. "Your father and I were friends before we married."

And look what your friend did to you, Josie thought.

Jane thrust out her bulldog jaw, as if she'd read Josie's mind. "I know our marriage didn't have a happy ending, but we had many good years together. You can't deny that."

Jane was the queen of denial. She'd been deliriously happy with her country club life in Ladue. She'd had the perfect life. She told everyone that Robert worked late because he was a good provider. When Josie was seven, Robert provided himself with a younger, blonder wife.

Jane got minimum alimony and child support and a two-family flat in Maplewood. She nearly died of shame. Maplewood was so low-rent Jane couldn't admit she lived there. She told her Ladue friends she lived "on the border of Richmond Heights." They knew better.

Josie, who started like the privileged little girls at the Barrington School, grew up to be a public-school kid in Maplewood. As a child, Josie told herself she didn't miss her father. She hardly ever saw him. Maplewood had seemed more fun than stuffy Ladue. She'd only wished her mother would quit crying.

Jane got a job at the bank and went to work like a martyr mounting the scaffold. She had one goal: Josie had to recapture her dream.

"Mom, I know you were happy, but I'm not cut out to be a corporate wife."

If Josie had followed her mother's plan, she would be just like Alyce—and just as trapped. Josie knew that now, and on some level she must have known it then.

"You didn't try," her mother said. "One minute you were engaged to Andy. The next, you ran off with that man." Jane couldn't bring herself to say his name.

Josie knew it must have looked that way to Jane. But it wasn't what happened. She'd been unhappy with Andy. Nathan made her understand that.

Josie knew one other thing: She loved Amelia's father the moment she saw him. She loved him still. But there was no way Amelia was ever going to meet the man.

Josie could still recall the way Nathan had looked the first time she saw him. She'd been sitting with her business school friends at O'Connell's Pub. Josie felt sophisticated drinking half-and-half —half Guinness stout and half lager—and eating a bloody-rare burger and fries.

She was half listening to Andy with the beautiful eyes and the adding-machine soul. In the dark pub Andy whispered in her ear, "It's my job to convey the bottom-line benefits to my customers."

That's when Nathan walked in the door. Josie saw his dark blond hair, the color of wild honey, his brown eyes, his leather jacket, and his swagger.

A woman at Josie's table waved and said, "Hi, Nate. Come sit by us."

"He's a helicopter pilot," she whispered to Josie.

That explained his absolute confidence, Josie thought. He needed it. One miscalculation and he'd be flying a rock.

Nate squeezed in next to Josie, swiped one of her fries, and started talking about flying.

Before the night was over, he'd taken her on a moonlight helicopter ride along the Mississippi. Josie saw the silver light shimmering on the Arch and knew she could never listen to another bottom-line lecture from Andy. She gave him back his "investment diamond."

A week later Nathan was her high-flying lover. He had a downtown bachelor apartment with black satin sheets and a view of the Arch, a white Porsche Boxster, a Harley, and an Infinity sound system. Flying a copter must pay well, Josie thought. Nate was Canadian and flew regularly between his hometown of Toronto and St. Louis.

"You changed overnight," Jane said, bringing Josie back to her man-free bedroom. "You threw away everything—your career, your scholarship."

But, oh, what I gained, Josie thought. Nate took her to New Orleans for jambalaya, to the Grand Canyon to see the sunrise, to the Grand Caymans to scuba dive. He took Josie everywhere except Toronto. He always made those flights alone.

Josie's grades slipped. Her teachers lectured her about the future. But Josie didn't care. She had a marvelous man who never talked about "win-win negotiations."

One night, Josie and Nate made a pitcher of margaritas, lit a hundred candles and got gloriously drunk. When she woke up the next morning, Josie saw the box of condoms by the bed had never been opened.

"I knew it wouldn't last," Jane said. "I knew that man didn't have staying power. He abandoned you when you were pregnant."

"I left him!" Josie said. It was the one part of her past she could never get her mother to believe.

Six weeks after their candlelit night, Josie knew she didn't have the flu. She was pregnant. She also began to wonder where Nate got his money. He had lots of it, in cash. When she was hunting for a CD, she found the bag of white powder stashed in the cabinet. Josie knew the man she loved didn't make his money flying helicopters.

She couldn't go back to school with the bottom-line boys and her expanding belly. She couldn't marry a drug dealer, either. Josie decided she wasn't cut out to be a wife. But she did want to be a mother.

She was going to tell Nate about their child when he was arrested in Canada for drug smuggling. Nate went to prison and was barred from reentering the United States. Josie cut off all contact with him. She never told Nathan he had a daughter. She never told Amelia she had a father in a Canadian prison. For her mother's sake, Josie said she was the widow of a copter pilot who'd died in a crash. It was almost true.

She dropped out of college to have Amelia, then went to work as a mystery shopper. Josie thought she lived fairly happily ever after. She loved her daughter. She liked mystery shopping. Only Jane saw Josie's life as a failure.

"That man ruined everything I worked for," Jane said. "He left you a college dropout, with no marriage prospects."

"Andy still wanted to marry me," Josie said for the hundredth time. "I didn't want to marry him. He found someone else. Andy's happy. I'm happy."

Her mother looked smaller than Josie remembered. Older, too. Suddenly Josie was filled with love for this little woman, who picked up the pieces of her collapsed dream and trudged off to the bank every day. She only wanted the best for Josie. It's just that Josie and her mother had different definitions of best.

"GBH, Mom," Josie said, and this time her mother came into her arms without reserve.

"I just want you to be happy, Josie," she said.

"I am happy, Mom. Please don't get your hopes up about Stan. He's a nice guy, but I don't think he's right for me. Now, if you'll excuse me, I have to finish dressing for my date."

Stan didn't say where they were going to dinner. But now that Maplewood had become hip, there were dozens of places. Josie hoped it would be the Monarch, a ravishingly romantic restaurant. But she knew the couponclipping Stan would never shell out for the Monarch. He wouldn't even go Dutch. Besides, any man who wore wash-and-wear shirts would not eat black bass rolled in hazelnuts.

But there were other affordable choices: Arthur Clay's, the Schlafly Bottleworks, even the special at Spencer's Grill in Kirkwood.

Stan showed up at five thirty on the dot. Josie's mother opened the door and gave Stan a smile fit for a

future son-in-law. Josie groaned inwardly. Stan was
wearing self-belting polyester pants and a knit shirt that
clung to his torso. The man had bigger breasts than
she did.

While Jane waved from the porch, Stan opened the
car door for Josie. He drove a tubby white Chevy with
plastic seat covers.

"I have two early-bird coupons for the Big Buckaroo
Barbecue," Stan said. "It's all-you-can-eat. That's the
best dinner value."

They were the only people under seventy in the restaurant. It looked like a barn and was just as romantic.
It even had a cow—a giant plastic bovine with a salad
bar on its back. As they stood in the "chow line" Josie
sneaked a look at her watch. Six o'clock. It was going
to be a long night.

Josie and Stan carried their trays to the plastic picnic
tables. "If you can't think what to say, ask a man about
himself," Jane used to tell her. It was still good advice.
Josie asked, and Stan poured out his troubles.

"I'm in risk management at the hospital," he said.
"I'm the best in my field, but I'm not taken seriously.
No one in management pays attention to me. I wish I
knew why. What do you think, Josie?"

"It's your shirts," she said.

Stan looked at her in surprise. He quit gnawing on
the Big Buckaroo rib special.

"You wear drip-dry shirts with short sleeves," Josie
said. "That's why no one takes you seriously. You also
need a good suit and tie."

"That's ridiculous," Stan said. "It's so superficial."

"Yes," Josie said. "But it's how the world works. I
shop for a living. I know where the sales are. I can buy
you designer shirts and a good suit at bargain prices.
They'll change your appearance, and that will change
your supervisors' attitude. They'll look at you in a whole
new way."

"No, thanks. Kmart is good enough for me," Stan
said.

That was the problem, Josie thought. Stan would settle for what he had, rather than try something better.

She looked at her watch. Six fifteen.

Josie talked about the weather, her job and her dying air conditioner while Stan gnawed plate after plate of greasy ribs. The bones were piling up, but the minutes were not.

"For dessert there's butterscotch pudding, chocolate cake, or soft-serve yogurt," Stan said.

The pudding had a thick skin on it. Josie chose a stingy square of sheet cake. It was six twenty-two.

"Would you like to go for a drive after dinner?" Stan said.

"How about a drink somewhere?" Josie said. "My treat."

"Bars are so noisy," Stan said. "I have to get up early tomorrow."

"Then let's drive," Josie said. With the high gas prices, Stan couldn't afford to drive around for hours. But what were they going to talk about?

The door to the big white car shut like a prison cell. In desperation, she began telling Stan about her mother and the Home Shopping Network.

"Stan, I can't tell you how scary it is," Josie said. "Every closet is stuffed with boxes. Most of them were never opened."

Josie knew how much Stan liked her mother. She expected him to dismiss her worries.

Instead, he looked serious.

"This sounds bad. Could be depression," Stan said. He had a small speck of barbecue sauce on his chin. "It's a problem in older people. It could also be obsessive-compulsive disease or even a borderline personality problem. Can you have her checked?"

"I couldn't get Mom near a shrink," Josie said. "She belongs to the generation that thinks only crazy people go to psychiatrists."

"Would she see a doctor or a priest?"

"I think her internist, Dr. Randall, feels the same way

she does. But Father Keller might be some help. She likes him and he's younger."

"There's a priest who does counseling at the hospital," Stan said. "I'll get you his name. There's one other thing: She might need her medicine checked."

"What?" Josie said.

"My mom was acting strange," Stan said. "She's seventy-one and she started talking vague and sleeping too much. Some days she didn't make sense at all. I was afraid she had Alzheimer's. I got her to the doctor. Turned out she'd been on this diet—Atkins, I think it was—and lost thirty or forty pounds. She was taking several different kinds of medicine and overdosing herself. When we got Mom's medicine adjusted, she was her old self."

So far as Josie knew, her mother hadn't lost or gained any weight. She took only Zocor, for high cholesterol.

"A lot of older people self-medicate, you know," Stan said. "They take their spouse's medicine or a friend's pills 'because I have the same symptoms.' Or they don't tell their internist they're taking a prescription from a specialist. Or they don't mention their over-the-counter medications. Add in a dramatic weight loss and it can make a real difference."

Josie knew her mother had a healthy respect for medicine. But someone else thought he was smart enough to prescribe for himself. And he'd had a sudden weight loss. Serge! Serge had lost fifty pounds on the Atkins diet, and bragged about it in the paper.

Nobody killed him. Josie's heart rose at the thought. Serge killed himself. He poisoned himself because he was too cheap to go to a doctor.

Serge had calibrated his weight against a fat rat. But when he lost fifty pounds, he didn't change his dosage. Josie would bet anything that's what happened. Patients didn't think about that. That's why they went to doctors.

Josie would do some research on the Net, but she knew the answer already.

"Stan, that's it! You've been a big help. I could kiss you."

"That would be nice." Stan's ears turned red. He was such a sweet man, Josie wished there was some spark between them.

She gave Stan a sisterly kiss on his cheek. It was like smooching the seat cover.

Chapter 24

"What were you doing in my closet, Josie?" her mother demanded, hands on her hips.

"I was looking for a cup of sugar," Josie said.

"I don't keep sugar in my bedroom—or the hall closet." Jane's eyes snapped and sizzled with anger.

"You don't keep it in the kitchen, either," Josie said. "There's no room with all the Home Shopping Network boxes."

"How I spend my money is none of your business, Josie Marcus. Why aren't you working? You're always gone by nine."

"Today I'm staying with you," Josie said. "We have to talk. I don't care how you spend your money, Mom, but I do care how you spend your life. This is—"

The doorbell rang. Her mother started for the door, but Josie blocked her path. "I'll get that, Mom."

"It's my house. I'll answer my own door."

Jane was determined to push past her daughter. But Josie was an August-white-sale veteran. She'd shopped at eight p.m. on Christmas Eve. She'd bulled her way through the crowds at Loehmann's to buy designer suits knocked down 90 percent. One small woman couldn't stop her. Josie shoved her mother aside and opened the door.

The UPS deliveryman had a boyish grin and guileless blue eyes. I'd order a dozen toe rings to have this hunk on my doorstep, Josie thought. Why couldn't Mom fix me up with him?

The deliveryman held out three packages and smiled fetchingly. He had a dimple.

"Sorry, but we don't want them," Josie said. She wrote, "Refused."

The driver shrugged and left.

"Josie, what are you doing?" Jane sounded frantic when the driver departed with her packages.

"No, Mom, what are you doing?" Josie said. "Why are you buying this useless stuff? It's crazy! Who is this for? Amelia doesn't play with dolls anymore." She held out the frilly $159 doll.

Jane said nothing.

"And this?" Josie picked up the lip-finishing stick.

More silence.

"And this?" Josie grabbed a handful of ankle bracelets. The gold daisies and fake amethysts tinkled sadly.

Jane put her face in her hands. "I don't know. But I can't stop."

Josie put her arms around her mother and kissed her. Jane's gray head settled on Josie's shoulder. She saw her mother's hair was thinning at the crown, and felt even sadder. Jane wept bitterly. She hadn't cried like that since Josie's father had left her.

Josie held her mother and rocked her. She could feel Jane's angry body loosening. She saw the flabby arms, the age speckles on her skin, the creases in her neck, and loved her mother more for them.

"It's going to be all right, Mom. It really is. I have the name of a good—"

"Oh, no," Jane said, as if warding off a blow. "No shrink."

"He's not a shrink. He's a priest who counsels people."

Josie almost said that Stan gave her the name, but she stopped. Jane would be humiliated if she realized Stan knew about her shopping mania.

"Mom, please call this counselor," Josie said. "If shopping made you happy, I wouldn't care. But you're not happy. Promise me you'll make an appointment."

"I promise." Jane dried her eyes and put on a too-cheerful smile. "Well," she said. "That's that. I appreciate what you've done, but you're a busy woman, Josie. You run along and I'll watch some TV—"

She's going back to the Home Shopping Network, Josie thought.

"Oh, no. I'm not leaving until you make that appointment, Mom. I'm also driving you to the counseling session."

"I won't be a prisoner in my own home." Jane stuck out her lower lip like Amelia.

"You're already a prisoner. When's the last time you went out with your friends, Mom? Your life revolves around the Home Shopping Network."

"And waiting on you and your daughter," Jane snapped.

"Mom, I know I can't live without your help. That's why I want you to make that call."

Josie started cleaning the kitchen while Jane got on the phone. She hated spying on her mother, but she picked up the extension to make sure Jane got an appointment. An hour later, the dishes were done, the floor was mopped, the living room was dusted, and the soiled slipcovers bundled for a drop-off at the dry cleaner.

"Good-bye, Mom," Josie said.

Jane's only answer was an angry silence. At least she wasn't watching the Home Shopping Network. Josie carried the stinking garbage out with her. She was exhausted, and it was only ten thirty in the morning.

Mom's taken care of, Josie thought. Now all I have to do is solve Serge and Danessa's murders. She gave a slightly hysterical laugh.

Josie wanted to research warfarin, the drug that killed Serge. She had a perfectly fine computer at home, but Josie didn't want to hang around the house, in case her mother was looking for a fight.

Josie went to Has Beans to use the coffeehouse computer—and see Josh, too, if she was being honest. Last night's date with Stan had been depressing. The high point had been their conversation about his mother's medicine. The evening struggled along until nine thirty, when it finally died. Even Stan knew there wouldn't be another date.

As he walked her to the front porch he'd said, "Josie, this hasn't ruined anything between us, has it? You'll still be my friend?"

"Always," Josie said, and meant it.

Stan embraced her awkwardly. Josie could feel his wobbly breasts under his knit shirt. She pulled away and saw the hurt in his face. It stayed with her all night, haunting her dreams, along with the staggering stacks of Home Shopping Network boxes.

Her bad date with Stan was wiped away by the sight of Josh the next morning. He looked wickedly lean. No boobs on that boy, Josie thought. No old man's pants, either. When he bent down to get the coffee filters, his khakis cupped his rump nicely.

"Josie! What can I do for you?" Josh said and smiled.

You've already done it, she thought.

"Double espresso," she said. "A big fat brownie. And your computer."

"It's all yours. Sit down at the computer and I'll bring the rest over."

Josie typed in "warfarin" and looked for the symptoms of an overdose. They included fever and diarrhea. Yuck. Even a cheapskate like Serge would get himself to a doctor if he had those symptoms. Wait, what about these? "Unusual bruises or heavily bleeding wounds." Didn't Mrs. Perkins say he'd bled to death from a head wound because he'd had too much warfarin?

Serge should have had bruising on his body as he lost weight. Josie went through the newspaper archives online. In the photos Serge usually wore turtlenecks and had a full beard. There wasn't enough skin visible to show any bruising.

Josie couldn't get the autopsy report in an ongoing

murder investigation. She was a suspect. Who else had seen Serge's body?

Amy the Slut. She'd seen Serge's body, all right. She'd had it in her bed for a thorough examination. She'd know if he'd showed heavy bruising. Josie would ask Amy.

Josie didn't want to drag Alyce into this inquiry. Her friend had to live in Amy's subdivision, and the suburban siren could be malicious. I'll call her myself and keep Alyce out of this, Josie decided.

Has Beans actually had a phone directory with the pages intact. Amy was in the phonebook—but then, she would be, Josie thought. How else could the men find her?

She took a seat on the coffeehouse couch, which felt like it was stuffed with old basketballs, and called Amy.

Amy wasn't home, but her housekeeper gave Josie her cell phone number. From the sounds when she answered, Amy was in her car and well on her way to being wasted.

"Josie," she said. "This is a surprise. Is Alyce on the other line?"

"No, just me," Josie said. "I had to ask you a personal question."

"Oooh, those are the best kind," Amy said. Her speech was slightly slurred.

"Did you notice that Serge had a lot of bruising on his, uh, his body?" Josie was grateful there were no other customers nearby.

"You mean the parts not usually on public view?" Amy said. "Come to think of it, he did have a lot of small bruises, even a couple of big ones, but I took that as a tribute to my expertise. Why do you want to know?"

A horn blared angrily in the background. Josie wondered if the drunken Amy had wandered into another lane.

"Because Serge dosed himself with rat poison," Josie said.

"Sure did," Amy said. "Every night at seven thirty. He even took it in his champagne, and I don't think you're supposed to mix it with alcohol. But what's that got to do with anything?"

"Unusual bruising is one sign of a warfarin overdose," Josie said. She didn't say that she thought Serge had poisoned himself.

"Still investigating the murder with your trusty side-kick Alyce?" Amy said. Josie could hear the sneer.

"Of course. She's been very helpful."

"I bet," Amy said. "It's the best cover when the murderer is part of the investigation."

"What do you mean?" Josie said hotly. "Do you think I murdered Serge?" She looked up and saw Josh staring at her. She waved and he smiled tentatively. Josie longed for an old-style phone booth.

"No, silly," Amy said. "But your little friend Alyce had a good reason. She could tell you as much about Serge's body as I can."

Amy laughed nastily. "Oh, don't look so shocked."

"You can't see me," Josie said.

"I don't have to," Amy said. "I know exactly how a good little Maplewood girl would react. You're so loyal."

Amy's contempt was like acid. "You don't think a highflyer like Jake is faithful to Alyce the good frump?" she asked.

"Alyce is—" Josie said.

"Your best friend and you won't hear a word against her," Amy said in a singsong voice. "But she is a little dreary, even you must admit that. You don't have to say it. But you are thinking it, aren't you, Josie? Jake may complain about her clothes, but he wants Alyce to look that way. He's an old-fashioned guy, with the Madonna and the whore syndrome. Alyce is Jake's Madonna. Jake likes the perfect home and child, but a man needs his fun. I don't feel too guilty when I'm with Jake because I know Alyce had her fun with Serge."

Josie nearly dropped the phone. It can't be true, she

thought. Alyce would have told me if she had an affair with Serge. She's my best friend. She tells me everything, including her problems with her husband. Josie wanted to hang up on Amy's poison, but she couldn't. She had to hear the rest.

"Serge and Alyce had a fling," Amy said. "Didn't you know that? Well, I guess she doesn't tell you everything after all. I certainly don't blame Alyce for jumping Serge's bones. Jake was working hideous hours—at least that's what he told wifey—and Serge came on to Alyce pretty strong at a party. I saw the whole thing. I guess Russians like strapping women. Good for working the collective farm and all that."

"Why are you telling me this?" Josie said coldly.

"To help you solve your murder." There was another horn blast and Amy said, "Oopsy. You need a motive, darling. I'm giving you a big, juicy one. Serge romanced Alyce, then dumped her. She was furious. You don't treat a woman like Alyce as if she's some cheap tart. She killed him."

"But—"

"Let me guess. You're going to ask if Alyce knew that Serge took rat poison. Of course. All his women did. It would be so easy for any of us to increase the dose. Just another little spoonful, and it's lights out. Knowing Alyce, she put it in a soufflé with special ingredients from Williams-Sonoma. And yes, she had access to his house. People in Wood Winds don't lock their doors."

"Alyce would never kill Serge," Josie said. "That's ridiculous."

Was it? Josie wondered for a disloyal moment. Yes, it was. "Anyway," she said, "why would she murder Danessa?"

"Because Danessa found out, silly." Another blare of horns. "Drivers are so crabby today," Amy said. "Alyce couldn't risk a public scene with Danessa. Jake would dump her instantly. No more baby boy and custom kitchen."

Josie's head was spinning. This couldn't be true. Alyce

wasn't like that. Then Josie remembered Alyce's barb at their lunch. This was Amy's revenge.

"Nice try, Amy," Josie said. "But I'm not buying that story. You're mad because Alyce mentioned your little encounter with Danessa. That bitch-slapping scene was better suited to a Festus trailer park than the Wood Winds country club."

Josie decided it was time for a payback. "Besides, I heard Serge asked Kate to marry him."

"That horse-faced simp?" Amy shouted. Josie heard the rage in her voice. Score one for the good girls, she thought. "Never. Serge would never marry her. Kate lives in a romance novel. She was a pity fuck, that's all. She meant nothing to Serge."

Suddenly horns blared again. There was a screech of brakes, then a loud silence.

"Amy?" Josie said. "Are you all right?"

"I'm not good at staying on the straight and narrow. People get so upset."

Josie wasn't sure if Amy was talking about her driving or her life.

"Now, where were we?" Amy said, malice dripping like honey. "Oh, yes. Your little friend Alyce—except she's not really so little, is she?"

"Enough," Josie said.

"I admire loyalty," Amy said. "Even misplaced loyalty. Well, all right, since you think I'm a biased bitch, I'll give you another candidate to consider. The PR child. The one who followed Danessa around like a baby duckling. What was her name? Sandy? Stacy? Oh, yes, Stephanie. Such a long name for a little nothing. Why does Stephanie buy her suits two sizes too large? Does she think she'll grow into them? Serge got her out of them fast enough. I gather it was fairly easy. What better way to have revenge on an evil boss than to screw her lover? I don't blame the PR child. Danessa was her first major client at a big-deal public relations firm, and she had to be a horror show. Stephanie had so much more to lose than the rest of us. If she was discovered,

Danessa would make sure that Stephanie never wrote another press release."

Josie wouldn't give Amy the satisfaction of saying that this scenario made sense.

"There. You have two to think about, but I still say Alyce is the best. Tell me this, Josie. Why did Alyce act as your lawyer? Detective Yawney told me she came running to the police station with a briefcase. Her husband's, no doubt."

"Alyce said there was a big lawyers' conference," Josie said. "She couldn't find an attorney for me on short notice."

"In Wood Winds? Sweetie, we grow them here like crabgrass."

Amy's long, loud laugh was drowned out by a hellish chorus of horns.

Chapter 25

"Amy said what!? I had an affair with Serge? I love it," Alyce said.

"You do?" Josie said. Was there something wrong with her cell phone? She shook it.

Alyce was still talking when Josie put it back to her ear. "Oh, Josie, do you know how long it's been since anyone thought I was anything but Justin's mother? I'm so boring. Do you know why I can't go mystery-shopping with you this afternoon? I'm on the wives' dinner-dance committee at Jake's law firm. We're trying to decide if we should spring for chair covers for the hotel ballroom. How dull is that?"

"Doesn't the firm have secretaries to do that?" Josie said.

"Secretaries are too important for that kind of work," Alyce said. "Wives are not. Please, please say I'm a scarlet woman. Makes me feel like a hottie. Do you think someone will tell Jake?"

Her voice sounded sad and hopeful at the same time. Any lingering doubts Josie had about Alyce were gone. Only an innocent woman would act this way.

"What do you think of Stephanie, the PR woman?" Josie asked. "Could she be a killer?"

Josie was glad she'd moved to her car before she called Alyce. She sure couldn't ask that question in Has Beans.

"You can talk to her if you want. But Josie, if Amy

lied about me, she'll lie about Stephanie, too. Amy's whole life is one big falsehood."

"But isn't that what Stephanie does for a living?" Josie said. "She lies professionally. She was paid to make that nasty Danessa look good. Besides, Amy was right about Kate."

"That's the problem with drunks," Alyce said. "They're so unreliable. Gotta run. I'm so sorry I'm not going to Down and Dirty with you. Say hello to the fish sticks for me."

You could buy anything from fish sticks to fake legs at Down and Dirty Discounts.

The artificial legs hung in rows from the ceiling, right next to the fake arms. The fish sticks were easy to find, too. You followed the stink. It overpowered the odors of motor oil, dust and hot popcorn.

Josie wished her friend was along on this assignment. "I think those fish sticks are older than I am," Alyce would say when they entered a Triple D.

"Somebody must buy them, or they wouldn't keep them in stock," Josie would say.

Somebody bought the purple toilets and the bile-green bathtubs stacked in the parking lot. Somebody purchased the mustard-yellow paneling and the orange wallpaper. That never ceased to amaze Alyce, or Josie, for that matter.

Harry had given her Triple D as a punishment. It would seem that way now without Alyce giggling and making silly comments.

Alyce regarded Triple D as another country, and in a way she was right. It was the kingdom of the poor and the hopeless, a foreign country to Alyce and Josie. In rural areas, Triple D customers were sharecroppers and dirt farmers who barely scratched a living from the land. In the cities, the store was the province of the newest unskilled immigrants.

At the Triple D she had to shop today, Josie heard every language from Russian to Spanish—everything but English.

In truth, there was nothing funny about the stores. Triple D survived on slavery. Its cut-price goods were made by Third World slaves. Its cash registers were run by minimum-wage serfs. The dispirited staff moved through the murky light of the Triple D stores like strangers in a drug dream.

The only way to get waited on was to throw yourself in front of someone wearing a Triple D vest. Even then, there was a 50 percent chance the staffer would not speak English.

Josie wondered why Triple D bothered with mystery shoppers. She always gave the stores low ratings and nothing ever changed for the better.

This Triple D was in a run-down neighborhood on the city's South Side. The area had once been the home of house-proud Germans who'd scrubbed their steps with Old Dutch cleanser and trimmed their lawns with mani-cure scissors. The newer immigrants, from war-torn Bos-nia and Russia, had no interest in fanatic home care. Groups of dark men sat on their peeling front porches and glowered at strangers.

Josie parked in the Triple D lot and read the first question on the mystery-shopper survey form: Does the store present a pleasing aspect?

Squiggly gang graffiti decorated the redbrick walls. The dead bushes in the planters were infested with plastic bags. Josie picked her way past a full diaper steaming in the parking lot. She knew how to answer Question One.

Inside, the store was a welter of clashing carts, blaring announcements and Muzak. Something sticky had been spilled on the concrete floor, but shoppers walked through it, tracking pink liquid prints through the store.

Josie was supposed to ask the staff about the lightbulb special. She stopped the first employee, a woman so thin and sickly she looked like she'd escaped from a chemo ward. Her name tag said KARINA.

"Excuse me," Josie said. "Can you tell me about the Triple D lightbulb special?"

"No. I know nothing." The woman's voice was from a newly opened tomb.

Josie didn't have the heart to report this specter.

Gregor, the second employee, was a hugely cheerful man with bushy black hair and red lips.

"Lightbulbs!" he said, smiling happily and rubbing his hands. "Yes. We have lightbulbs for selling to you today. Go to the end of Aisle H, make a left and then a right."

Josie followed his directions and wound up at a concrete wall with a bulletin board. YOUR NEIGHBORHOOD NEWS it said. Dingy business cards and homemade signs in several languages were tacked on it. Two flyers caught her eye. One was in the Cyrillic letters of the Russian alphabet, the other in English. Both had the same photo of a blond woman.

HAVE YOU SEEN THIS WOMAN? the flyer asked.

It was Marina—the woman Danessa claimed didn't exist. The woman Josie swore had waited on her. The woman who nearly cost Josie her job.

The flyer had Marina's description, too, and it was just the way Josie remembered her: "Six feet two inches tall, 175 pounds, blond hair, age 30. Missing since September 16."

Josie knew that date. It was the night of Serge and Danessa's murders. Serge. Danessa. Olga. Marina. How did they fit together?

The flyer's next words made Josie feel good for the first time in a week: "Last seen at the Danessa store, Plaza Venetia."

There it was: proof that Marina existed. Josie hadn't made her up. Better yet, someone else was saying that Marina had been at Plaza Venetia. Josie had no idea what the Russian giant was doing there. The flyer didn't say that Marina was a Danessa employee. But she was real. Now Josie had her picture and description.

She wanted to show that flyer to the police. She wished she could shove it under that lying Danessa's nose. Well, she'd definitely show her meat-eating boss,

Harry. She had her proof that Marina was a real person. He couldn't take her job now. Unless she got arrested.

Who was looking for Marina, Josie wondered? The flyer had no name, only a phone number.

Josie slipped the flyer into her purse and sprinted for her car. She locked the door, then dialed the number on the flyer. A woman answered. Her voice was dry and cracked. She sounded old and a little confused.

"Hi, I'm calling about the missing woman, Marina. I wondered—"

"No spik English," the woman said.

"I'm sorry. I don't speak your language, either. Can I call back when someone else is home?"

The woman hung up.

Someone wants Marina as much as I do, Josie thought. That's why this flyer exists. She would keep calling that number.

Josie checked the time. It was twelve thirty. She had to take her mother to the counselor in half an hour. She hadn't seen Jane since their confrontation yesterday. Josie wondered if still more Home Shopping Network boxes had arrived and where Jane put them.

When she pulled up in front of her house, Josie was surprised to see her mother standing on the front porch. Jane wore her pink pantsuit, but now it was spotless. Her hair still straggled, but she'd made an effort to style it. She had on gold earrings shaped like stars and a matching pin. Josie hadn't seen them before. She wondered if the new jewelry was from the Home Shopping Network stash. She didn't know if that was good or bad.

Jane yanked open the car door and plopped down heavily. She held her big black pocketbook on her lap like a shield. Her jaw was set in the bulldog position.

"I'll go this once," Jane said. "But I'm not making any promises."

"Fine, Mom. That's all I ask."

The counselor's office was in a medical building next to the hospital. Jane and Josie entered a waiting room just big enough for two chairs and four *Smithsonian* magazines. Josie hoped the man wasn't treating anyone for claustrophobia. Jane looked like she might jump out of the chair and bolt for the door. Josie paged through a *Smithsonian* magazine from 2000. Both women were afraid to say anything.

They heard the counselor's office door open, and then the door to the waiting room. A tall, stooped man with thinning white hair and a long, pale face smiled at them. Josie was relieved to see his Roman collar. Jane could tell herself she was seeing a priest.

"I'm Father Fellows," he said.

Jane stood up, squared her shoulders, and followed him into his office. Josie thought her mother's straight back looked both brave and pathetic.

Josie was reading a *Smithsonian* magazine from 2001 when her cell phone rang. She wasn't sure if the tiny waiting room was soundproofed, so she stepped into the hall.

"Josie, it's me, Alyce."

"Alyce!" Josie said. "How was your meeting?"

"We're still debating whether to have surf and turf or stuffed chicken breast. I slipped out to the ladies' room to give you a call. Bunny Zarris is here, and she gave me more gossip about Amy the Slut."

Who? Josie started to say, and then remembered. She'd heard Alyce mention Bunny's name before. She was one of the interchangeable little blondes who infested the subdivision. Bunny had two sons and a chirpy disposition. She was a joiner, a team player, a committeewoman.

"Bunny says Amy had a real hang-up about Serge."

"She was in love with him?" Josie said.

"I don't think that's the right word. Amy has the emotional depth of paint," Alyce said. "She's slept with half the men in West County. But she's always in charge. She starts it, she finishes it. She really gets off on the control. But Bunny says Serge broke off the relationship with Amy. She didn't get to end it this time. He dropped her. That's when Amy started stalking Serge."

"How does Bunny know this?" Josie said.

"She overheard them at the country club. It was a few days after Danessa's slapping session there, but this time it wasn't so public. Serge apparently caught Amy spying on him and dragged her into the coatroom. Bunny heard the argument. She just happened to be passing by."

Right, Josie thought. And she just happened to glue her ear to the door.

"Serge was vicious. He told Amy to stay away from him, it was over and he didn't want to see her skinny ass again. Those were his words. Serge said Amy should go back to her husband, if she remembered which man he was."

"Oooh. That was cruel," Josie said.

"You bet. Serge was brutal. Amy wasn't used to that. It would be easy for her to kill him. A spoonful of rat poison, and he'd be dead. She'd have no problem getting into his house."

"Right," Josie said. "Serge didn't lock his doors. Amy told me that. She also said she had an airtight alibi."

"But she doesn't," Alyce said. "She was at the Wood Winds Mothers Club meeting. It lasts until almost midnight, but the meeting breaks into subcommittees about seven o'clock. Nobody checks to see if all the committee members are in their sessions after that. Some women leave for a while to set out refreshments, get coffee or check their cell phones. Amy could have slipped in and out and no one would have noticed. Serge's house is five minutes away."

Josie was silent for a moment.

"Are you still there?" Alyce said.

"What about Danessa? Why would Amy kill her?"

"I don't know, Josie," Alyce said. "That's all I know. I better get back before they choose something with goat cheese. One more thing. There's a memorial service for Danessa and Serge tomorrow at the Chapel at Wood Winds. All the neighbors have been invited. We can bring a guest. Jake can't make it. Would you like to go with me?"

"Yes," Josie said. "I'd like that very much. And Alyce, thanks. This is really helpful."

Now Alyce and Amy were even: They'd each accused the other of murder.

Amy had a good motive to kill Serge. She was the woman scorned. Josie suspected she'd been following Serge and had seen him with Kate. That must have been bitter for Amy. She'd been ditched for a woman Amy considered no match for her. Amy had raged at the mention of her rival's name.

Amy might kill Serge. It would be easy, as she told Josie.

But would she kill Danessa, too? Maybe. Danessa had publicly humiliated her. The Wood Winds public, anyway. But what about Olga? Did she try to blackmail Amy? Could you blackmail the town pump? Only if Olga saw her drop an extra dose of rat poison in Serge's drink. And if Olga let Serge swallow the rat poison, then she was as liable as Amy was.

Besides, Josie wasn't sure anyone had killed Serge. There was a good chance he'd killed himself, thanks to his own cheapness.

Josie tried to solve the puzzle of Serge, Danessa and Olga. But she couldn't make the pieces fit. Maybe the key was Marina, Serge's sister—or lover—or sister-lover. Where was she? Why did she disappear? Would she inherit Serge's fortune? Was she dead, too?

Then Josie had a brilliant thought. The idea was so bold it zapped through her brain like an electric shock. What if Amy killed Serge and someone else killed Danessa?

Who would have a better reason than Stephanie, the PR child, as Amy called her. Poor little Stephanie, with her owl glasses and oversized suits. She had to know an affair with a client's boyfriend was a career wrecker. If Danessa found out, she'd blacklist Stephanie. But how was Josie going to get the young PR woman to admit she'd had an affair with Serge?

Josie thought she knew.

She called Stephanie's office. Reichman-Brassard was the biggest firm in St. Louis. Stephanie was at her desk— but then she would be. It was one p.m. and minions at her level didn't get long lunches. Stephanie answered her own phone, more proof that she was at the bottom.

"It's Josie Marcus," she said. "You remember me. Your late boss barged into the Suttin office and threatened to sue me. We need to talk. I'll meet you at the bench by the fountain in front of your building. If you know what's good for you, you'll be there. I know about you and Serge."

There was a short, frantic silence, then a scared gulp. "What time?" a small voice said.

Guilty! Josie thought.

Chapter 26

"I don't want to discuss it," Josie's mother said.

She marched out of the counselor's office with her bulldog jaw at its most belligerent angle. Josie saw tear-stains on Jane's face and a wad of tissues in one clenched fist.

Poor Mom, she thought. She must have had a rough first session.

"I'm entitled to my privacy," Jane said, as she climbed into Josie's car.

"Of course, Mom," Josie said.

"And I'm perfectly capable of driving myself to my next visit." Jane slammed her door.

Yes! Jane had another appointment with the counselor. Josie tried not to sound pleased. "If that's what you want, Mom."

"It's exactly what I want," Jane said. "What are you doing on Spoede Road?" She pronounced it "Spay-dee" in the St. Louis manner. "This isn't the way home."

"I have to pick up your granddaughter at school."

"Well, don't sit at that STOP sign all afternoon, or you'll be late."

"I'm not sitting, Mom. This is called stopping. It's what you do when you see those red signs with the white letters."

"You don't have to get sarcastic, Josie. I don't know why you park at STOP signs. You must get that from your father. You're going to get rear-ended driving that way. Real St. Louisans don't stop. They sort of slide on through at an intersection. I don't know what's wrong with you."

"You must have picked up a baby from Minneapolis at the hospital," Josie said.

"I'm serious, Josie," her mother said. "Look out! Watch that black car there. The driver is making a right turn, but he doesn't have the signal on."

"If he had his signal on, I'd know something was wrong," Josie said. "St. Louisans don't use that, either."

Josie listened to her mother correct her driving all the way to the Barrington School and bit her lip to suppress a smile. Jane was seeing a counselor. She was going to be okay. Life was good.

Except for those murders. Suddenly Josie's troubles came crashing back down on her. She remembered the feel of the lie detector's sensors on her skin. She remembered that horrible moment when Olga's hair flew away. She saw the homicide detectives sitting in her living room. She could still wind up in jail.

"Josie, be careful. Your daughter is running straight for this car."

Amelia came tearing out of school as if a pack of pit bulls was chasing her. She jumped into the backseat and pulled her backpack in after her.

"Okay, I want to make it clear right now," Amelia said, "before anyone gets to you. It wasn't my fault."

"What wasn't your fault?" Josie said.

"Trey," Amelia was talking very fast, so Josie knew her daughter had done something wrong. "He's ten years old and bigger than me. Way bigger."

Josie remembered Trey. He was a hulking bully. He thought he could do as he pleased because his parents were doctors. All the kid did was walk into the room, and Josie went on full mom alert. Trey was triple trouble.

"Trey took my notebook and wouldn't give it back. So I hit him." Amelia's words skidded to an abrupt stop.

"And?" Josie said.

"And what?" Amelia looked way too innocent.

"What happened after you socked the kid?"

"He fell down," Amelia said.

"You knocked down a ten-year-old?" Josie tried to keep the pride from her voice.

"He wasn't going to give my notebook back," Amelia said.

"Was he hurt?"

"No, except the other kids laughed at him because he got hit by a girl."

"Did you get detention for fighting?" Josie said.

"No, it just happened, Mom. We really need to go."

"Why didn't you tell your teacher that a big boy took your notebook?"

"Because then I'd be a baby."

"And hitting someone is grown-up?" Josie said.

"Mom, can we go, please? Otherwise, we're going to have to sit in Mrs. Frederick's office for hours."

Josie didn't think she could take Mrs. Frederick's social-worker lectures about inappropriate responses. Because she was the mom, she said, "Amelia, I'm disappointed that you used fighting to solve the problem."

"I asked him nicely and he said no."

"That still doesn't mean you can hit him. What if you broke his nose? If that boy tells his parents—"

"He won't complain," Amelia said. "He won't tell them he got hit by a girl."

Thank God for ten-year-old sexism, Josie thought. "Guess he's just learned a girl can hit as hard as a boy," she said.

"Harder," Amelia said and grinned. "The boys are afraid of him."

"Don't encourage her," Jane said. "Fighting is not ladylike."

"A lady knows how to defend herself," Josie said. "But she doesn't look for trouble. Say hello to your grandmother, Amelia. You jumped in this car without a word of greeting." Josie put the car in gear and started out of the school drive. She checked the rearview mirror. Mrs. Frederick was not in pursuit.

"Hi, Grandma," Amelia said. "You're wearing the star earrings you bought on TV."

Sometimes Amelia had a positive genius for saying the wrong thing. Josie could feel her mother stiffen.

"Are you going to wear the star ankle bracelet?" Amelia said.

Josie tried to change the subject. "What would you like for dinner, Amelia?"

"I'm not going to wear the ankle bracelet," Jane said.

"Can I have it?" Amelia said. Even food couldn't distract her.

"No. Ankle bracelets are tacky," Jane said.

"But you—" Amelia said. Josie gave her tactless child such a glare even Amelia shut up.

"I bought a lot of things I don't need," Jane said. "I'm going to send them back if I can. If not, I'll donate them to the church charity for the homeless."

Josie had a sudden vision of the city's homeless holding up WILL WORK FOR FOOD signs, their arms, necks and ankles glittering with gold jewelry.

She looked over at her mother. Jane had dark circles under her eyes, as if she'd been beaten. "Would you like to have dinner with us, Mom?"

"Thanks, Josie, but I'm a little tired. I'd like to rest."

As they pulled up in front of the house, Josie saw that the old sycamore trees were shedding their leaves. Big brown leaves the size of dinner plates covered the lawn and sidewalk. They crunched through them to the house.

After her mother wearily climbed the stairs, Josie said, "Amelia, can you do your homework for an hour? I have to run an errand. I'll be back by four thirty. Then we'll do something fun."

"Guerrilla gorilla?" Amelia said.

"Better," Josie promised, as she grabbed a Coke from the fridge.

Stephanie's PR firm was ten minutes from Josie's

house. Reichman-Brassard had four floors of a square blue-glass skyscraper. Stephanie was sitting on the marble bench by the fountain, smoking a cigarette with wary watchfulness, as if she expected a school monitor to bust her. Josie, carrying her Coke, sat down beside her. They looked like two colleagues on break.

Stephanie looked small, wilted and resentful. "You didn't have to blackmail me," she said. "We weren't going to sue you. I knew those stores were a mess."

Josie had already worked out her strategy. She would be sympathetic and pretend to know more than she did. "It must have been difficult having to cover up for Danessa," she said.

"It was a nightmare," Stephanie said, and pulled down the sleeves of her too-big jacket. But not before Josie saw the pink rash on her wrist. Eczema. "I thought it was my big career break and didn't understand how someone right out of school could get such a terrific gig. After one week, I realized everyone else was too smart to touch it."

"Danessa made scenes, didn't she?" Josie said.

"She screamed at everyone except the media." Stephanie took a deep, comforting drag on her cigarette. Josie wondered if her firm represented the tobacco company.

"I lived in terror that she was going to blow up at some media biggie, but she controlled herself around the press. Eventually, word of her temper would leak out, and we'd have image problems. It was my idea to have her donate money to local charities. I remembered from my classes that's how robber barons like John D. Rockefeller and Andrew Carnegie rehabilitated their names. It didn't take much for Danessa. A check for five hundred here, a thousand there, enough press releases and photo ops, and Danessa got ten thousand dollars' worth of publicity. The media loves feel-good stories about major advertisers. I made her St. Louis's sweetheart."

"Most people never guessed what she was really like," Josie said.

"They didn't have a clue." Stephanie sucked in more smoke, then blew it out. "And that was a good thing."

"You said the stores were a mess. The purses weren't good, either," Josie said. "Danessa was buying cheap junk and passing it off as handmade." Josie said it as a fact, but it was a wild guess.

"That started about three months ago," Stephanie said. "I think she was in financial trouble, but she never said anything to me. I saw it and kept my mouth shut. I hoped the crash would come soon so I'd be free. No one else seemed to notice. Danessa lived a charmed life."

"So when did you start the affair with Serge?"

"About six months after I was working for her. He was nice. I was lonely. Also young and stupid. It didn't last long." Stephanie scratched her neck. Josie saw the bright pink flare up there, too. "We hooked up a few times. It wasn't a big deal. He was too old, but I liked him anyway. He made me laugh, and I didn't get many laughs around Danessa."

"Why did you stop?"

"Danessa almost walked in on us one day. I realized I'd lose everything, including my job, if she caught us together. I broke it off. Serge understood. He was a gentleman. Besides, I got the feeling he was serious about someone else, but I didn't know who." Stephanie seemed relieved to talk. She'd even stopped scratching.

"Any idea who killed Serge or Danessa?" Josie asked.

"Not a clue. I think about it a lot. I can't believe they're both dead. Serge was so alive. Danessa was a force of nature, like a tornado."

Stephanie looked at Josie. "I know what you're going to ask next. You're looking for her killer, right? The cops must suspect you, after she ragged on you at your office."

Josie nodded.

"I didn't kill her," Stephanie said. "But I'm glad she's dead."

She stubbed out her cigarette and stood up. It was a chilling epitaph for Danessa.

Josie was back home by four thirty, as promised. She

rummaged around in the toolshed, found an ancient rake and said, "Get your jacket, Amelia. Let's go outside."

Amelia eyed the rake and said, "I thought we were going to have fun."

"We are."

Amelia stood with her hands in her pockets while Josie raked the leaves into a pile nearly as high as her head.

"This is a good fall," Josie said. "We haven't had much rain. These leaves are fat and crunchy. In the olden days, we'd burn them. Now that's against the law. But this isn't."

Josie yelled, "Fall into fall," and jumped into the pile of leaves.

Amelia hesitated for a moment and Josie held her breath. Would her daughter turn into a teenager, too grown-up for childish games?

Then Amelia belly flopped into the leaves. For the next half hour, mother and daughter rolled, jumped and ran through the leaves, crunching them into little pieces. When they demolished the pile, Josie and Amelia raked the leaves into bags "because Grandma isn't feeling good." Amelia would do things for Grandma she wouldn't do for her mother.

Dinner was beef stew with s'mores for dessert. Real fall food.

It was almost eight o'clock by the time Josie finished cleaning up the kitchen and checking Amelia's homework. She dialed the number for the HAVE YOU SEEN THIS WOMAN? flyer. The last time, Josie had talked to an old woman who had trouble with English. Josie thought someone else might be home after work.

The flyer's phone number rang four times before a woman answered. "Hello, who is calling, please?" Her accent sounded Eastern European. Russian, maybe? Her English was excellent.

"I'm calling about the flyer for the missing woman, Marina," Josie said.

"Who is calling, please?" the woman repeated.

"I saw your flyers for the missing woman—"

"She is not missing," the woman said. "She has been found. There is no problem. We thought we had taken down all the flyers. We are sorry to trouble you."

"Marina has been found?" Josie said. "That's wonderful. Where is she? Could I talk to her? Are you a friend or a family member? Hello?"

The line went dead.

The call didn't answer any of Josie's questions. It gave her more. Was Marina really found—or was someone pretending that she was safe? Was Marina as dead as Olga? If she was alive, why was Marina hiding?

Chapter 27

"In the midst of life we are in debt."

The first time Josie attended a Protestant funeral that's how she heard the famous words from the Book of Common Prayer. They seemed more accurate than "in the midst of life we are in death."

Now, at Danessa and Serge's memorial service, that thought came to mind again. The crowd who packed the Chapel at Wood Winds looked rich. But Josie sensed something unstable about these sleek and pampered people, as if they were one mortgage payment, one job, one divorce from disaster.

The wealth on display was staggering. In the pew in front of Josie, at least twenty thousand dollars in black Danessa purses hung from slender shoulders. She wondered if her sturdy Coach bag was a faux pas.

Maybe it's my imagination, Josie thought. Maybe it's my own life that's unstable. She was nervous, jumpy, expecting the police to arrest her any moment. She looked around for Detectives Yawney and Waxley, but didn't see them.

I've made a mistake, she thought. I shouldn't be here. I never met Serge. The only time I saw Danessa we had a vicious fight. The homicide detectives will think I'm a killer, come here to gloat over my victims.

"Relax," Alyce whispered and patted her hand. "You're safe. Your mouthpiece is with you."

Alyce could often read Josie's thoughts—or in this

case her nervous twitches. Her friend seemed pale and thinner in her black dress. She also looked unhappy. Josie hoped it was because she was at a funeral, not because there were troubles at home.

Josie and Alyce couldn't even go for coffee and a good talk when the service was over. Alyce had yet another committee meeting afterward.

Josie had expected Serge and Danessa's memorial service to be as extravagant as their lives. She saw their sable-draped coffins in a Russian Orthodox church glowing with gold and czarist jewels.

Instead, the couple had a quiet Protestant memorial service in the austere white chapel. On the altar was a bouquet of white waxy lilies and portraits of Serge and Danessa. Already, their photos had the remote look of the long dead.

The organist played something so cold and classical the notes hung like icicles in the air. Only the crowd of newspaper and TV reporters was the same. Eager photographers lined the sidewalk, filled the vestibule, and spilled into the church. Josie had heard that the police videotaped funerals of murder victims. She wondered if any of the folks behind the cameras had badges. She checked the church again. Still no sign of the homicide detectives.

Stephanie the PR child sat near the front in a figure-hugging dark suit. Now Josie saw what must have attracted Serge. She had a sleek little figure. The owl glasses were gone. Perhaps when she worked for Danessa, Stephanie had dressed down so she wouldn't be a threat to her client.

Josie couldn't miss Amy the Slut sashaying up the aisle in a butt-hugging, breast-baring black number. She gave Josie and Alyce a pert little finger wave. Alyce stared back.

Saint Kate also arrived alone. Her lank hair was pulled into a stylish chignon that made her long, toothy face seem distinguished. Her black dress emphasized her fashionably lean body. Mourning became her. She took a seat behind Amy and bowed her head.

"Kate looks good," Josie whispered.

"Her house is under contract," Alyce said. "They're getting five thousand less than the asking price, which is nothing short of a miracle."

"I guess burying Saint Joseph worked again," Josie said.

Almost all the mourners were women. Josie wondered how many had slept with Serge. Next to Kate were three small blondes in black. Any of them could have been Bunny with the sizzling gossip. The little blonde had given Amy an excellent motive for killing Serge.

The minister finished the first round of prayers. The eulogies began. A stocky woman in a gray suit stepped up to the microphone. She was the director of a women's shelter. "Serge and Danessa were two of the most generous people in this city," she began.

The tributes continued until Josie felt as embalmed as the subjects. Director after director thanked their dead benefactors, and no doubt prayed that their organization was in their wills. Josie noticed two things: None of Danessa's employees praised her. And no one cried for Serge or Danessa.

Amy was flirting with the man next to her. The guy's wife had daggers in her eyes.

Saint Kate sat regal and composed, but dry-eyed. Maybe she'd already done all her crying.

Stephanie looked relieved.

Serge had stirred violent passions—but no one had really loved him.

Josie looked at the photos of Serge and Danessa on the altar. They made a perfect couple, equally matched in flamboyance and flaming temper. So why wouldn't Danessa marry the man? They belonged together. They died together on the same night.

Who killed them?

Kate? Amy? Stephanie?

Josie thought Amy had the best reason for seeing Serge dead, but she didn't like the woman.

And where was Marina, the six-feet-two Russian blonde? Josie scanned the crowd once more for her, but she wasn't in the church. Danessa had declared that Marina didn't exist. Why did she lie? She had to know that Marina was at her store. Maybe Danessa didn't want Marina to exist.

Who was Marina? Serge's sister? His lover? His incestuous lover?

What did she have to do with Serge's death?

Suddenly Josie knew. She knew it all. She knew how Serge died, who killed Danessa and why. She knew how Olga the shotgunned saleswoman fit into the picture, and why she didn't wipe Josie's fingerprints off that snakeskin belt. She knew who killed Olga.

Josie knew everything except where to find the mysterious Marina. But she did have a phone number. Now she needed a cross directory so she could match the number to an address. The people there would lead her to Marina. Once Josie located the Russian mystery woman, she'd be ready to go to the police and clear her name. After the funeral, she would go to Has Beans and use the computer to find the address.

Now there was a plan. Get some hot coffee. See some hot Josh. In the midst of death, we are in life. . . .

"St. Louis lost its two most generous spirits—" a man in a somber navy suit was saying, when the long song of a cell phone stopped him cold. He frowned into the congregation.

"What idiot forgot to turn off her cell phone?" Alyce whispered.

"Er, I think it's me." Josie switched off the noisy little device and checked the display. Her mother was calling. It could be important. Josie grabbed her purse and slid out of the pew in red-faced disgrace, feeling the glares and stares of the mourners.

The vestibule was packed with people who couldn't

get into the church. Josie walked toward the parking lot as she speed-dialed her mother.

Jane must have been waiting by the phone. She picked it up on the first ring. "Josie? Is it you?" Josie could hear her mother's anxiety. "That fancy phone you have is useless. It has every function except how to get you to answer. That police detective—Yawney—wants to talk to you. He's called three times already."

"Oh, God," Josie said. "Did he say what he wanted?"

"No, just that you need to call him right away. It's important."

Josie saw an unmarked police car driving into the parking lot. She ducked around the side of the church and took a longer look. It was Detective Michael Yawney. He'd come to arrest her.

Josie had to talk fast. "Mom, do me a favor, please. I think they may try to arrest me. But I can prove my innocence. If Detective Yawney calls again, say you don't know where I am. And please pick up Amelia from school. Can you do that, Mom?"

"Josie, what's wrong?" Jane said.

"I'm going to stay away from home until I find out something. But don't worry." The three words that made every mother worry. "It will just be overnight at the most. I promise. You'll make sure Amelia does her homework?"

"Josie—" her mother said. Josie snapped her cell phone shut.

Detective Yawney was marching up the sidewalk toward the church, his face grim. Josie backed farther around the corner, out of his line of sight, and bumped into a woman peering through the church window. The woman's eyes were red from weeping. Her face was wet with tears.

There was something oddly familiar about her. Her outfit was strange. She had on thick-soled old-women's shoes, a shapeless blue coat, and a Danessa bag with the distinctive diamond clasp. Josie was close enough to see it had the usual Danessa quality problem. The strap was badly sewn and the stitches were crooked.

The woman's black hair was crooked, too. A few strands of blond showed at the hairline. She was wearing a wig.

She could change her clothes and her hair, but nothing could disguise more than six feet of height.

"Marina!" Josie said.

Chapter 28

"I am not Marina," the woman said. "You are mistaken."

She was lying. Josie knew it. She'd heard that voice before.

"I am not," Josie said. "I know who you are."

Marina did look like a different person. The chic blond Russian was gone. Now her hair was stringy and shoe-polish black. The harsh color turned her face a sickly yellow. Her lumpy coat gave her a hunchbacked look. Her sturdy shoes made her legs seem thick and old.

But Marina's hands were strong and young, and her nails were long and polished.

"I talked with you on the phone last night," Josie said. "I called your home twice. I got the number off the flyer I found at Down and Dirty Discounts. An old woman answered in the morning. You answered at night. I know your voice. You waited on me at the Danessa store. Remember the snakeskin belt?"

"No! I do not," the woman said and started to move away.

Josie grabbed a hunk of Marina's flat black hair and yanked. The wig came tumbling off. Marina's own blond hair was scraped on top of her head, anchored with bristling bobby pins.

Marina lunged for the black wig and missed. Her hand clamped on Josie's arm like a steel band, and Josie felt the young woman in the old woman's clothes.

Josie chopped at Marina's hand with her heavy Coach bag. The Russian let go in surprise, shaking her wrist. She kept coming for Josie, anger lighting her eyes.

"Give me that wig," Marina hissed. She should have looked ridiculous with her bad hair and her baggy coat. Instead, they made her seem feral, a creature who didn't abide by ordinary rules.

Josie stepped back, holding the black wig like a dead rat. "Touch me again, Marina, and I'll scream. There are several hundred people in that church, including a homicide detective. I'll have him out here in no time."

And he'll arrest me, Josie thought.

"No, no police," Marina said, suddenly cooperative. "What do you want? I don't have money."

"I don't want money. I just want to ask you a couple of questions."

They could hear a cold swell of organ music from inside the church. The memorial service would be ending soon.

"We can't talk here," Marina said. "We must go now."

Josie agreed. She didn't want Detective Yawney to find her.

"We'll go to my house in South St. Louis," Marina said.

Too dangerous, Josie decided. Too isolated. Anything could happen in one of those old brick buildings. The thick walls smothered sounds. The neighbors heard nothing. Josie wanted to meet this woman safely in her territory. She wouldn't take Marina to her house in Maplewood, but there was another place where Josie felt at home.

"We'll go to a mall," she said. "Pick one."

Josie knew them all. She'd walked every inch of every mall in St. Louis. She knew where to find their hidden passages, security guards and emergency exits.

"Plaza Venetia," Marina said.

That choice surprised Josie. It also pleased her. Plaza Venetia had the sort of shoppers who whipped out their cell phones and called 911 at the slightest hint of trouble. She couldn't think of a more secure meeting spot.

"Where should we meet?" Josie said.

"There is a bench for sitting behind the chocolate shop on the second floor," Marina said. "It is near a little fountain and a side staircase. It is a private area where we can talk. I will meet you there."

That site would have been Josie's first choice, but now it made her uneasy. Did Marina know something she didn't?

Josie reviewed the spot in her mind. She saw the wide staircase with its white banister, the wrought-iron bench, the marble fountain surrounded by ferns and flowers. On the wall behind the bench she also pictured a red fire alarm and a fire extinguisher in a glass case. Both could be used as protection in an emergency. Josie also had her trusty Coach bag, which weighed twenty pounds fully loaded.

"Good," she said. "I'll follow you there. And don't try anything. I know what you drive."

"You are lying." Marina turned those feral eyes full on Josie. Lynx eyes. They made her shiver, even in the warm fall sun.

Josie scanned the church parking lot, which was paved with pricey vehicles: Mercedes, BMWs, Lexuses, Hummers and other high-end SUVs. There were a few modest but respectable cars like her Honda. One rusting monster, a 1972 Cadillac, stood out like a bum in a ballroom.

"That's your car," Josie said, pointing to the junker Caddy. "The brown one with the rust and the loose rear bumper."

Marina looked startled. "How did you know?" she said. "You did not see me drive in."

"Americans know cars," Josie said. The people in that church would hitchhike before they'd drive a rust bucket like Marina's, however luxurious it used to be.

"We also know license plates," Josie said, "so don't try to get away from me. The minute I don't see your car on the road in front of me, I'll call the police." She held up her cell phone. "Stay off the highway and take Clayton Road all the way to the mall. I'll follow you."

The first mourners were leaving the church. "We must go," Marina said. Josie saw a flicker of panic in her eyes. She felt it herself.

Josie sprinted for her car, still holding Marina's black wig. She threw it on the seat in disgust, wondering why she hadn't given it back.

Marina tore open the heavy door on her Cadillac. Josie could hear its dry creak across the parking lot. The Russian woman peeled out of the lot, Josie following. Marina drove fast and hard, but she did not try to evade her pursuer.

Nice work, Josie told herself, as she followed Marina. But now that you've got her, what are you going to do with her?

As she dodged in and of traffic, Josie plotted how to save herself. She didn't just want to talk to Marina. She wanted to record their conversation. She knew Marina could exonerate her. Okay, she didn't know. But she hoped she could. Josie couldn't carry a tape recorder to their meeting. For once her silly cell phone might come in handy. It had a recording function.

Josie wished she could call Alyce for help. But her friend was still at the funeral. She'd have to depend on her mother this time. She knew Jane would make her life miserable for this. There was nothing she could do about that. Josie braced herself for the conversation with Jane, as she tried to keep track of Marina's car speeding through the traffic. She took a deep breath and dialed her mother.

"Josie, are you in jail?" Jane said.

"No, Mom. I think I can get the cops off my back. All I have to do is record a phone conversation with my cell phone."

"Are you finally going to get some use out of that overpriced gadget?" Jane said.

Josie struggled not to say something sarcastic. Her mother might hang up on her.

"Yes," Josie said. "My phone will be worth every penny if it works. Mom, I've got you on the phone now because I want to start the recording. Don't hang up, no matter what you hear—I need to record all of this call. It's really, really important. And don't get scared. I won't be alone. I'll be at Plaza Venetia with lots of people around. Okay?"

"I guess so, Josie," her mother said. "But what do I do when I leave to pick up Amelia?"

"You can go. Just don't hang up your phone whatever you do. And don't worry."

Josie instantly regretted those words. Jane would have her ear glued to the phone. Well, Josie needed a witness.

"Josie, this sounds dangerous. Shouldn't I call 911?"

Marina pulled into the Plaza Venetia lot. Josie followed her. "Mom, please. I'm running out of time. I need to record this meeting. Promise me you won't hang up, no matter what."

"I promise, Josie," Jane said and hung up the phone.

"Mom!" Josie screamed into the dead phone. She speed-dialed her mother, but the line was busy. Jane was probably trying to call her back. Josie took a deep breath and dialed again. Her mother answered on the first ring.

"I'm sorry," Jane said. "I got nervous. I'll remember this time."

On the drive to the mall, Marina had brushed out her long hair, put on her makeup and shed her ugly coat. She must have had some stylish shoes stashed in her car. A striking blonde emerged from Marina's car at Plaza Venetia. Once inside the mall, Marina would blend in with the clientele.

Josie was glad the Russian had changed her appearance for another reason. Marina's black turtleneck and pants were too tight to conceal any weapons. Her dinky Danessa purse was too small and fragile to hold a gun. Josie felt safer.

Marina may have looked like the other shoppers, but Josie could feel the rage radiating from the woman. The big Russian raced through the mall with long, furious strides. She could see Josie struggling to keep up with her, but Marina would not slow down. As she charged past a cookie store, Josie's stomach growled. She hadn't eaten since last night.

"Would you like to stop for coffee or a sandwich?" Josie asked.

"No. I do not want to eat with you," Marina said.

I have to face this woman on an empty stomach with no caffeine, Josie thought. They sprinted through the mall in silence until they came to the back staircase, decorated with banners that said CELEBRATE FALL IN PLAZA VENETIA STYLE. Each banner hung on a spearlike brass standard. The banners had muted orange and yellow leaves. Autumn's flaming colors did not exist at Plaza Venetia. Neither did the end-of-the-year sadness that gave this season its special beauty.

Marina loped up the stairs. Josie followed, panting like an old dog. She was looking forward to that bench by the fountain. On a better day she would have admired the bronze mums planted around its splashing, soothing water. The sweet smell of chocolate wafted from the shop around the corner. Josie's stomach growled again.

The fountain alcove was a good choice—isolated from most mall traffic, but not completely deserted. An occasional shopper wandered by.

"Are you wearing a wire?" Marina asked.

"No," Josie said.

"Before I talk, I will pat you down and check your purse."

"Only if I can do the same to you," Josie said. She hoped security didn't come by and see two women feeling each other up.

Josie looked in Marina's bag. It was too small for a wallet. She saw a lipstick, credit card, driver's license, small brush and a black cylinder.

"Perfume?" Josie said.

"My inhaler," Marina said. "I have asthma."

Josie tried to look innocent while Marina searched her Coach bag. The Russian looked disgusted at the wad of used Kleenex Josie had packed on top as a distraction. Marina gave Josie's cell phone only a cursory inspection. She never noticed it was on.

"So," Marina said. "We are here." She looked hard and arrogant. "What is it you want to know?"

"What is your relationship to Serge?" Josie said.

"What do you mean?"

"Look," Josie said, "if we fence around this way, we'll be here all day. Serge was your husband, wasn't he? You were married in Russia."

"How do you know that?" Marina said.

"Most people thought you were his sister. But Mrs. Perkins saw you kissing him. She thought you had an incestuous relationship with your brother."

Marina's laugh was like a rusty gate. "That old woman has a dirty mind. She was always snooping where she didn't belong."

"That's why Danessa wouldn't marry Serge, wasn't it?" Josie said. "It's what you fought about in the stockroom. She knew Serge already had a wife. She wasn't going to commit bigamy. How did she find out about you two?"

"She spoke Russian. Not a lot, but enough to hear Serge address me as his wife. She was already suspicious because Serge did not always act like a brother around me."

"How could you stand Danessa living with Serge?"

Marina's laugh turned derisive. "Danessa was gay, you fool. She was in love with Olga."

"Urk!" Josie said. She couldn't help it. She was surprised.

"Did Olga love her?" Josie said.

Now Marina's laugh was like sandpaper on skin. "Olga loved money. Danessa had it. She loved to stay at Danessa's mansion. Her own place was not a palace."

Josie remembered the dreary little avocado green

kitchen and the feasting bloody flies. She didn't want to talk about Olga.

"Was Danessa in on the osmium-187 scam?" Josie said.

Marina shrugged. She didn't ask how Josie knew about it. "Danessa said she wanted nothing to do with it, but she knew. I was the one who had to unpack the boxes. She didn't want her fingerprints on anything. So I did the dirty work. But Danessa took the money Serge made from it." Her contempt was corrosive.

"Serge told her there was no risk," Marina said. "It wasn't real nuclear weapons material. It was fake. The problem wasn't the osmium-187. It was the people he sold it to—terrorists."

"Did they kill him when they found out he'd scammed them?" Josie asked.

"No. They were killed first. In a car bombing in the Middle East. All four of them. Serge thought he was invincible then, a child of the gods.

"Then immigration started in after him. The officials started asking where he got his money. They suspected he was using Danessa's store to launder it. If they knew he'd been selling to terrorists, even if he cheated them, they'd deport him. Serge had most of it hidden. He quit giving Danessa money. He tried to pressure her to marry him. He thought if he didn't give her the money to keep her stores going, she'd say yes."

"Is that when she started ordering cheap goods?" Josie said.

Now Marina's eyebrows did go up. "How did you know that?"

"I saw the beading on those purses," Josie said. "Plastic beads cost less, but they don't catch the light. They look dull. And those so-called Italian leather bags were poorly sewn. Who put the fake MADE IN ITALY tags in those inferior purses?"

"That was Danessa's idea," Marina said. "When Serge's money dried up, she cut back on the quality of the stock. She did not think anyone could tell. She said

customers were stupid to pay her prices in the first place.
'The more I charge, the better they think it is,' she said.
Danessa paid me to put in the new tags. She wouldn't
soil her hands with the actual dirty work."

"And you'd go against your own husband?"

"I wanted him to take his money and disappear with
me. We could go anywhere in the world. But he would
not leave. He liked the celebrity life. He liked the"—
she paused to search for the right word—"the limelight.
That's why I was at the store that day you mystery-
shopped us. Another shipment had arrived and I had to
unpack and tag it. Danessa denied I was there because
she was afraid someone would find out about the
cheap purses."

"You did the dirty work," Josie said. "You lived in a
slum while Danessa lived in style. You took all the risks.
Danessa got everything. But she wouldn't help out Serge
and go through with a bigamous marriage. Couldn't he
get a Russian divorce?"

"It would take too long. Serge declared himself single
when he came to America. He lied. Immigration would
not look kindly on this. I had to stay out of the picture.
He had to marry an American soon or he'd be sent
back, no matter how powerful his media friends. A quick
marriage to an American woman was the only thing that
would save him. And Danessa wouldn't do it."

Her eyes looked away from Josie for the first time.
She's lying, Josie thought. Was there some reason Serge
had to stay away from Russia? Would it be fatal for him
to go home? Or did he give his real wife a healthy chunk
of that hidden money?

Did Marina know about Kate and the other women?
Did she care? Or had that side of their marriage died?
She was the only woman who had cried at Serge's
funeral.

But Josie thought Marina was shrewd. Unlike her
spouse, she kept a low profile and stayed off immigration's radar. She could hide out in the Russian community, take Serge's money, and run if things turned rough.

"Did you know Serge took rat poison?" Josie said.

"Of course."

"You found his body before the police did, didn't you?"

Marina's face was a mask of hate. "Yes. That bitch killed him. That miserable bitch."

"Who?" Josie said.

"Danessa."

"So that's why you killed her," Josie said.

Chapter 29

"You killed an innocent woman," Josie said.

"No!" Marina's voice was low and fierce. Josie had never heard such desperate denial in one word.

"I was there," Marina said. "I saw Danessa bring my Serge's orange juice with the dose of medicine in it. She gave it to him with her own hands. I saw Danessa murder my husband, only I did not know it. No one else could have tampered with his drink. Mrs. Perkins was not home. He had no other visitors that evening except me. Danessa gave him his juice and then she left for the stores about seven twenty. She said she had to visit them for damage control. That was your fault."

This trail of death started with me, Josie thought. I mystery-shopped the Danessa stores and gave them a bad rating. Danessa stormed into Harry's office and threatened me. She was killed that same night and I got blamed. It seemed so long ago, like some historic battle.

"Why didn't Serge fix his own medicine?" Josie said. "Danessa never struck me as the sort of woman who waited on a man."

"No, but Serge loved to be pampered. Danessa was extra nice to him because she thought her deal with the Creshan Corporation was going to fall apart. So she prepared his medicine drink and he died. My husband would be alive except for you." Marina seemed to burn with hatred. Josie could feel its passionate heat. It was so out of place in the beautifully bland Plaza Venetia.

"Oh, no," Josie said. "I'm not taking that guilt trip. You can blame yourself. If you'd waited on me better, I would have given your store a higher rating and none of this would have happened."

"That worthless Olga was supposed to be minding the store," Marina said. "She wandered off for coffee without telling me. She did as she pleased. Danessa never disciplined her. Olga could do no wrong. My Serge was just an accessory for Danessa, a man to wear on her arm when she went to her charity events. She used him for his looks and his money. He financed the stores. I used to read the news stories that called Danessa the St. Louis Martha Stewart and laugh. She could not balance a cash register, much less run a chain of stores."

"Mrs. Perkins told me Serge was the real brains of the operation," Josie said.

"She was right about that at least," Marina said grudgingly.

"But he needed Danessa, too," Josie said. "He used the stores to launder money from his scam."

"Danessa never cared where the money came from," Marina said. "She needed more and more. The stores were not doing well. They swallowed money in greedy gulps. She also liked to see herself as the great philanthropist. She lived for the news stories where she was Lady Bountiful helping orphans and battered wives. Charity can be an expensive vice.

"The Creshan deal would have given even Danessa enough money, for a while at least. Then you ruined everything with your bad report. A little nothing like you toppled Danessa's mighty plans. I wanted to laugh. I thought that was the end of her ambitions. But Danessa saw a way out. If Serge was dead, she would not need the Creshan deal. She would inherit all of Serge's money."

"Wouldn't you get it?" Josie said.

"Ah, I lied, too. I am an unmarried woman to your immigration. Serge and Danessa took out big insurance policies and made wills when they moved in together. She insisted. He thought it was a joke. Serge never thought he would die."

"Serge gave you cash, didn't he?" Josie said. "He didn't name you in his will, but he made sure you were well provided for."

Marina didn't answer. "Serge died first, so his money became part of Danessa's estate," she said. "There was also a nice bequest for her faithful Olga. She can spend it in hell." Marina's laugh was straight out of a horror movie.

Josie looked around nervously, afraid they were drawing curious stares. But no one seemed to notice them. Two women, loaded with bags from expensive stores, stopped at the fountain. One was big and blond. The other was small and dark. They seemed to be friends. Just like Alyce and me, Josie thought, and wished with all her heart that she was shopping this afternoon.

"Thank God those pointy-toed shoes are going out of style," the brunette said. "They kill my feet."

"But what moron designed open toes for fall?" her blond friend said. "My feet will freeze." She held up a chic store bag.

It's not the moron who designs them, Josie wanted to say. It's the moron who buys them.

"Make a wish," the brunette said as she tossed some coins into the fountain.

"I wish I could eat all the chocolate I wanted and it wouldn't land on my thighs," her friend said.

"I wish I could find mums that color bronze," the brunette said, admiring the fountain plantings.

I wish my life would go back to normal, Josie thought. I wish I'd never heard of Serge and Danessa. I wish I'd never found Marina.

The two women shoppers moved into the peaceful world of the mall, with its soothing music, splashing fountains and pretty trifles for sale.

Marina regarded the pair with withering contempt,

then went back to discussing murder by the mums. Josie longed to check her purse and see if the phone had been recording the crucial confession, but she didn't dare.

"So you believed Danessa had killed Serge. And you drove to Plaza Venetia and killed her," Josie said.

"It was the best thing I ever did," Marina said. "Danessa is dead and I am glad. She was an evil woman."

"Evil?" Josie said. The single word escaped.

The only evil woman she saw was Marina. Hate had transformed her face. She had a skeleton's grin and a lost soul's empty eyes.

"Now answer my question," Marina demanded. "Why do you say that Danessa did not kill Serge?"

"Serge killed himself," Josie said.

"He would never commit suicide!" Marina cried.

"I didn't say he did," Josie said. "Serge was too cheap to get a prescription for warfarin. Instead he calibrated the dose from rat poison."

"It was the same thing!" Marina said. "Americans love to throw away money on doctors, like old rich women. There was no need to get warfarin from a doctor when Serge could buy it at the hardware store for one-tenth the cost."

"You don't just pay for the prescription," Josie said. "You pay for the doctor's knowledge. Serge lost fifty pounds on his diet. A good doctor would have adjusted his medicine and given him a smaller dose. Serge didn't change the dose when he lost weight, did he?"

"He was a big man!" Marina said.

"I'm right, aren't I?" Josie pressed.

Marina's silence said everything.

"Didn't you see the bruising on his skin?" Josie asked. "That's a sign of warfarin poisoning."

"I thought it was from other . . . things."

Other women, Josie thought. Marina knew her husband was unfaithful.

"You found his body, didn't you?" Josie said. "Before the police discovered it."

"He passed out in front of me," Marina said. "He hit his head on the marble coffee table and died as he fell to the floor."

"According to Mrs. Perkins, the police said your husband bled to death."

"He was dead, I tell you. I know what death looks like. You Americans do not know about death and destruction."

"Dead people don't bleed," Josie said. "And I haven't heard that the police found any bloody fingerprints or footprints near the body."

"You think I killed him, fool?"

"No, I think you let him die. I think you were angry with him because he was unfaithful with so many women. It was just an impulse to let him lie there and bleed to death."

Marina had gone a peculiar gray. Her breathing was shallow and she was sweating. Did guilt do that to her?

"I do not have your silly American views about marriage," Marina said. "I am a woman of the world. I knew Serge must go with these other women for his image. I knew he had to marry one to stay in this country. I was lucky. If there was a problem I could disappear and immigration would never find me. But Serge was not what you call low profile. He would be easy to find. He had to marry an American to save himself."

Her eyes shifted. She was lying again. A few minutes ago, she'd said she wanted Serge to take the money and run away with her.

"He didn't have to have affairs with everyone who wore a skirt," Josie said. "He didn't have to fall in love with Kate."

"Serge did not love her." Marina's rage ignited again. "He only thought he did. He would tire of her soon enough. He liked women of spirit. Kate was boring. He would have come back to me."

Come back. So Marina knew he had left. She was so pale, Josie was afraid Marina might pass out. Yet she seemed compelled to make her terrible confession. Keep her talking, she thought. You have one more murder to clear up. Josie prayed her phone was still recording. Marina's revelations might have melted it by now.

"Olga," Josie said. "What about Olga? She was blackmailing you, wasn't she?"

"Danessa ordered her to clean the store after she got your report. Olga did everything but reassemble the snakeskin belt display. She was not clever with her hands. Olga said you made her take the display apart. That was petty of you. It takes an hour to set up that display."

"I'm sorry," Josie said. She was, too. She would have never been mixed up in a murder if she hadn't insisted on trying on that silly snake belt.

A mother with twins in a sports stroller raced by. Josie was glad the mom moved so quickly. She didn't think this conversation was fit for infant ears.

Marina shrugged. "I liked it that Olga had to work for a change. She put the belt in the back room. Danessa was going to do the new display herself. After she killed Serge—"

Marina would not admit that she'd made a mistake and killed Danessa for no reason. She looked at Josie, daring her to say something.

"After Danessa killed Serge," Marina repeated, "I could not let her live. I left the house, driving like a madwoman. Why I was not stopped by the police, I cannot say. It was nine thirty. I told Olga to go home early. She took her purse out from under the counter and left without another word. There was no one on the floor. I went into the stockroom. Danessa was unpacking a shipment from Prada. I had on gloves. I planned to strangle her with my hands. But when I saw the snakeskin belt, I knew it was meant for her. Her death was not as quick as Serge's, or as painless."

Marina gave her death's head smile and Josie's stomach twisted in terror. *I am sitting with a double murderer—maybe a triple killer—in a shopping mall. All*

I have is a cell phone to save me. Mom is listening in. She'll be frantic.

Marina started talking again. She couldn't resist telling Josie how clever she was. Marina wasn't a loser duped by an unfaithful husband. She was a criminal mastermind. "Olga knew, or guessed, what I had done. She blackmailed me. At first, I could pay her. She only wanted her rent money. But then she got greedy. She was tired of that dingy city apartment. She missed Danessa's mansion. She wanted a palace of her own. She asked for more money. She said she would go to the police and collect a reward for finding Serge and Danessa's killer. The reward was twenty-five thousand dollars. She wanted me to give her fifty thousand. Instead, I disappeared. I did not tell my friends or family where I was. Russians are good at hiding. If Olga had left me alone, she would still be alive. It was not my fault I had to kill her.

"Olga went to my old grandmother with some flyers she'd made, saying I was a missing person. My grandmother was worried about me. She thought Olga was a friend, trying to help. They put the flyers all over the neighborhood. I had to do something then. Someone would find me and turn me in."

"So you shot Olga," Josie said.

"I made it look like a break-in, except the police did not believe that. I moved in with my old grandmother, but I still had to keep out of sight. I could not even attend my Serge's funeral. I am the widow. But I cannot mourn my husband after that woman killed him."

"Danessa didn't kill him," Josie said. "Serge killed himself. And you killed her for nothing."

"Liar!" Marina said. "Liar, liar, liar—" Her voice was cut off by a terrible choking wheeze. "My inhaler. Please. I need my inhaler."

She was scrabbling for her purse, but her fingers didn't seem to work. They moved helplessly around on the bench like lost creatures.

"I'll get help." Josie was afraid Marina might die right there.

"No. Inhaler. In purse." Marina's voice was a horrible gurgle.

Josie popped the purse open.

Suddenly Marina's fingers were swift and strong. She reached in, grabbed the black cylinder and aimed it at Josie's face.

Josie could smell the pungent odor.

Pepper spray, she thought, as Marina pressed the nozzle.

Chapter 30

Josie felt like her hair was on fire. She wanted to claw her head off.

She'd ducked just before Marina let loose the burst of pepper spray. Josie caught most of it on her scalp, but a tiny drop hit the corner of her mouth. Now her lips and tongue burned like she'd eaten a million Mexican dinners. Josie was afraid to open her eyes. If they filled with stinging pepper spray, she would be blinded.

I'm letting a killer get away, Josie thought. But she couldn't chase Marina through the mall. She wanted to rip off her scalp. Josie had to stop the searing pain or she'd go crazy.

Water. Water would wash away her agony.

Josie, eyes still closed, felt blindly for the fountain. Her hands found the rough clay pots lining its rim. She shoved the bronze mums out of her way. The flowers toppled to the marble floor with a terrible clatter. Maybe the noise would bring help. Josie could smell the plants' bitter scent even over the pungent pepper spray.

She knelt down and plunged her burning head into the fountain. Ahh. Relief. The water felt icy cold. The flames on her scalp settled into a slow, bearable sizzle. She rubbed a handful of moist dirt on her head. It was a soothing poultice, absorbing the burn. Better and better. Josie slowly opened her eyes in the water. They didn't sting. She could see. She wanted to shout her relief. She wasn't blinded by the pepper spray.

Josie felt long, strong hands on her back and neck. Help had arrived.

Then those same hands shoved her head under water and Josie's stomach lurched. It wasn't help. It was Marina. The Russian giant was trying to drown her. Marina wasn't going to run away—not until Josie was dead.

I know too much, Josie thought. She has to kill me. And I've made it easy for her.

Josie thrashed and kicked at her attacker. She got her head up out of the fountain, choking and spewing water, taking in great lungfuls of air. But before she could fight all the way free, Marina plunged Josie's head back under the water, then landed on her body, slamming it against the hard marble edge of the fountain. Josie's chest felt crushed and she was momentarily dazed.

She tried to rake her nails along Marina's arm, but it was protected by her sweater. Josie fought and gasped and swallowed half the fountain. Sometimes she could thrust her head above the water for a quick, painful breath, but Marina shoved her back under. The big, muscular woman weighed a good thirty pounds more than Josie.

Josie's lungs were bursting and black dots danced before her eyes. When those dots completely filled her vision, she would die.

Free. She had to break free. But Josie was so tired. All she wanted to do was—

See her daughter again. Amelia, with her sweet cinnamon sprinkle of freckles. Josie had to survive. She had to see her daughter grow up. No one was going to take that from her. Josie fought her way to the surface once again, breathing in great gulps of air. They burned her lungs, but they felt good.

Why wasn't anyone stopping Marina? Couldn't they see she was trying to drown a customer? Why weren't shocked shoppers calling 911? Josie wasn't sure how long she could hold on. Marina was going to force her head under the water again.

Josie's hands scrambled frantically for a weapon to break Marina's hold. In the mum muck around the fountain, she found a long, sharp shard of clay pot. She thrust it like a red dagger into Marina's foot. The Russian wasn't wearing stockings, and the shard knifed through her bare skin. Josie's anger gave her the strength to push it in deeper. She thought of her orphaned daughter and twisted it.

Marina shrieked. Surely that scream would bring some help.

Josie broke free from Marina at last, rolling away from the nearly fatal fountain. She sat up, breathing heavily, painfully. She pulled herself up by the bench. Help. She had to get help. Now was her chance. Marina seemed momentarily stunned. Blood spurted from her foot. She started hobbling away from Josie, but slipped on the wet, muddy marble floor, and belly flopped. Josie's slick leather-soled shoes slid out from under her and she landed on Marina with a loud "Oof!"

Josie's arms flew straight out from her sides. Her left hand felt something leathery and familiar. The strap of her Coach bag. The all-purpose weapon. Josie swung her heavy purse like a bolo and hit Marina's head with a solid *thwack*. Marina grunted and then lay still.

Josie looked into her attacker's face. Marina's eyes were closed. She was out cold.

Good. Josie sat up on Marina's broad back and wiped her streaming eyes with her wet blouse. All that did was smear more mud around her face. At least her head wasn't burning any more from the pepper spray. She blinked and regarded the fountain area through bleary eyes. It was a welter of mum mud and water. But no shoppers were around. No moms with cell phones and baby strollers. No power-suited executives slipping out on their lunch hour. No ladies who lunched and called 911.

Did they close the mall? Was Josie invisible? How long had she and Marina been wrestling in the fountain?

It seemed like years, but it might have been only a minute. Rational time lost all meaning when you were fighting for your life.

"Help!" Josie called. "Help me!"

"Yiiiii!" Marina screamed and leaped to new life. She was now an electric, writhing creature who twisted and turned. She bucked Josie off her back, then rose up to her full height, like some movie monster crawling from an open grave. Marina's blond hair stood out in crazy wet clumps. Her face was dark with dirt and rage. Her chic black clothes were torn and streaked with mud.

Weirdest of all, her dainty little Danessa purse dangled down her front, like a name-tag holder on a conventioneer.

If Marina realizes she still has that purse, she'll shoot me with her pepper spray again, Josie thought. And this time I won't be so lucky.

But Marina wasn't thinking. She wasn't even human. There was a wild light in her eyes. Her lips were drawn back in a cruel snarl.

"You!" she said, and pulled Josie up by the collar. Josie could hear her blouse rip. Marina's hand hooked around Josie's wrist like a steel cuff, and she dragged her toward the back stairs. Josie slid along behind Marina in her slippery leather-soled shoes, unable to stop. She swung her heavy Coach bag at Marina's back, but it bounced off the woman as though she were made of kryptonite.

Marina threw Josie against the back staircase like a load of dirty laundry, knocking the breath out of her. Then Marina reached down, grabbed both of Josie's feet and started to tip her over the rail. Somebody has to see us, Josie thought.

Josie screamed and clung to the rail. She slammed her feet against Marina, but it made no difference. Marina was a woman in an altered state. No matter how hard Josie kicked and punched, the Russian would not stop.

The world tilted, and Josie saw the marble mall floor rush up at her, then the ceiling with its bowl-shaped

Venetian glass chandeliers. Josie tried to strike out at Marina, but it only sent her tipping farther over the rail. Her attacker's strength seemed to double magically.

Josie looked down and saw her body hanging more than halfway over the rail. Panic flooded her, then fierce determination. She clung to the rail with all her strength. I'm not going over, she thought. I cannot die. I will not die. But as she tilted out over the mall floor, she thought, I will not die alone.

Josie swung her body back and hooked her hands onto Marina's waistband, hoping that could pull her to safety. Marina gave one more crazed cry and pushed Josie as hard as she could.

Josie could feel herself going over the rail's edge. She dragged her attacker along with her. They tumbled over.

She let go of Marina, her arms windmilling wildly. Then one hand caught a brass spear that held the CELEBRATE FALL IN PLAZA VENETIA STYLE banner.

My fall, Josie thought.

She hung by one hand. Then she heaved her other hand up. Now both clutched the brass standard. It bowed ominously. She dangled fifty feet above the marble mall floor. Her hands were slippery with sweat and mud. Her arms ached. Her battered ribs screamed their pain. But Josie heard only a dreadful stillness as she looked down at the hard mall floor two stories below. If she fell, she would be a bag of broken bones.

Josie couldn't see Marina's shattered body on the floor. Then she realized the Russian was hanging on another banner standard, five feet away. Josie's pole gave a harsh, horrible creak, and lurched downward. The top had pulled out of the wall. Five brass toggle bolts were all there was between Josie and death.

Marina gave a sudden heartrending shriek and then hung very still, and Josie knew that the Russian's banner standard was also pulling out of the wall.

She could see a crowd of horrified shoppers below, pointing and screaming. A security guard was talking on a radio. Another was pushing people out from under

Josie and Marina. So our bodies don't kill someone when we land, she thought.

"They're going to fall," a woman shrieked and threw her sweater over her child's head so he wouldn't see the awful accident. The little boy began to cry. People were running in circles and yelling useless commands: "Get help!" "Get a ladder!" "Get the police!"

"Hang on!" a security guard shouted up at Josie. She thought that was the most pointless advice she'd ever heard. Her grip was the only thing between her and certain death.

Then the brass standard lurched again, and another toggle pulled out of the wall. Two down. Four to go. Josie knew that help would not reach her in time. She had to find something that could support her weight better. Salvation was some three feet away. One of the huge Venetian glass chandeliers was solidly anchored to the ceiling with four sturdy chains. Each chain was as thick as Josie's arm. They were designed to withstand tornadoes, earthquakes and other disasters, natural and unnatural. Josie tried to reach the chain, but her arms weren't long enough.

The brass standard gave another dizzying downward lurch, and another toggle bolt pulled out of the wall. No time to think. Josie tried to lasso the chandelier's heavy silver chain with the strap of her Coach bag. She missed.

A woman cried out far below. Josie could feel the brass standard coming loose. A little avalanche of powdered concrete and wallboard fell on the crowd. More screams.

Josie swung the purse a second time. This time the strap snagged a heavy anchor chain. The bowl of the Venetian chandelier tilted insanely, but Josie was secured by her purse strap. She wrapped it around her wrist just as the brass banner standard pulled completely out of the wall and fell to the floor with a hollow, bouncing clatter. More shrieks from below.

Out of the corner of her eye, she saw Marina was doing the same thing with her Danessa purse. The athletic Russian looped her bag around the chandelier on the first try, and her hand reached out for the safety of the heavy anchor chains. That's when the skinny strap on the obscenely expensive bag snapped.

Marina's flailing body plummeted to the floor with a terror-filled scream.

Josie knew that she would hear it for the rest of her life.

Chapter 31

Marina looked like a sacrifice to a savage god. Her broken limbs formed a graceful X. A banner of long blond hair hid her smashed face. Even the deep red pool that haloed her head had a cruel beauty.

Josie stared down at the woman who had tried to kill her, fifty feet below on the cold marble. She felt an electric flash of anger. Marina had destroyed two women to avenge a murder that never happened. Such a freaking waste. If only Serge hadn't been so cheap. So unfaithful. So destructive. Josie almost wished Danessa had murdered the SOB. He deserved it.

"Hurry!" a security guard barked down below. "What's taking so long? Get help. This woman can't hang up there forever."

You took the words right out of my mouth, Josie thought. She had an odd urge to giggle, but her battered ribs ached too much to laugh.

Besides, there was nothing funny about what happened.

I'm supposed to feel terrible. I guess I will later. Right now I am triumphant. I want to beat my chest like Tarzan. I should have died, but I didn't. I solved the murders. I saved my own life. If I was still hanging on that banner standard, I'd do one of those three-hundred-sixty-degree turns, like an Olympic gymnast.

There was a stir in the pointing, staring crowd below.

A small woman marched across the mall, pushing security guards out of her way. Police officers pursued her, but she shrugged them off like yappy pups. The determined woman did not stop until she was standing under Josie.

It was a Fury in a pink pantsuit. She shouted up, "Josie Marcus, you get down from there right now. What were you thinking? You told me recording that phone call was safe."

"Sorry, Mom," Josie yelled back. Her words echoed against the marble.

"Sorry won't cut it," Jane said.

Josie could see her mother's bulldog jaw two stories down.

"I couldn't pick up Amelia at school because of you," Jane said. The echoes intensified her martyred tone. "Your daughter is at that overpriced school on extended playtime. I had to put the twenty-five-dollar fee on my own credit card. You will pay me back, young lady."

Shoppers stared slack-jawed at Jane, shouting at the woman dangling over their heads.

That's my mom, Josie thought. She was secretly proud. She knew Jane was trying to hide her own terror.

"Alyce is driving out from Wood Winds to pick up Amelia at school," her mother said. "What were you doing, running after a killer on your own? Have you gone completely nuts?"

"I think so, Mom." What else could Josie say? She was hanging from a tipped-up chandelier in the fanciest mall in town.

"You!" Jane said to the security guard. "Find out what's taking so long."

"Help is right here, ma'am." The guard pointed to a power lift chugging toward them.

"Well, tell them to step on it," Jane said.

The guard spoke into his walkie-talkie and the orange machine moved a fraction faster.

The power lift was worth waiting for, Josie decided.

It was staffed with two studly maintenance men. They were so hot they sizzled. That was the other thing Josie noticed about surviving your own death. You felt frisky.

As the power lift ascended to the ceiling, Josie studied her rescuers. One was blond and muscular with wide shoulders and tight buns. His sunburned arms had little golden hairs. He was the sort of man who would barbecue with beer, she decided, and make a woman laugh. The other was lean and had long brown hair in a ponytail. He looked worried. That man would be an intense lover, slow and deliberate. Two men, two moods. No wedding rings.

"Careful," Ponytail said as they maneuvered the lift under Josie. "Watch it. She's heavy."

"I am not," Josie said.

"Not you, miss," Ponytail said. "The power lift."

The lift was directly under Josie now. If she fell, she'd land on either the blond or the brunette hunk. That would be a real thrill for those guys, she thought ruefully. I look like I've been mud wrestling. The hair brushing her shoulders was stiff with the potting soil she'd rubbed into it. Terrific. I gave myself a mud mousse before meeting two hunky men.

Their strong hands reached out for her.

"Ouch!" Josie said as the men clutched her ribs. She flinched and felt their hesitation. "Don't stop. Get me down from here."

Finally Josie could let go of the chandelier. It swung wildly, then settled into a stately pendulum swing.

Ponytail wrapped her in a soft blue blanket, covering the worst of the mud. Josie couldn't feel her fingers. They were red and numb.

The jolly blond took her hands in his and began rubbing them until they started tingling. Other parts of Josie were also tingling, a lot more pleasantly than her fingers.

"That will get the circulation back," the blond said. "I'm Mike. I'll be your copilot today. Our pilot is Christopher. If you feel dizzy, grab onto his ponytail."

Josie started laughing, then winced.

"Broken ribs?" Mike asked sympathetically.

"I think so." Josie studied her reddened fingers. They were surprisingly clean. "There was hardly any dust on that chandelier." She sounded like a demented housewife.

"Thanks. That's our job," Ponytail said. "We keep the lights clean."

"We usually don't get a hands-on inspection," Mike said. Josie liked the way his neck was sunburned.

Josie rubbed her head. Her semiclean hands came away covered in dirt and blood. She must have a cut up there somewhere. The crowd on the marble floor was coming closer. She figured they had about twenty feet to go.

"We're almost there," Mike said. "That your mama in the pink pantsuit?"

Josie nodded.

"She's pretty worried," Mike said.

"She's gonna kill me," Josie said.

"Not until she knows you're okay," Mike said.

Josie understood his logic perfectly. He must have a mother like Jane.

They were less than four feet from the floor now. Lean Christopher gently guided the lift and they touched down with a slight bump.

"Nice landing, Captain," Mike said. Muscles bunched along his arms as he helped Josie off the power lift.

The crowd applauded. Jane elbowed everyone aside and threw her arms around her daughter. She cried and held Josie with a fierce strength, hugging her daughter's battered ribs until she cried out.

"Ouch, Mom, that hurts."

"Good," Jane said. "Maybe it will squeeze some sense into you."

Detective Yawney was waiting beside her mother. God, he was handsome. Josie decided the fight with Marina must have knocked something loose. She was horny as a teenager. Her eyes traveled from Yawney's slim hips to his wide shoulders. Very nice indeed. Then it got to his glowering face.

Josie looked at him and said, "I didn't do it."

"That's what I wanted to tell you," Detective Yawney said. "If you'd bothered returning my calls."

"You knew who the killer was?" Josie said.

"That's my job, ma'am," he said.

Josie couldn't tell if he was joking. He seemed angry, but she thought she caught a hint of a smile around those sculpted lips. It could have been a trick of the light. Of course he'd solved the murders. Josie should have known a suburban mom couldn't beat the cops at their own game. Except she had.

"I got a confession from Marina," Josie said. "She killed Danessa and Olga, too."

"You nearly got yourself killed while you were at it," Detective Yawney said.

Josie's mother glared at her daughter, then said, "You told me that phone call was safe!"

Josie was glad when the paramedics rushed forward with a stretcher and firmly shooed her mother out of the way. She was saved twice in one day. Suddenly life seemed wonderfully safe and warm. Josie was so tired she could no longer sit upright. She settled onto the gurney. It felt good to lie down.

As the paramedics strapped her to the stretcher, Mike the macho maintenance man whispered in Josie's ear, "I like a woman with spirit. Can I have your phone number?"

"Sure," she said.

Maybe I should use a mud mousse more often, Josie thought dreamily as the paramedics wheeled her away.

The next day Josie felt like her arms had been pulled out of their sockets. It hurt to breathe. It hurt to walk. She had two cracked ribs and five stitches in her scalp. A chunk of her hair had been shaved off, and she was afraid to see if it showed. Her hands were bruised. Her life seemed hopeless.

When she sat up in bed, her ribs screamed for mercy. Her stitches itched. Her conscience hurt. Josie blushed with shame when she remembered how she'd eyed the men like a drunken hooker at a sales convention. Mike the Maintenance Man had actually asked for her phone number. What kind of example was she setting for her daughter?

Josie tried to fall back to sleep, but every time she shut her eyes she felt herself falling over the railing, saw herself swinging far above the bone-breaking marble floor, heard Marina's final scream. The video ran endlessly in her mind, until she opened her eyes and stared at her cracked ceiling.

Then Josie would cry for no reason.

Actually, she cried for a good reason. She'd killed a woman. If only she'd taken Detective Yawney's call, Marina would still be alive. Josie no longer felt triumphant at her attacker's death. Any sense of victory was gone. She would give almost anything to bring Marina back to life. She kept remembering the moment she dragged Marina over the rail to her death.

The tears started again, leaking onto her pillow. Josie reached for a tissue and winced at the pain in her side. She'd told herself again and again that Marina's death was justifiable, even deserved. The Russian had tried to murder her. But Josie still felt like a killer.

She'd showered three times when she came home from the hospital. She got the mud out of her hair, but not her soul.

Josie looked at her bedside clock. It was eleven o'clock on a Saturday morning. She should have been up hours ago, but she didn't have the energy. Heavy weights pressed her back into the bed.

She could hear her mother and Amelia talking in low, urgent voices in the kitchen. She could smell burnt toast and fresh coffee. Even the thought of caffeine didn't tempt her to get up.

There was a knock on her door. "Mom," Amelia said.

"What?" Josie said. It came out as a bark.

Amelia hesitated, then pushed open the door. She was balancing a tray that tilted frighteningly to one side. Josie held her breath as Amelia carried it to the bed.

"I brought you breakfast," Amelia said proudly, as the tray made a three-point landing on the bed and hot coffee slopped over the covers. Josie narrowly missed second-degree burns on her thighs.

"Oops," Amelia said. "Well, there's still some coffee in the cup. And it missed the toast."

Too bad, Josie thought ungraciously. The toast looked like two buttered charcoal briquettes. A bouquet of the hated orange mums was crammed into a yellow plastic cup. In the middle of the tray was an outlandish pink bottle with a sickly sweet smell.

"What's that?" Josie pointed to the bottle.

"It's your birthday present early," Amelia said. "I bought it with my own money."

The ultimate sacrifice. Amelia guarded her allowance money like a miser.

"It's mango-guava bubble bath." Amelia held out the small, smelly pink bottle. "It's cruelty free. No animals were harmed in the testing. You always said a hot bubble bath could cure anything. Why are you crying now, Mom?"

"Because I'm happy," Josie said, and gathered her girl in her arms. Marina had tried to take this away from her. That was why Josie fought her to the death. She'd do it again, too.

"I'm going to be fine," Josie said, to her daughter and herself.

Epilogue

"Do you really think Marina killed Serge?" Josh said.

"I don't think she meant to," Josie said. "But I think she let him die. It was an impulse. She was angry with him. I don't know how she stood Serge as long as she did. It was so unfair. He lived in luxury with Danessa and his harem while she did the dirty work."

"If you ask me, living with Danessa didn't sound like much fun," Josh said.

"Serge and Danessa were two of a kind," Josie said.

"So were Serge and Marina," Josh said.

Josie and Josh seemed to be a lot alike, too, now that they were away from the Has Beans coffeehouse.

They were sitting at a table in the Schlafly Bottleworks, the new brewery in Maplewood. They'd admired the gleaming tanks of beer, guarded by shining glass, gilded by the warm fall sun. Beer making seemed so clean. Josie was recovering from her battle with Marina, but she still took too many showers. Josie wasn't sure what she was trying to wash away. Her ribs didn't hurt quite so much, and if she combed her hair carefully you couldn't see the stitches in her scalp.

They'd ordered Josie's favorite meal—offbeat appetizers. She forked into the red quinoa crawfish cakes slathered with lemon sour cream. Josh raided the spicy chorizo and sopressata sausages on the farmer's platter. He was a neat eater. Josie never saw him stuff his face. His plate was simply suddenly empty.

An afternoon with Josh was nothing like her date with Stan. No early-bird specials and food fit for dentures. Josh was an adventurous eater. He'd suggested the goat cheese dip, the lamb skewers and the venison chili.

She liked the way he ordered. Josh never looked at the price of anything on the menu. Josie hated tightwads.

She liked his clothes, too. No sad shirts and old men's pants for Josh. His navy sweater and khaki pants hugged him in all the right places.

Best of all, there were no awkward silences, no desperate "what do I talk about next?" thoughts. The topics stacked up like airplanes on O'Hare runways, then flew off in all directions.

"Yum. What's that glaze on the lamb?" Josh said.

"Apple mint," Josie said.

"I'm impressed. You're quite the foodie," he said.

"I read the menu," she said. "It's served over curried raisin-almond couscous."

Josh laughed. "Another beer?" he said, as he signaled the server.

"Think I'll try an oatmeal stout," Josie said.

"There's something sexy about a woman who drinks beer," Josh said.

Josie tried to take ladylike sips, but the strong-flavored stout was too good for that. Josh watched her guzzle with little speculative looks.

"And now for dessert," he said, when she had drained her glass.

"I'll have the sticky toffee pudding," Josie said.

"That, too," he said. "But there's my masterpiece." He opened his backpack and brought out a manuscript, thick as a phonebook, and handed it to Josie. She took it reverently. It seemed fat with promise.

"Josie, will you read this and tell me what you really think? I want the truth."

She studied his face. It was strong, but not conventionally handsome. His goatee was wicked. His hands, holding the manuscript so hopefully, were long and sensitive.

"I will," she said. Why did she feel like she was committing to more than reading his novel?

"They have a film series here on Wednesdays called Strange Brew," he said. "Cult films. They're showing the Martin Scorsese movie *The Last Waltz*. It has these incredible performances by Muddy Waters, Joni Mitchell, Bob Dylan—"

"I'd love to," Josie interrupted.

"Really?" Josh seemed surprised. "The last woman I asked said she didn't want to see a bunch of old guys who were famous before she was born." Josh took Josie's hand. There was that delicious tingle again.

"Coffee?" the server said, as she brought them their sticky toffee pudding.

"Thanks," Josie said, "but I've had enough coffee."

"It's time for something stronger," Josh said and kissed her. He threw down some money and they left their desserts untouched on the table.

"So did you . . . you know?" Alyce said. Her slate-blue eyes were bright with questions. Her white-blond hair did that expensive floaty thing.

Alyce and Josie were at Spencer's Grill, where the waitress poured them their usual bottomless cups of coffee. Generations of St. Louisans had drunk from the grill's thick china coffee cups. There was a permanence here you couldn't find at a fast-food joint.

"Did I what?" Josie said, straight-faced.

"Did you go home with Josh?" Alyce blushed.

"Do you think I'd do something so trashy on the first date?" Josie said, with a sly smile. "I don't know anything about the man."

"I know Josh is a hottie," Alyce said. "Any woman would go home with him if she had half a chance. Besides, it wasn't a first date, not really. How long have you been flirting with him over coffee? You saw him first thing in the morning, too. You can tell a lot about a man in the morning."

"I love it when you rationalize," Josie said. "Which is more important—sex or rationalization?"

"Sex?" Alyce said tentatively.

"Rationalization. Just try to get through the day without it."

"You're not going to tell me what happened, are you?" Alyce said.

"A woman needs a few secrets, even from her best friend," Josie said.

"Then I won't tell you my secret," Alyce said.

"You're dying to tell me. Spill," Josie commanded.

"Jake surprised me with a cruise for our anniversary. We're sailing on the *Queen Mary 2* right after Thanksgiving. The new nanny will take care of the baby for a week."

"New nanny?" Josie said.

"The old one quit," Alyce said. "I hired this one from a different agency. She's a lovely woman. Excellent references. Mature and experienced. Also fat. Fatter than me."

"Not fat—a woman of substance," Josie said. They clinked coffee cups.

"Now I have a secret for you," Josie said. She leaned in to confide in Alyce and lowered her voice. "You won't believe this. Detective Michael Yawney stopped by Saturday afternoon to 'clear up a few things.' I thought he was going to give me more details on the case. Instead he hit on me."

"That man is such a slut," Alyce said. "He's worse than Amy."

"Do you really think he slept with her while he was working the case?" Josie said.

"Who knows? Who cares?" Alyce said. "Amy can't remember who she's slept with anymore."

"Detective Yawney isn't going to make Husband of the Year, that's for sure," Josie said. "He said he and his wife had an 'understanding.' They were staying together for the sake of the children."

"He expected you to swallow that old line?"

"That and a few other things."

"Josie Marcus," Alyce said, "I am shocked."

"At me or him?"

"Both of you. But I'm glad you turned him down." Alyce looked so happy. She didn't just float when she walked, she seemed to levitate slightly in the booth. Josie was delighted her friend's marriage was over its rough patch.

"So when's our next shopping assignment?" Alyce said when the waitress brought their check.

"My boss, Harry, is supposed to call around noon with a new one," Josie said. "I should get home and do some laundry while I have the chance. Now that the doctor gave me the okay, I'm going to be a wage slave again."

"Harry had better give you a good job," Alyce said. "Or he'll hear from your lawyer."

Josie's home was wonderfully quiet. Her mother's TV was mercifully silent. Amelia was at school. Josie reveled in the quiet for half an hour, then went to work. She threw a load of laundry in the washer, cleaned the kitchen, then vacuumed and dusted the living room, making sure to remove all the cobwebs she'd studied during her interrogation by the homicide detectives.

She was dumping wet clothes into the dryer when the doorbell rang. The UPS driver with the blue eyes and boyish grin was back on her doorstep. The man was definitely eye candy.

I wonder if he delivers? Josie thought.

"Package for Mrs. Jane Marcus," he said. "Will you sign for it?"

Josie looked at the return label. It said HOME SHOPPING NETWORK.

"Nope." Josie wrote "Refused." The driver shrugged.

At least Mom is at her appointment with her counselor, Josie thought. I guess that's progress.

Harry called an hour later. Her meathead of a boss

had been superfriendly since she'd been cleared of Danessa's murder. You got more respect when your lawyer talked to your boss, Josie thought.

As Harry talked, Josie heard the sounds of a hyena gnawing an antelope carcass.

"What are you eating now?" Josie said.

"Prime rib," Harry said.

Chomp. Slurp.

"This Atkins diet is the best," he said. "I've lost two pounds."

Josie noticed he didn't say "another two pounds." He kept losing those same pounds, over and over.

"Shit!" Harry said.

"What's the matter?" she said.

"Spilled the au juice on your assignment. Wait a minute, where's my napkin? I got another job for you at Plaza Venetia."

"Harry! I can't go back there. Not for a while."

"Why not?" Chomp. Slurp. Double slurp. Harry was drinking something—the au jus? Josie hoped he wasn't licking it off her assignment sheet.

"No one is going to recognize you. You weren't on TV," he said. "You never made the paper. You were damn lucky."

Chomp.

"It's not like people were looking at your face when you were dangling over their heads, you know what I mean?"

Thank you for that picture, Josie thought.

"Besides, it's a nice assignment," Harry said.

Chomp. Slurp. Snuffle.

He's working too hard to sell this assignment, Josie thought. Something is wrong with it.

"What is it?" she said.

"I want you to shop a shoe store. Very upper-upper. Seems they've got a little problem. They want you to ask for a salesman named Mel. He's really into ladies' feet, if you know what I mean."

"You want me to investigate a pervert?"

"He's not dangerous, Josie. The worst he'll do is give you a foot massage. Might feel good on your tired toot-sies. Consider it like a bonus."

"A bonus! Harry, tell me you're joking."

"Of course, I'm joking," Harry sounded as slippery as his grease-covered fingers. "Listen, this Mel may not even be what they think he is," he said. "The store own-ers are a little suspicious, that's all. They've had a couple of complaints from lady customers and they don't know how seriously to take them. Women can be crazy, you know what I mean?"

Josie could feel the anger rippling through her. She wanted to reach through the phone and stuff that prime rib down his fat throat. Of course, that would only con-firm Harry's opinion of women.

He chewed for a while, unaware of her silence. "They don't want to fire the guy and risk a lawsuit until they know for sure," Harry said. "He likes brunettes, which is why I picked you. So go try on the nice shoes at the nice store."

Slurp. Chomp.

Josie groaned.

"Hey, don't give me that," Harry said. "It's not that bad. They pay twenty-five dollars extra. You'll do it, right?"

"The game's afoot," Josie said.

Josie's Shopping Secrets

Like all good shoppers, Josie gets her information the old-fashioned way—by milling around the malls. She's also picked up some good ideas from consumer advice books, the Internet and news stories. Here are her favorite shopping tips, designed to take the mystery out of shopping.

It's your bag: Long to tote the same bag as a big star? Maybe you can't buy a designer bag that costs more than your rent. Fashionistas like Gwyneth Paltrow are photographed with Fendi satchels, but the star is also reported to carry a tote from New York's legendary Strand Book Store.

The Strand's large black canvas tote is $12.95, which fits nicely into most budgets. The small tote is $5.95. To order, call 212-473-1452. Or order online at strandbooks.com.

Best time to bag the best bag: If you want service, Josie and other experts say to shop weekday mornings. Josie finds the ideal shopping hours for her are between ten and eleven o'clock, Monday through Friday. There are fewer customers in the stores and salespeople can spend more time with her. By midafternoon, the help is harried. Weekends are hopeless.

At some department stores and boutiques, shoppers can call in advance and make an appointment with a sales associate. Tell her the type of clothes or accessories that you want, and they will be waiting for you. That saves your time and energy.

Tripping over bargains: Feeling guilty because you splurge on designer purses, shoes or suits on your business trip or vacation? That may be the best time to buy. You may not have to pay that hefty sales tax if your purchase is shipped home from another state. Often, the hitch is the store cannot have a retail outlet in your state if you want to beat the sales tax. Check with your sales associate before you buy to make sure you'll get a sales-tax break.

Ask and you may receive: As Josie can tell you, serious shopping takes nerve as well as skill. If you are spending major money, ask the store for a discount. Don't bother if you're buying a nine-dollar T-shirt. But if you're going into four figures, it's worth a try. You may get 10 percent or so off the price. The worst the store can do is say no.

You can also ask if there's a discount if you pay cash. Small independent stores are more likely to say yes to this. They get hit hard by credit-card fees.

Learn to wait: Shopping can be a cat-and-mouse game. If you can't quite afford that designer dress or handbag, go back at the end of the month. Many stores have monthly sales quotas. The store may give you a discount as that deadline looms—but only if you ask. Of course, your item could be gone by then, but in that case you'll save even more.

Another way to wait and save is to shop the last day of a sale. The store may give you an extra break to get the sale item off the shelf.

Undercover shopping: When J-Lo wore her dress cut to there, no one noticed her handbag. But they did wonder about her other accessories. Where do you buy the right bra for a backless or frontless dress? Models make their foundations out of gaffer's tape, but that's hardly a romantic look. You can order Braza adhesive bra cups online. They are waterproofed and have air holes to prevent unfashionable sweating. Check out www.brazabra.com.

Best time to buy: The monthly retail sale guides say Memorial Day weekend is a good time to look for low prices on summer bags. Fall and winter markdowns start in November. And wallet prices are lowest in December, because they're often given as holiday gifts.

Bagging a bargain: Can't afford those fabulous Dooney & Bourke bowler bags? Wish you could own a classic Kate Spade? Resale shops in upscale neighborhoods are the best place to find deals on designer bags. I picked up an authentic Kate Spade purse for an amazing price at a South Beach resale shop.

Resale shops are also the ideal place to buy evening bags. Often, these are the least-used items in a woman's wardrobe, so you'll find bags that look nearly new.

Save yourself time and shoe leather and look for designer handbag bargains on eBay and other online auctions. eBay forbids the sale of fake designer goods. But in online auctions, watch for the weasel words "inspired by" Gucci or "replicas made of real leather." Those are codes for "fake."

One good site for bargains on new bags is bluefly.com.

Designer prices leave you dizzy? Some shoppers keep their money in their pockets and buy the sleek Isaac Mizrahi collection at Target.

Old and New York: Fashion mavens rave about Fine & Klein, 119 Orchard Street, on the Lower East Side. For some sixty years, it's had handbags to die for. Customers from Paris to Beverly Hills buy their bags. Like many places in the neighborhood, Fine & Klein is closed Saturdays but open Sundays. Stop by the Lower East Side Tenement Museum while you're in the area.

Tokio 7, 64 East 7th Street (between First and Second Avenue), may have some of the best designer resale bargains in Manhattan.

Don't expect rock-bottom prices at the good resale shops. Classic Gucci, Vuitton and Chanel can still cost a couple hundred dollars. Know what the bag costs new and you'll know what kind of a deal you're getting.

Faking it: In New York City, Canal Street is known as the place to buy fakes. Designer fakes are controversial. When you buy a good counterfeit bag, are you stealing the designer's quality and talent? Or are designer prices the real crime? That's for you to decide, but there is some evidence that buying fakes feeds gangs, crime syndicates, even terrorists.

Fakes used to be easy to spot. Nowadays, some are so good, you may not be able to tell them from the real thing. The bags have authentic-looking logos with the designer name spelled correctly—no Guchi purses. The clasps, straps and handles are sturdy and well made. The good fakes may even come with serial numbers on the inside tags.

Not sure if your bag is a fake? If you're buying it from a street vendor, out of a car trunk, or in a bar after midnight, its origins are doubtful.

If the price is unbelievable, don't believe it.

If your $25 Gucci bag has a "Made in China" label, it's a safe bet you're not buying a genuine designer purse.

Cruising for a bargain: If you can't make it to New York, St. Thomas in the U.S. Virgin Islands is the top-rated place to buy designer purses. This island's capital, Charlotte Amalie, is packed with boutiques. Scuttlebutt says the best fakes are at the blue-plastic covered outdoor market by the harbor where the cruise ships dock.

Go shopping, not slumming: There is no Down and Dirty Discount chain, but there are stores like them.

Some well-heeled shoppers think it's fun to go to there. Don't do it. You can get robbed, car-jacked, or worse.

What are the telltale signs? If you see gang graffiti, trash-strewn parking lots, warnings that the lot is patrolled by security cameras, metal detectors and guards at the doors, this isn't a shopping experience you want. If you are driving the most expensive car in the parking lot, leave immediately. These are the signs of a crime-plagued business.

Here's the real shopping secret about these stores: You won't find many bargains. The cost of crime is passed onto consumers in higher prices.

A traditional mystery has to have a cat. We have a cat shopping tip: What do yacht owners, cat lovers and museums have in common? They all use Museum Wax. Museums use this clear wax to anchor art, glass and china on shelves, tables and pedestals. The wax, properly applied, does not mar many surfaces. It can be removed with fishing line or dental floss. Yacht owners use Museum Wax to keep their art, antiques and collectibles from sliding around in rough seas. Museum Wax is also popular in quake zones. Depending on the use or the surface, you may want to try Museum Putty and Museum Gel.

When I lost an art-glass lampshade to a leaping cat, the lamp store told me their cat-loving customers used Museum Wax. I waxed my antique china, glass and lamps, and I've had no more cat-tastrophes. When my cat climbed the seven-foot ficus tree in my living room and overturned it, I Museum Waxed that, too. (The tree, not the cat.)

If you don't travel in yachting or arts circles, where do you buy these anchoring products?

Home Depot, Lowe's, and Orchard Supply Hardware in the West Coast earthquake zones carry them. Online, try www.museum3pack.com. Or check your local art supply store.

PS: Museum Wax helps prevent disasters when you have rambunctious children, too.

Read on for a sneak preview of mystery shopper Josie Marcus's next dangerous adventure, coming in October 2006

"Josie, please, can I come in?" Josh was kissing her neck and her right ear.

Josie Marcus kissed him back. There was a deep silence, broken only by heavy breathing. "Sorry, Josh, it's a school night," she panted. "I have to be in by ten."

Josh unbuttoned the tiny pearl buttons on her shirt, then kissed the tops of her breasts. "I'll be very quiet," he said.

More silence. More kissing. More panting.

"My mother's upstairs," Josie said breathlessly. "She's got ears like a bat."

"Come to my place," Josh said. "There are no old bats. Just a big bed with fresh sheets and some very nice wine." He flicked open the front closure on her bra and said, "Oh my God."

Josie was glad the porch light was out. Her knees were weak. That must be why she was clinging to Josh. "I can't," she whispered frantically. "There's my daughter, Amelia. I have to be home for her." Josie refastened her bra.

"How about my car?" Josh said, kissing her again.

"It's parked under a streetlight," she gasped. When he kissed her that way, she could hardly stand up.

"We'll have the windows steamed up in no time," Josh said.

Josie almost said yes. Then she saw the curtains twitch

at the house next door. Now she felt hot, but it was the heat of anger.

"I can't," she said. "Mrs. Mueller will see us."

"Who," he said between kisses, "is Mrs. Mueller?"

"The neighborhood gossip. She'll tell Mom and my life will be hell."

"Josie, how old are you?" Josh said.

"Thirty-one."

"Why are we making out like horny teenagers on your front porch?"

"Aren't you glad I make you feel young?" Josie pulled away and buttoned her blouse.

"That's not how I feel," Josh said. "I may never be able to straighten up again. We're too old for this."

"No, we're exactly the right age," Josie said. "If we were teenagers, we'd be boffing like crazy. Only adults have these problems."

"Josie, please let me in."

"Josh, I really want to, but I can't." Josie tucked in her blouse. "We should have thought of this earlier."

"Are you kidding? It's all I've thought about tonight. But I wanted to take you to dinner like a gentleman instead of just jumping your bones. Look where it got me."

Josie laughed. Josh didn't. "Who the hell is this Mrs. Mueller and why is she so important?" he asked.

Josie studied him in the starlight. Josh was four years younger, smart, and sizzling. Her friends wouldn't believe she was telling him no. Josh had a sensitive poet's face, a dangerous walk, and expert hands. He wanted to be a sci-fi writer, but right now, Josh was the best barista in Maplewood, producing sensational espressos and cappuccinos on his gleaming machine. When Josh was with Josie, he pulled out all the stops.

She kissed his nimble fingers and tried to explain the constraints on her life. "Mrs. Mueller rules the neighborhood," Josie said. "She's convinced I'm a slut, and I haven't done anything but wear a couple of trampy outfits for my job. If I go to your car, she'll have proof. She might even take pictures. She'll tell my mother, who is also my landlord and my babysitter, and therefore has absolute power. If I let you inside, we'll wake up Mom and I'll never hear the end of it. Even if we don't wake up Mom, Mrs. Mueller will be standing by with a stopwatch. She'll watch the shadows on the window shades and listen for the bedsprings."

"She sounds obsessed," Josh said.

"Mrs. Mueller has had this thing about me ever since I was fifteen. She caught me smoking behind her garage and ratted me out to Mom. I got even by putting a bag of dog doo on her porch and setting fire to it. Mrs. Mueller stamped it out."

Josh burst out laughing. "Mrs. Mueller fell for the flaming dog doo of death trick?"

"You may think it's funny, but she never forgave me. My name is mud. No, it's worse than mud."

"Why do you care what she thinks?" Josh kissed her so hard that her last few wits nearly fled.

"I don't," Josie said. "But Mrs. Mueller runs all the major church committees and clubs in the neighborhood. She rules Mom's social life. Mom thinks the sun rises and sets on that awful woman. To make it worse, Mrs. Mueller has this perfect daughter named Cheryl. She keeps rubbing Cheryl's achievements in my mother's face until Mom can hardly hold her head up.

"Josh, you're single, so it's hard to understand. If it was just me, I wouldn't care, but Maplewood is like a small town. Gossip about me will hurt my mother and my daughter."

"I do understand," he said. "I just don't like it."

"Amelia has a sleepover soon. Maybe we can be together then," Josie said.

Josh kissed her again. They stood hand in hand on Josie's front porch, looking at the clear November night. The old sycamore trees rustled and the houses creaked in the warm wind. It was one of Saint Louis's famous freaky weather switches. The night was a springlike sixty-five degrees when there should have been frost.

"Look," he said. "A falling star. Make a wish."

Josie saw the curtains twitch again.

"I wish Mrs. Mueller would get hers," Josie said. "I wish she'd be so embarrassed she couldn't hold her head up in Maplewood—no, the whole Saint Louis area. I wish she'd fall so low, she'd have to look up to me."

Josie got her wish. Every word would come true.

And she would regret them all.

Mel held Josie's right foot, slowly rubbing her arch with his thumb. His stroking fingers inched toward her toes. Josie tried not to flinch.

"Pink nail polish is so feminine," Mel said softly.

"Thank you," Josie said.

Yuck, she thought. I can't yank my foot away from this pervert. I have to pretend to like this. I have a job to do. Some job—having my foot fondled by a freak. If my mother knew, she'd hit the roof. What if my daughter found out?

How is Amelia going to know? Josie's sneaky side said. Are you going to tell her? God forbid your daughter should do this for a living.

Mel had stripped the pointy red Prada heel from Josie's other foot and examined it closely. Was he looking at the stitching or sniffing her shoe? Josie's stomach lurched.

Mel stopped stroking her stockinged foot and set it gently on his sloping footstool. She buried it in the soft padding. If only Josh were massaging her foot. If only Josie weren't in the Soft Shoe, the most exclusive retro shoe shop in Saint Louis.

The Soft Shoe was a perfect copy of a 1950s women's shoe store, with powder pink decor and salespeople who sat on old-fashioned slanted footstools, slipped off your shoes, then brought you stacks of styles to try on. The store was a shoe lover's dream.

Mel was its nightmare. He gave Josie the creeps, and she couldn't say why. He was slender and well dressed in a beautifully tailored gray suit. Maybe it was the pink carnation in his buttonhole. It made him look like an old-style gigolo. Mel wore too much cologne and his carefully cut hair was a little oily. That was it. Mel was oily. His manners, his hair, even his manicured hands were slightly oily, and he kept rubbing them.

"I see that you have an appreciation for quality," Mel said. "Prada is well made. Sexy, too. Plenty of toe cleavage, which men adore. Smart women know that."

Many smart women didn't know—or care—about toe cleavage, the hollow between the big toe and second digit. But Mel's hand grew moist as his eyes drifted toward the tiny valley between her toes. Josie wished she were wearing her grandmother's black lace-up Enna Jetticks, which would conceal her feet completely. Except they might really excite Mel.

"You're looking for a high heel?" Mel smiled. All the man needed was a pencil-thin mustache.

"Yes," Josie said. "Something special." She smiled back. She hoped she looked winsome, and not like her feet hurt.

"I know all the styles that please men and make women feel pretty," Mel said.

Mel was the Soft Shoe's top seller nationwide. But the company suspected Mel might love shoes a little too much. They were in dangerous territory. If they falsely accused Mel, he could sue Soft Shoe. Plus the company would lose its best salesman. But if Mel really was a foot fetishist and the company let him prey on customers, there would be a nasty scandal—and more lawsuits. That was why Soft Shoe had hired Josie's company, Suttin Services, to mystery-shop the Saint Louis store and target Mel.

Josie's boss, Harry, had given her the Soft Shoe assignment this way: "The company wants you to ask for a salesman named Mel," he said. "He's really into ladies' feet, if you know what I mean."

"You want me to investigate a pervert?" Josie had said.

"He's not dangerous, Josie," Harry had told her. "The

worst he'll do is give you a foot massage. Might feel good on your tired tootsies. Listen, this Mel may not even be what they think he is. The company is a little suspicious, that's all. They've had a couple of complaints from lady customers and they don't know how seriously to take them. Women can be crazy, you know what I mean?"

Josie had not called her boss on his sexist remark. Harry was hopeless. Besides, Josie got a bonus for special assignments and mystery shopping paid little enough. But now that Mel was sitting on his sloping pink stool, oozing over her foot, Josie wondered if the extra money was worth it.

"You wait here," Mel said. "I'll be right back."

Mel had an odd crouching walk as he ducked through the pink curtains into the back room. So far, I have nothing suspicious for my report, Josie thought. What can I say? He held my foot a little longer than usual? He rubbed my arch in a suggestive manner? I'll sound like a nutcase. All I have is my feeling that something is off about Mel.

Still, other women must have felt the same way, or Josie wouldn't be there. She would have to try on shoes until she knew for sure. She owed it to her sole sisters, as well as to the company.

Josie couldn't bring her mystery-shopping questionnaire into the store, but she knew the questions by heart. Right now, Mel had a perfect score. Had he greeted her warmly when she entered the store? Had he introduced himself in a positive manner and mentioned the store name? Had he waited on her promptly? Had he offered to bring out the high-fashion stock? Yes, yes and yes.

Here he was now, carrying shoeboxes stacked up to his chin. The Big Bopper sang on the retro soundtrack about Chantilly lace and a pretty face. Josie's mother had danced to that tune when she was young.

"I have a sassy pair of open-toed Bruno Maglis." Mel took off the shoe box lid with a flourish.

Josie studied the shoes. They were cute. If she could

afford nearly three paychecks for shoes, she'd buy them. At least she was being paid to try to them on.

"I like them," she said. "But I have on the wrong stockings. Mine have reinforced toes."

"Where did women get this idea that men don't like reinforced toes?" Mel said as he slipped the shoes on Josie. Sweat had popped out on his forehead, although it wasn't warm in the store. He wiped it with a silk pocket square.

"Some of us men long for the good old days when women wore stockings with reinforced heels *and* toes," Mel said. "Unfortunately, pantyhose have taken over everything. They're so orthopedic. Women have lost their affection for high heels. Why don't women wear heels any more, like they did in the fifties and sixties?"

"Because they hurt," Josie said. She had to walk miles through malls in heels for her mystery-shopping. Spikes were torture.

"But heels do such nice things for the calf and leg. I'd think women would endure a little discomfort to look attractive," Mel said.

"Hobbling is unattractive," Josie said, and wondered if she'd blown her cover with her anti-heel remark. "I'll take the Bruno Maglis."

"May I show you a Kenneth Cole d'Orsay pump?" Mel was practically on his knees begging as he brought out a turquoise shoe with open sides.

"Sure."

Mel slipped the pair on her feet. Josie stood up and took a few steps to the long mirror. The open-sided shoe was sexy, no doubt about it. Her legs looked terrific.

"Adorable," Mel said. "I'll be right back." He disappeared behind the pink curtains again with that strange crouch.

Josie sighed. She was going to be here all day with nothing to show for it but mauled feet. If Mel was misbehaving, she hadn't caught him at it.

Mel returned a few minutes later with another precarious pile of shoeboxes. "I have a gorgeous little slingback with a stiletto heel," he said. "And an adorable ankle-wrap sandal."

Mel opened the boxes like a courtier showing jewels to his queen. Josie tried them all on, wishing she were wearing them for Josh instead of Mel. After nearly an hour, she was knee-deep in a welter of rejected shoes. All she could say in her report was that Mel had spent more time than usual with her, and that wasn't wasted time for him. She was buying three pairs of shoes—nearly a thousand dollars' worth of stock—or so he thought.

Damn. I'll have to come back here for another visit, Josie thought. Maybe then I'll figure out why Mel bothers me. There's something wrong about that man. I wish I could see it.

Mel packed her new shoes in elegant pale pink shopping bags while Buddy Holly sang about Peggy Sue. "You don't want to take these old shoes with you." Mel indicated her red heels.

I do, Josie thought. Because I'm returning everything I bought here today to another Soft Shoe in Plaza Frontenac. Josie wouldn't get to keep those gorgeous shoes. Returning recently purchased items to yet another store was one of mystery shopping's less glamorous assignments. It was an effective way to test customer service.

"Actually, I do want them," Josie said.

Mel looked sad. So did her resale-shop Pradas. Were they really so down-at-the-heels? Funny how shoes that seemed attractive when she walked into a store looked worn and dusty when she bought new ones.

"Then let me clean them for you," Mel said.

At least I'll get a free shoeshine, Josie thought. I can keep that.

Before she could say anything, Mel had her shoes in one hand and was heading for the pink curtains with that odd crouching walk. He reminded her of Josh on her front porch the previous night.

Suddenly, Josie knew what the salesman was going to do to her innocent Pradas. She ran toward the back room, flung open the pink curtains, and caught Mel crouching like a teenage boy behind stacks of shoe boxes.

"Unhand that shoe, you heel!" she thundered, and ripped her still-pure Prada from his grasp.

Josie had him. After her report, Mel would never molest another pump.